DON'T WORRY
EVERYTHING IS GOING TO BE AMAZING

Billy Moran is an award-winning television writer. He grew up in the West Country, where his teenage years were rudely interrupted by the Second Summer of Love. Since then he has been embracing mysteries, craving solutions and writing lots of lists. He lives in London and has two children, two cats, one football team and several favourite detectives. *Don't Worry, Everything Is Going To Be Amazing* is his debut novel.

BiLLY MORAN

DONT WORRY WORRY EVERYTHING IS GOING TO BE AMAZING

Sauce
Materials

Published by Sauce Materials

ISBN 978 0 9927678 1 5

Cover designer: Alex Kirby

www.misterkirby.com

Instagram.com/sauce_materials

Facebook.com/saucematerials

www.saucematerials.co.uk

Everybody in the place, let's go

PROLOGUE

THE FUTURE

The End

DIGK	'Police testimony of Stephen Patrick Runce. Those also present are: on behalf of Mr Runce, Ms Patricia Liversedge; myself, Detective Inspector Graham Kaye; and PC Tim Paphaedes. Please confirm your name for the tape Mr Runce and then we'll begin. Mr Runce?'
SR	'Mmm?'
DIGK	'Name?'
SR	'Oh. Right. Sweet – an easy one. So: Stephen Patrick Runce, just like yer probably said Boss Man, but call me Runcie, or MC Chester, or President of the Republic of–'
DIGK	'Date of birth?'
SR	'Well, it was one of them years…yer know – back a bit?'

DIGK   'Fine – have it your way. So, to confirm. Mr Runce: ahead of the inquest and any subsequent prosecution, you're here to tell us what you know about Chris Pringle, and events leading up to the fatal fire which occurred at No.7 Brunswick Villas. We know the basics. But there's a lot still missing. And for a number of reasons, Mr Pringle's accounts are...compromised. So that's where you come in: help us fill in the gaps. Take your time. There's no hurry. And please – let's start at the beginning.'

SR   'Right Boss. Fillin' the gaps. Takin' me time. Tellin' the tale. Got it. It's a journey mind, so clunk click: there's a bit of now, a bit of then, now-then, now-then – but yer'd like that, right? See – he had to make a choice: between keepin' things buried, n diggin' 'em up? He didn't have the answers – course he didn't. But he did have a plan, a crazy, stupid, ridiculous plan: to get involved. The trouble was, yer let him – n we all know how that turned out...'

PART ONE

WHAT A TIME TO BE ALIVE

1

NOW

Runcie

Me lids are closed.

I hear big letters makin' little words, very slowly. Then nothin'. Some wheezy breathin'. Some thinkin' – starin'. I know what'll come next though – eventually – coz I've heard it a million times: a mechanical whirr n a placcy clatter; a soft thud on the carpet; a whole new world of revelation slidin' out of its safe place; a placcy clatter n a mechanical whirr. N then a short wait. It's guesswork this bit, but I'm goin' with…Columbo?

Chicken dinner.

So I'm still not needed. Not yet.

N me engine remains on idle – purrin'.

• • •

BILLY MOR

Everythin' always starts on a Friday. Coz what it is right, Chrissy calls Friday *Action Day*. As in the day he sorta unfolds himself out of his recliner, sticks on his best tracky, n actually leaves his gaff. His day for detectin' – waddlin' around with his note pad – fine. N his day for jobs n navigatin' The Man – not fine. So I'll trudge alongside him all day like some baked, Cheshire Cat minder. Well, Salford Cat minder.

The telly's off, but so far we've only made it to the caravan in his back garden – which has only ever been in his back garden, coz he *doesn't have time for holidays* – where he's jammed in behind his shiny red table, considerin' a biscuit tin. He notices I'm considerin' it too, gives me a slow, owly Pringle look, n then returns to the job in hand.

I try not to ask Chrissy questions coz yer just get more questions back, so I plonk his Chronicle down next to him – another Action Day ritual – n mooch around, pokin' at stuff. After I've made the second brews of the day though – n wondered if Chrissy could ever be trusted with a kettle – I give in.

'What's in the tin Chrissy?'

He gives it a long, worried pause, n scratches the big, cosy gut of which we're all so fond.

'Why are you erm…asking?'

'Coz I'm fookin' starvin'.'

It's a lot to think about, but finally he nods, me explanation deemed acceptable.

'So – what's in the biscuit tin?'

'Photos.'

'What of?'

'Biscuits.'

Right. If there's an explanation, he'll only give it when he's good n ready. Here goes.

'When I was...younger? Erm. Yes. Younger. I used to collect biscuits. Packets of biscuits. Remember? But then Dr Cripps told me "stop." Remember? He said that because I was eating a lot of biscuits while I collected them, it meant blood pressure or something. So. Erm...'

This isn't over.

'So...because I loved collecting biscuits...but I couldn't eat biscuits...I decided to collect photos of biscuits. Instead. Safer. Remember?'

Nah man – I don't remember. Whole story needs fact-checkin' n all.

'In the end, I didn't stop eating biscuits.'

Exactly.

'But I liked the photoing, and the logging...of which biscuits made me happiest? Because that's the whole point isn't it – you know, scores out of ten? So I thought to myself, "Chris, carry on logging biscuits...and eating them." '

So he did.

'Mind if I have a look?'

He does his look-down-look-left-look-right-look-down-look-at-you thing – protectin' his world.

I chuck meself in.

'Yep, there we go: biscuits, biscuits, biscuits, all caught on camera. Jammy Dodger, Fig Roll, weird granny one with the coconut dust, borin' one. What's it mean on the back, *WW, D4, G6.1*?'

'Erm, right, so, just let me...remember. Mmm...yes...ok... yes...so...WW means it's a biscuit for wet weather...D4's just 4 out of 10 for dipping, not that dippable, a mid-range dipper…G means it's for general use, not a special occasion biscuit, and 6.1 is the final score. Which, if you think about it, really isn't that good for a biscuit. What is it? Oh – a Nice. French. Not the best.'

'Bob on Chrissy. The vino, the food, the women, the laziness, they've nailed it – biscuits though, they dunno what the fook they're doin'. Dunkable though Chrissy not dippable – surely?'

Looks-down-looks-left-looks-right-looks-down-looks-at the Nice. I put him out of his misery.

'Dippable's fine. Ooh look, Dark Chocolate Digestive. Was an 8.5, but yer've crossed that out n downgraded it to a 6. What's the story?'

He puts his head in his hands – it's a pretty fookin' dramatic gesture.

'The sugar. Sometimes it doesn't melt properly. Crunchy. Not good.'

'Good collection though Chrissy?'

He loves a collection.

'Procedure Runce – very important. Been doing it for years.'

'Yer've been doin' everythin' for years.'

Most punters think Chrissy's been doing nothin' for years. But most punters don't get it. Full of surprises he is – mostly based on snacks n TV detectives.

•   •   •

Me, here, now? Who's askin'?

Me?

Stephen Patrick Runce, much-loved community-facilitator, details could compromise - you ain't seen me, right? Winnin' smile! The only one who could give yer the full low-down is Chrissy, n he hasn't got the time or the head space – he's got biscuits to rate.

Here? Shit Town. Imagine takin' all village idiots, packin' 'em into one ugly, needlessly hilly compound, suckin' out their hopes n dreams, n then fillin' the void with lager n roundabouts. What did they think would happen? Welcome to Shit Town: a glass in yer face if yer look outta place. The Wild West Country: there's some fields over there, but no cows, no peace, no butter-cups. Just En-ger-land: shite.

Now? Well it's frigid, n like I say, Friday. A whole town of cock-nobbers lookin' forward to Happy Hour: get yer head stoved in for half the price. Don't panic though, yer safe with me. I give knuckleheads a wide berth. These days.

N Chrissy? Kidder's like me cousin. Not proper cousin – just his ma n mine, close-as from way back, so it's visits up n down the country, yer start callin' 'em *Auntie*, n then it just is, right? Bonded by their bad choices we were. He was down here, I was up there, but we were closer than cousins: brothers.

Back then he was the sidekick to me mad Dennis the Menace – but I always had his back, n although I failed, one all-important time, I always will. He needed someone. Big nog-gin, big everythin', gromits – which made him slow from the start – quiet, watchin' eyes n a wanderin' mind, it's always been a little bit like he's had a bang on the head. Bongo, The Beast, Thick Fat Chris, Special – names he got called, still does prob-ably. But a few of us know better. It's a secret to keep yer sane in a mad world: special might just mean he's a bit more special than you. Yer get me? Look, he's no Stephen Hawkin'. He's not even a Stephen Mulhern. He's a bit damaged. A bit loose. A bit screwy. He'll never hold down a job, he'll never have a missus, n if yer saw him in the street, there'd always be some part of him – plastic bag, keks showin', note pad, egg in his bum fluff – that would make yer think: simple. But he's not – not totally. There's summink there. Somehow, n I've stopped tryin' to work it out, he actually knows stuff. Understands stuff.

• • •

'I'm getting ready Runce.'

Action Day: Chris askin' anyone he bumps into a loada daft questions they never understand the reasons for – n a lotta waitin'. To be fair though, I can wait with the best of 'em. I exist on a different plane – I'm the Elvis of time-wastin'.

First, the Doc's.

'Check-up.'

There'll be a mission though – there's always a mission. Whatever. I like taggin' along – partly to keep an eye on him, partly for entertainment reasons. Coz I love the Doc's. Waitin' room punters love hearin' about alternative treatment plans, so it's opportunities for all, innit – but it's more about the interactivity, yer know, *what's he in for, which one's the timewaster, who's on the claim?* Trouble is, get stuck next to someone even nosier than you n yer fooked, n today, I've got an Australian – middle-aged unit, hair like a minger's minge, spreadin' himself across a coupla seats next to me without a care in the world.

'What are you blokes in for?'

Chrissy's head down, makin' notes in his pad, plannin' summink to fry the Doc's brains – so it's all on me. I set me stall out early.

'Not me Pal – I self-medicate.'

He don't have a Peter 'Ookin' clue what I'm on about though, so I play on.

'I'm with him. So go on then,' coz he's dyin' to talk about himself, 'why are you here? In fact, why you up here, when yer could be down there?'

'Ah look – retired mate. On the old big trip with the hand-brake: Europe, the States, see her family, do the sights, try not to get blown up by ragheads, you know the drill. Just landed yesterday. You got broadband?'

What the fook's he on about? N more importantly – back to the game – what's he in for? No thinkin' time today though.

'In your digs mate – have you got broadband?'

'Nah, always on the move me' I tell him, pullin' out a burner, big but not smart. I was hopin' me obvious disinterest in broad-band n Islamophobia would shut him up – but he's not bothered what I think.

'Well that's what I did mate – and they said it couldn't be done – laid a cable all the way across Australia.'

Bunions? Lumbago? Hernia? Mole check?

'Dicky ticker now though mate.'

Shite. I'm losin' me touch.

'So, now I get to kick back and enjoy your Great British weather! Although – if they don't crack on and give us my Warfarin, I'll be dead before I get to Stonehenge!'

Could be for the best.

'Chris Pringle?'

Disapprovin' Receptionist Lady doesn't like regulars, but Chrissy's different. He's jumped the queue, n I head out for a smoke before Paul Fookin' Hogan can start tellin'

me how shite the UK is. I ain't a part of it Pal, Blue, Fella –
strictly a republican. These days? The Republic of me, Chrissy, n
whatever's on his mind.

• • •

Chris

Dr Watts. He's a very good friend of mine.

'Good afternoon Chris. And how are you? Keeping warm?
How's the flat?'

'The flat is a bungalow Dr Watts. And how...is your...erm...?'
I look at his...erm...

'Stethoscope? Cold apparently. Or at least that's what–'

'Can I try?'

'Oh, well, have you been having issues with your, er–'

'No, you just said it was cold and that's a free...temperature.'

'Right, OK – well let's have a listen to your heart anyway.
Let's see. OK, so shirt up please Chris, and we'll pop that on.
Have you had yourself weighed recently?'

Asking more questions than Dr Watts is hard work.

'So who would do that? And why?'

'Remember I explained that your weight and body mass
should remain within a certain range in relation to your height?
You're what 5'11" so–'

'If I had a special girlfriend, I might have to do some lift-
ing up...which would be fine...but I don't...which is also fine.
I think?'

I stop to conduct a short interview with a key witness –
myself – to check that it is fine, and straight away I find out that

yes, it is. Case solved. I'm happy being a large, fat man. Fatty Pringle. Detective Fatty Pringle?

'Right, OK, well perhaps we'll get you to step onto the scales in a minute anyway, but let's have a listen first.'

'It's not that cold Dr Watts.'

'Goooood.'

It's quiet now. He's listening, finger on my wrist. In my head I copy him – it could be useful if I ever find a corpse. My pad's in my hand to make a note, but my pen's out of reach, so I search for a word that will remind me all about this later.

'Stethoscope.'

'What's that Chris?'

He's still listening – doing his job, while I do mine. I feel very calm.

'Dr Watts?'

'Mmm?'

'I was reading out there in the waiting room about "health profiles," and I wondered, what is my "health profile," and how many heartbeats should I have, in say…a minute?'

'Well, I strongly suspect that you wouldn't be willing to undergo all the tests necessary to give you a proper overall picture of your health Chris, but great that you're curious, so for an adult male, nearing the old half century…60 to 100 beats per minute would be considered normal. But really? I'd want a nice fella like you to be somewhere around 80!'

Dr Watts seems happy. I will try and make him even happier.

'Well – let's see if I can beat that.'

I begin.

'Invisible skipping rope,' I explain – it should be obvious, but Dr Watts is a doctor not a detective.

'Yes, well that number's what's called your resting heart rate Chris, although it is good to get that up during exercise.'

I feel puffy-breathy, already, but I keep skipping.

'Getting hot now Dr Watts.'

I take one hand off my invisible skipping rope to loosen my bottoms a little – get some air down there. Still skipping though.

'Dr Watts? Did Dr Cripps ever get you to shave your balls?'

'Are you saying Dr Cripps asked you to do this?'

'Yes – when I had my ball operation.'

Dr Watts is at his computer now – I have a good view of the top of his head, with all the dusty spaghetti cheese sprinkled on the see-through bits. My tummy rumbles. Hungry and skipping.

'Ah. Here we are, 1999, embolisation of a varicocele. And Dr Cripps himself prepared the area?'

'No, he just wanted to check I'd done it right. He was always like that – helpful. He used to inspect Mum's bathroom for mould. With the door locked. Are you going to ask me how my memory is doing?'

I stop skipping.

'Well, OK then: how's it doing?'

I hand him my note pad, with the bullet points I'd prepared.

- Balls?
- Memory?
- Go

'A good detective asks more questions than he answers. I expect it's the same for doctors. Something to work on perhaps? Can I go now?'

• • •

Job Club.

That's what Runcie calls us. But this is the Job Centre. Job HQ. Where the people with no jobs go, to find that there are no jobs. That they would ever want to do.

Today I've got the nice lady. She's a very good friend of mine.

'So Mr Pringle, Chris – one month until your annual review. Do you understand? The week of – well anyway, it's a big moment for you. So, word to the wise: let's just try and keep things on track, nice and simple, yes? So. What have you done in the last two weeks to look for work?'

'Nothing – I'm on a case.'

She's put her pen down. She's leaning in. She has something she wants to tell me. I lean in too.

'Chris. You know how it works: I ask you what you've been doing to look for work, you say "a lot" and give me some actual examples. I say "Well done, have you thought about applying for this seasonal job down at the turkey farm?", you give me some confusing reason why you can't, I tick a box and – bingo – you go home. OK?'

'Is there a job at the turkey farm?'

'There will be.'

'What are the hours?'

'Flexible – don't you want to know what the job is?'

Do I?

'OK.'

'It's breeding season – so, helping with that. Breeding.'

'Not killing?'

'No. Someone else does the killing. Later. In time for Christmas.'

Mmm.

'Who does the feather things...the plucking?'

13

'That happens later too. After they've been killed. It's a happy farm I think, which the turkeys prefer.'

I doubt that. I've never met anyone who's dead and happy. I've never met anyone who's dead – but if I do, I have to be ready. At the moment though, I can only see turkeys. Looking at me. Sadly.

'I've had to shave my balls twice. Once for an operation, and once when I got scrot rot on a coach.'

'OK, I don't think we need to talk about that again. You understand the job though? The turkeys will either be alive, or not even born – they don't kill them until Christmas is just around the corner.'

Oh dear.

'Mean. Killing a turkey, just before Christmas?'

She's thinking. She decides.

'Right then. "Religious objections." Have a good weekend Chris. See you in two weeks. And then two weeks after that. You need to show you've been looking for work, or they'll withdraw your benefits: so stop telling people you think you're a detective.'

Why?

• • •

I can go home now. I say goodbye to Runcie and get on the bus. Searching for clues.

I write down two names.

I have a case, and I am getting ready to solve it.

Because before.

Back then.

I wasn't…

2

THEN, 1992

Chris

It will be dark. The air will be white dust. Faces, spinning round and round. I'm not in yet. Not in Utopia. Not in The Republic. But I can remember. I won't see, and I won't hear.

I look up at letters: THE PAVILION.

First we were in a car. Now we are in a queue. Which is outside. Not inside. With lots of other people, who are hopping up and down. Talking, talking. Swapping places – which is not how it is supposed to work, but it's OK because everyone knows each other, even though they don't.

I have questions in my head, but they stay there so other people can ask their questions, which are "Who's here, where you from, what you on?"

Runcie explains. He always explains.

'It's excitement Chris, fookin' mad excitement. Entry euphoria – it's the best bit!'

I move slowly. I always move slowly. Runcie has asked me if it feels fast, but it doesn't. I'm not hopping – I'm just sort of…stepping…tipping slowly, from side to side. But I'm not even here. I am outside – I can smell the sea – but I can't hear the sea, because everything's getting quieter, because I already feel inside. The Pavilion. The Republic. The weekend. Utopia. On a ghost train. Slow, bumpy, rolling along. Where everyone knows me and everything is quiet.

But I'm stuck on a thought.

I'm stepping, slowly, from my right foot to my left foot, from my left foot to my right foot. I only do what Runcie and the music tell me to. I can hear more questions, like "Is Runcie the first person ever to take a spanner to a rave?"

Thump, thump, thump, thump, thump, thump, thump, thump, spanner.

I feel the thump.

I remember the spanner.

It's here for two reasons. The first reason is that if they find the spanner, they might not find the pills, because they'll get distracted by the second reason. This is Runcie's plan. I don't get asked about plans, I get asked about spanners – but if you did ask me about the first reason for the spanner, I would say "I find this confusing."

The second reason for the spanner is so that it can be used. The water in The Republic always gets turned off. Everybody will be thirsty. Runcie's spanner will release the water. Everybody will love Runcie. Everybody will buy pills off Runcie. It's the better part of the plan.

Runcie loves being in queues. He's chatting to everyone. Blowing smoke rings. Jumping. Singing.

'Meetin' n greetin'. *I feel it in me belly, I feel it in me toes.* It's the best bit this!'

I don't get asked about plans, but I do get jobs in plans and I've done this job before. The job is to take my shirt off and dance on a podium when Runcie tells me to.

'Yer creatin' a distraction Chris.'

He asked Julie Duke to paint me, while he sat on the bed putting things in pockets and packets and shoes.

'Same as last time Julie – fluoro on his chest there, green, swirlin' around like a whirlpool. Orange boobs…a vortex thingy…n then *Chris* on his back. Sorted! Look at yer? Now, give us a kiss yer mad, gorgeous, painted genius.'

And then he kissed me and popped a treat in my mouth.

I remember where I am – outside. Outside the quiet that's inside. Cold. But sweating. Is that good? I have tassels on my nipple bits and a dummy in my mouth. When I get on the podium, everyone will cheer and the bouncers will look more confused than normal. Should they join in? Should they tell me to get down? Should they punch my face in?

'That's way too many things for 'em to think about Chris, coz they're total fookin' dopes right – so that's when I strike.' That's what Runcie said.

Chris? Chris? Chris? There's an echo.

'Chris? Got the backup spanner, right?'

'Yes.' It's in my pants. A place that no-one ever goes. It's part of the excitement.

'Give it me now then. No trouble for Chris, right – not on my watch. We're goin' in.'

•   •   •

Marching. Through March. 1992. I'm standing in the middle of the Exmouth Pavilion, because that's what Runcie asked me to do. Right in the middle of the Exmouth Pavilion. I asked Student how and he said "triangulation." So...

I am not alone, which Student said would have made the triangulationing easier. There are a lot of other people too, a really big...number...so it's "excuse me"..."thank you"... "oops"..."thank you"..."excuse me" and they're all stepping up and down and around and marching along with me, to the same place. It's dark and I can't hear and there is sweating and Vicks, but I might be the only one with an actual cold. It's impossible to say how long we have been here. Impossible. Because this is Utopia. Rat Pack Utopia.

My eyes are closed. If I open them, I open them a bit. I look down at the feet and there's a path through the dark. Between the feet. But it's better to stay still. It's better to close your eyes, and I'm turning now and holding my hands out, and everything around me is speeding up, but my eyes are closed and I'm hugging the roof. I am Chris.

You should never mess around at the farm, because you can fall into machinery, but in The Republic, you fall through the machinery and it's a long journey through, with piano, so much machinery, then a chipmunk and boof-boof-boof-boof-boof, scribbling, with crayons, up and down and around, all the colours in my head, because my eyes are closed.

'The bass n the beats Chris – that's all yer need, the bass n the beats.'

That's what Runcie says. You march, forever, together and you think, this can't be the way to the secret? But then you discover the secret and you know: the machinery just wants you to be happy.

The bouncers haven't discovered the secret. And they haven't discovered the pills or the spanner.

'I'd love 'em to discover the secret right? But they mustn't discover the pills or the spanner first?'

What is the secret? Am I at the beginning of something or the end? The questions can last forever, so you smile when you finally understand: you don't need to know the details. It's the feeling that's the important thing. I see Runcie, far away in the corner, surrounded by more new friends.

'A sea of smiley faces in an ocean of love Chris,' he said.

He winks at me. It might mean the taps are off.

But I'm stuck on a thought.

• • •

I drift. I am trying to find the Chill Out Room. I don't think it should be this hard, but I don't mind. I give a small man with a black eye a hug because it is important to be nice, and he says "Normally I'd smash your fat head in, but not tonight mate," and more damp men hug me. Ladies smile, but don't hug me.

Now here's a bar. The music has changed. It's a bar with shutters that come down when the bar doesn't want to sell grown-up drinks any more. Behind the bar, they're also here when Showaddywaddy come to play, or it's bingo, so they look shocked and surprised. And it's what I've remembered I was looking for: the Chill Out Room.

You can't chill out in the Chill Out Room, because it's hotter than any room ever and not relaxing in any way. But everyone in the Chill Out Room – apart from the men and ladies working behind the bar who look shocked and surprised

– seems very happy, about everything. Runcie tells me not to look for answers when there's no need for questions. And everything drips.

I hear only Runcie.

'It's all about the weekend, n it used to be lager n darts n Roxette, n that's all there was, but now it's pills n plannin' n dancin' n drivin' until the party's over. N it's not over Chris – nah man, n I'm not even bothered about Roxette, in fact, if I met 'em tonight, I'd probably give 'em some pretty fookin' positive feedback, know what I'm sayin'? The side of me head's gone well numb.'

He takes a deep breath which may never stop. It stops.

'Fookin' loved up. Loved fookin' up. Love fookin' up.'

His arm pulls my head.

His head touches my head.

But I'm stuck on a thought.

• • •

Runcie

After Utopia.

'Where are we?'

Chris asks. He always asks.

Empty air hangar, woody glade, new age farm or wacky warehouse, heads flingin', lights blindin', jaws lurchin, guts dippin', noses breathin', hands touchin', love loopin': after party.

We're in The Republic. That's all we need to know.

• • •

Another zombie dawn. A different kinda glow. Yer can feel it – breathe it in through yer schnoz. We're pacin' down lanes, arms raised to the sky, chucklin' at the wonder of it feelin' this fookin' good, every single time, until yer body – finally on yer side n at one with yer mind after all these years – tells yer to get to a beanbag n a bucket. Top one. Nice one. Sorted. Deep travels always send me home, so I'm duckin' n divin' n givin' it the full Browny, n me survival gene's sayin' *look around yer, sell, sell, sell*, n I have to remind meself *that's not it*. We're in it together, we're lookin' for our wheels, this is The Republic – n I'd give up everythin' for The Republic.

The majestic Julie Duke, aka the Fat White Duke: stops to talk dirty Welsh to every man she meets. But shaggin's not on the menu, coz all this actually carin' about other punters' feelins is a full-time job, so yer don't have time to think about shaggin'. Unless yer Julie.

Student: analysin'. Don't think it, feel it.

Chris: stops to dance, which is a problem coz there's no music. We're damagin' him.

There's a nice little vibe to just walkin', walkin', walkin' – we're keepin' the vibe alive. What we doin'? Oh yeah: wheels.

• • •

The Republic: of the weekender, of partyin', of rave. We're spangled, mangled, n news comin' in, Roxette have just been strangled. Actually nah – everyone's welcome, even them, just keep the noise down right, both of yer? We've got nothin' in common, but suddenly we've got it all in common: the possibilities are endless.

On the way here: lanes, lanes, slidin' down lanes, the convoy stopped, n it was mystical arcs of frosty piss in the headlights, firin' into the grassy banks, last stop before paradise. I remember that.

We've found the Courgette – Student's hangin' green Chevette – abandoned, like we had no intention of returnin', which to be fair, we didn't, coz where we were goin', we didn't need cars. Plus, that is one rank motor. Now though, I love it, coz, well, I love everythin'.

Gettin' Chris in's an operation. Another night of no routine n a loada free pills, n the big lad's proper wonky. Still marchin', won't stop, can't focus. We have to push the last bits of him in, n then we're movin', n we've got choons, n smokes, n we're gettin' the power of speech back, n life is sweet.

But Chris is quiet. Always quiet in The Republic he is. But this? *Stuck on a thought* he calls it. Tryin' to remember: what though? The secret? Nah – coz yer never remember the secret. Yer feel it – it's just a part of yer – but when it's slippin' away, givin' yer a little wave, yer start tryin' to bank it, stayin' awake to find an order for it all that'll still be with yer tomorrow, the next day, n the next day. But sleep just dissolves it all away, with technicolour dreams n then nothin': warm, flat, fuzzy, white noise, forever. N when yer wake up, what yer knew last night, with absofookinlute certainty – the secret – has gone. All that's left is knowin' there is a secret: that it's The Republic, not just the pills, that it's about findin' yerself, not losin' yerself. I remind everyone of all of this, as we're vibratin' happily along the blurry A30. But Chris, who needs it most? His brain is roadkill.

• • •

All back to Student's. Yer never really know where yer goin' or how long it will take, but when yer get there, yer try to stop someone playin' Enigma, maybe have a brew. Chris eats all the biscuits. N then I always take him out for walkies before bed. We're *24 Hour Garage People*, n I try to get him to remember the list, keep his mind on the straight n narrow – but all he can come up with halfway up the hill is Hubba Bubba, skins, n a chocolate banana, which he thinks means two milkshakes.

'I fell asleep once and did a wee – a wee I hadn't…planned.'

'I remember, but forget about that – checkit.'

I show him a bank card I libboed from a Land Rover on our long walk to the present. Force of habit, it's in me genes, I'm Robin Hood me – borrow from the asleep, lend to the awake. Chris don't approve though – he's good for me – so I toss it.

'We don't need it though do we Chris – coz what's in yer bum bag?'

'Money Runce.'

'Lots of money.'

Chris: Mani/tracky/bum bag combo. His ma gave him his special bum bag, says Algarve 85 on it – I dunno why, coz he never went to the Algarve in '85, never went anywhere. His ma stuck an i-SPY book in there when she got him it n all, so he still has one: On the Motorway. He gets it out, even though we're only walkin' along a B road.

A boy racer screams past.

'Nice hat fat boy!'

A nearly-empty can of Budweiser hits the ditch, n a GTI death-trap of Jive Bunny cowards bombs into the distance. Me protective instincts kick in n it's a buzz killer.

'Amazin' innit? I mean, the Pav was full of all sorts: old birds, homies, lads n crusties, party kids: 137 bpm, lift-off, n everyone's cool. Out here? There's always some towny wanker who wants to stamp yer brains out coz yer wearin' a mint hat. Back in there, no problems – all sorts.'

'All sorts.'

I focus on rememberin' the secret. We're on one. All night. All weekend. Movin' on up. Together. Deeper into The Republic.

Chris though, is stuck on a thought.

3

NOW

Chris

I am in. In my bungalow. The council gave it me. My job is to remember. To understand the rules. To solve the case.

The detective looks for clues, thinks about them, then looks for more clues. There are clues everywhere. Some disappear and then you notice they've come back again. Often this reminds you that they are clues, because if you don't notice them, they probably aren't. That's how the detective brain works. "The Way of the Detective." That's what Runcie calls it.

I remember. Dr Watts asked me another question.

'Are you lonely?'

But are the people who ask me if I'm lonely actually the lonely ones? Mmm. Maybe. But Dr Watts can't be lonely – he sees me all the time.

Where was I? Oh yes – where I should always be. Detecting.

When I am alone, I am not alone – I'm alone with my thoughts. My thoughts are my friends. Runcie isn't here, but I tell him anyway.

'Each of your thoughts is a friend, but "you have to give your friends room to grow." Julie read it me from a magazine.'

'That's nice Chrissy – brew?' the not-here Runcie says back. I put the fingers of my hands together – like Mum praying, but also, like wise people do.

• • •

I love detectives. I love my case studies. I love my files. I love my chair and my bath. I love five people. I don't need to solve good mysteries such as:

- Why are biscuits brilliant?
- Why are slippers best outside?
- Why do I admire Frost so much?

Because he's an amazing detective: so, case solved. You don't need to detect good change. You just need to detect bad change. Problems. The perfect murder.

But. But. But. "Practice makes perfect."

So I'm in the Incident Room. Which is the caravan. It's always been the caravan, but now it's going to be the Incident Room as well – or instead. Allowed in the caravan: Chris, Runcie, Julie and Student. That rule will stay the same – but stricter. There's a picture of Mum up on the wall. Does that make her a witness? If so, what to?

The rest of my detective work takes place in my bungalow. Or in my head. Or on the bus. Or when I go for a walk. When I'm on surveillance. But usually in my bungalow. In the

Interview Room. Which was the lounge, before it became the Interview Room.

I put a sign above the lounge door: it says "Interview Room" on it. I tried it on the door itself, but Runcie pointed out that the door is usually open.

'No-one'll see yer sign. Yer'll end up having to explain it's yer Interview Room, n that's a distraction yer can do without. Yer wanna be on top from the offski – with yer suspects shittin' 'emselves. Who yer gonna be interviewin' anyway?'

He's right – details. I look at my note pad. It says: "phone."

I went to the phone box again today – our old phone box, where we used to go. But that's not it – it's time for me to make a call.

'Yes, hello?'

'Mum. It's Chris. Your son.'

'Yes, I know that dear. Is Stephen with you? Oh no – it's early. Has he been buying you vegetables? You can get frozen peas you know?'

I screw my eyes shut, because I mustn't get distracted by peas.

'Are you OK Mum? I just want you to be OK.'

'I know dear. Me too. Are you sticking to your routine?'

'Erm? Mmm. So Mum, I've been thinking. And I wanted your advice.'

'OK, this is a first, but fire away.'

'You've seen Taggart, haven't you?'

Phones reveal sighs very clearly – and that, there, was a very long, slow sigh. Mum usually has a small, kind, hurty smile she begins sentences with. This time, I don't think it's there.

'Oh Christopher.'

She hasn't seen Taggart.

'Really? You've never seen Taggart?!'

'No, but Christopher, that's not–'

'You've never seen Taggart?'

'No…?'

This is bad.

'I have a lot to do Christopher. I'm on doubles at Morrison's this week, I've got Brendan and all his business. I'm sure it's really not that amazing that I've never seen Taggart.'

'Amazing and surprising Mum – is what it is. I mean. You've had a television for several years – aren't you even a bit…? Brendan used to be a police man! It just doesn't add up. He's even Scottish.'

'Well dear, that's that. I've never seen Taggart. Maybe everything would be better if you'd never seen Taggart?'

That – that's just too big to think about.

'Is Brendan there?'

'Yes?'

'I would like to talk to Brendan please – as part of my enquiries.'

Mum's special friend. Brendan. A "good man."

'OK. It's 8:30 am and you want to talk to Brendan as part of your enquiries. Well, Christopher. I will hand the phone over now. But please think about what you say. As you, well, pointed out, do try to remember that he was an actual policeman. OK?'

'OK Mum. Bye bye.'

I bet Brendan's seen Taggart.

'Hell–ooo?'

'Is that Brendan?'

'Yes?'

'It's Chris – Mum's son.'

'Yep, hell-ooo Chris, I gathered that–'

'Brendan, have you seen Taggart?'

'Yes of course. "There's been a–" '

'Thank you! Right. You've seen Taggart. You've been a law enforcement officer, out on the street. You know how to take down a perp, handle a snitch, taser a–'

'I worked mainly on Barra remember Chris. Remote island communities like that – they're not that gritty really.'

I shake my head, sadly.

'Try telling that to Bergerac.'

'Yes. Look Chris, I'm hoping you can come over to lunch again one Sunday, your mum would like that.'

'That is certainly not…impossible. But I do have…cases. The quicker you can help me with a couple of questions sir, the quicker that will be.'

'Riiight?'

'OK. So. When I'm detecting, should people call me "Pringle"?'

'Why?'

'Because Taggart was a dull, Scottish man, like you really, but he was…where is it…"feared and respected"? If he'd had a suspect and he was all like "Hi there, I'm Jim" – well it wouldn't have been the same? He was "Taggart." So I'm thinking I should be "Pringle." '

'I think the respect he got came more from him being an experienced, high-ranking detective Chris. He was good, Taggart.'

Good?!! Wow…

'You could say that Brendan yes. He was Glasgow's premier Detective Chief Inspector, and he just said "Taggart, Taggart, Taggart." Mmm.'

'Yes, but really, he would have been known as Detective Chief Inspector Taggart.'

'That's not what happened.'

It's not surprising Brendan didn't make detective.

'Yes, but it was just a TV show Chris.'

I give him silence. Total silence. 109 cases Brendan! Although he was dead for most of them.

'So you think I should be DCI Pringle? It's a bit formal.'

'No, you can't do that Chris. To wear any kind of police badge there are minimum requirements. A life in uniform – it may seem like pen-pushing to you, but there's years of training.'

I have a quick chuckle about this – I'm sure that can't be true.

'Look Chris, I think I best be off. Lunch though, right? It would make your mum happy.'

I like making Mum happy. And I would like to make Brendan happy.

'Yes Brendan. Oh, Brendan?'

'Yep?'

'What were you doing between 4 and 7 on Saturday?'

'Bye Chris.'

Click.

I write "Brendan?" on my pad. Then cross it out.

You have to be ready. That's the main thing. You have to be ready.

• • •

Runcie

Sleep like a cat, me – just like that, exactly when I want, which is often in the mornin'. But the big man's got more wonk on than usual, n I need to be all over it, so here I am, pullin' up at Chrissy's when I've not even tapped up the Honey Monster. I can feel me bloodshot peekers.

Me man from Hilltop's picked me up, n I give him a teenth n a Yorkie to sit tight, while I check on a 48-year-old unemployed man who wishes he was Columbo. But before I can even get up the path to his battered front door, the *I'm not racist but* next door neighbour is on me case. Shiny shirt, crap tat, Brummie-builder type, with a gut so big, every slash is a gamble. His *job*? Standin' outside, smokin' a No.1, surveyin' his manor, n pointin' out the fookin' obvious.

'Here to see Chris are you?'

'Smokin' a fag?' I ask in return.

He don't care though – he's at war, but not with me. With the next one along – who just happens to have that foreign-lookin' skin they don't like round here in Engerland, total fookin' coincidence I'm sure.

'You tell Chris I'll come. But it's back to how things used to be now – our rules. So that fella disrespects me over my fence one more time, I'll give him a slap.'

I stroke me chinny-chin-chin to convince the daft fooker I'm takin' his comments incredibly seriously – a proven Runcie technique which allows me to enjoy his idiocy in peace from behind me mirrors.

'And yes, I'll bring a sock.'

A sock?

Satisfied, he rasps his way back to his front door with the straight armed walk of yer standard fat bully, where he turns for a quick final sweep, just to make sure no other Poles or darkies pose an immediate threat to his own sweet corner of this once proud nation. Whatever Chrissy's cookin' up, I'm 'avin' one of them Spike-Lee-at-the-Knicks front row seats: coz free entertainment, is the best entertainment.

Inside Chrissy's lounge – now Special AKA the Interview Room – he's kinda melted into his recliner, listenin' to rave – loud, old school rave – starin', mouth slightly open, like a frog waitin' for a fly.

'Alright kid? Are yer winnin'?'

He isn't. So I've got what I came for, proof he's wobblin': fiddly diddly he calls it. N there's nothin' I can do about it. Not yet. Coz this little set-up says he's away, puttin' a little distance between the here n the now n…him. The clang n the thud takes me to a far off place n all – womb-like memories of The Republic of Rave. Not such happy memories for Chrissy though, coz that far off place mashed him right up. Thinks it holds the key to his one, all-consumin' mission n all: his *job*. Does it? Fook knows – but it did save him from the only real one he ever had.

• • •

The Little Chef, 1989: that was the last time we worked – as in, doin' summink rubbish, wearin' summink bogus. Since then? Well, I'm a hard worker, active in the community, yer get me? I look after meself, take care of Chrissy, n I'd never give them pinch-faced Daily Mail prunes the pleasure of callin' me a bludger – so there's no signin' on for The Runce. But since the Chef? Nah – no job. N as for Chrissy? Well – he's had even less of a job. I mean, he's tried stuff – Trolley Wally at Safeway, dinked a 4x4 on day one whilst buildin' a snake. But there's nothin' doin': so of course he signs on. Proper, full-on, Job Club: a friend on benefits. N before the Chef? Well that's a galaxy far, far away. When we were kids – proper kids.

We'd send packages – pen bro's. He liked *Mike Read, Mike Read, 275 n 285,* n I was all about Steve Wright in the Afternoon. I'd get Mike Read tapes from him, listin' all the songs, ratin' 'em, n reasons why Steve Wright weren't funny. Turns out he was ahead of his time of course – he weren't funny. That's Chrissy all over.

N then every summer – coz me ma had long-since popped her pumps, n life was fookin' bobs – I'd pack meself off from Manc to meet him at a Radio 1 Roadshow, an annual comin' together of two different schools of thought, n then go on n stay at his for me holidays. With Auntie Mo. *Just call me Maureen.* The sweetest, chattiest, biggest-hearted little molly-coddlin' mum in the Mid South West – always graftin', always cuddlin', always cookin', always worritin', always lookin' after yer. Never took a holiday, never pissed up a penny. She was at work. Or she was droppin' in on oldies, runnin' errands or checkin' up on whoever'd been hit by tragedy that week – everyone in Shit Town knew Chris, n through her I got to know everyone I wanted to in Shit Town, which came in handy later. But mostly, she was at home – with Chrissy.

So, she looked after me each summer, n in return, I helped Chrissy understand stuff: like that weird can be alright. Coz he was weird, n the whole set-up was weird. Two completely different worlds: when his dad was there, n when he weren't. I had one life that was shite, he had two, both proper odd, but both cosy n free – n I told yer, I love free stuff.

When Frank was around, him n Chrissy's ma got on fine, in a sorta whispery, gentle way. But mostly – coz he was all about his disappearin' act – she'd be off, puttin' in the hours, payin' the bills while she could. He'd bring shit gifts, that was his contribution – the sort grannies get, yer know, kind but fookin' hopeless? But maybe they had some screwy Pringle logic attached to 'em, coz Chrissy always lapped 'em up, his way. Just a nod, n then he'd play with it, whatever it was – miniature cricket bat without a ball – for like two hours, methodical. N yer'd just have to entertain yerself, n his old man would sit there quietly n all, watchin', waitin' for the clock to hit 12, so he could head off to the pub, returnin' only when the job was done.

He was never a mean drunk or violent. Sometimes we'd watch him wobblin' down the path in the dark, tryin' really hard not to fook it up, n if he found out we were still awake, he'd wanna get us out of bed n chattin' about grown-up stuff we weren't interested in, *Fair play to you lads, fair play to you*, like his mute button had done one, n he'd want Chris to sit on his lap, right up to when he was gettin' pretty big, 12, 13 – 'til Chrissy's ma shooed us all to bed. Then he was always first up in the mornin', sittin' at the little kitchen table again, drinkin' his sugary brew, smilin' n just not sayin' much. It was a house where nothin' ever got done – if there was a blocked sink or a mirror got broke, it stayed that way – but I loved it. To me it was peace, yer get me? N Chrissy was *happy and kind, because that's all you have to be* – coz that's what Frank always said. He didn't do sober jibber-jabber, but he did like a sayin': *You can't be brave unless you're afraid*. That was another. Deep.

So anyway, all that, n then one day, he'd just be off. No dramas – Maureen'd calm down the hours a bit, be a bit more around, fussin' n scoldin' n *I give up*-in', n everythin' would chug along, n Chrissy chugged along happy enough too. But I could tell his little eyes were watchin' – seein' more than me. Tryin' to work stuff out – already.

Coz when yer look back, no doubt he had the sore guts of a boozer, Frank: but there was a haunted look about him that was more than that. Not a bad bone in him – but he was a wreck. Nervous. I probably did see it, but when yer a kid, normal's normal innit?

'Til it's not.

Coz one summer, '85, Chris n I were what, 14, I was down for me hols, n one mornin' Frank weren't up 'til Mo was out the door – shoulda seen the signs. We left to go to the Rec or summink – he took his coat, just his coat, n went. Never came back.

Gone.

N bad news like that? At school? It sticks to yer like chewy-on-the-shoey. Chrissy was different anyway. But to be all that n also in the free lunch queue coz yer alchy old man's not there to stand up for yer? Well that was askin' for it, n it seems he got it, yer know, relentless: the usual. Names. Chuckin' his daps on the bus stop roof. Books ripped up. Bein' tipped into a wheelie bin. All that stuff, with only Julie n Briefcase Stu to back him up, 'til I kinda knew I had to be there: coz yer don't hurt punters right, n yer never hurt punters like Chrissy. N by sixteen, things had changed for me anyway, life had gone from shite to shiter – bad geezers in the hood, bad prospects, aggro. So I ducked – Chrissy was at home doin' nothin', that sounded sweet, so I shipped meself off to Shit Town to live the Wild West Country dream. *Let's just make the move official* said Maureen: muck in with her n her Christopher, fill a hole, n *just say no* to a life of crime. Didn't exactly work out like that of course – but I'm not the bad guy.

Bein' around more though, I started to realise that Julie got stuff out of yer – n him too. Better at bein' human, girls are – n Julie's the best. Connections n memories. N one day, Julie fills me in: she says Chrissy believes, really believes, that his dad will come back, that one day he's gonna ride back in on a shiny stallion, sober, sorted, back for good. It's all he thinks of. He's waitin', waitin', doin' fook all.

But when he turns 18, Maureen's had enough. Time to see if he could look after himself – with my help of course. We had to get out of the house – or at least start enterin' it with a bit of cash. And so: the Chef.

At first it was alright. I mean, they knew to keep Chrissy away from hot surfaces, so all he had to do was take orders, in return for money, n free Magnificent Seven Burgers. Good bunch of kids workin' there, all was doodlin' along nice n easy: we were fine. 'Til one day, a mysterious stranger chips up n says to me: *Don't worry, everything is going to be amazing.*

Nothin' starts with an E – right? The love had to be in yer, waitin' to come out. But we didn't know about any of that. We were driftin' towards a regulation existence n then, just like that, it's an ordinary day at the Chef, I'm 'avin' a cheeky smoke out the back, n some mystical dude from Essex blazes up n changes everythin'.

Now I'm a talker, but he was givin' it the full chatty geezer act, *oi oi, M25, blah, blah, blah, Sunrise, loved up boys and girls, do your mind a favour Son.* N he gives me a flyer: free party. We'd been to parties, n most of 'em were free, so I didn't have a fookin' Scooby what he was wangin' on about, but what I'll always be is a champion blagger, so obviously I said *Cool, see yer there,* n the next thing yer know, we're doin' it: it's the weekend, n we're off in the Courgette. Phoned the number he told us to, went to the services it told us to, followed a convoy when someone told us to, n took the first thing someone told us to, n then, well – those angels from above, came down n spread their wings with Doves.

Eight hours in a cow shed with a loada strangers who were different. Make up by Zippo light, wardrobe by pattern-happy, colour blind crazies, with hats n hankies n dummies n shirts off n smileys n smocks n sunglasses, n hot girls with messy hair n short shorts – all without bad vibes. Lotsa hugs – I've always liked 'em – n everyone was smilin'. There were rumours Ian Beale from EastEnders was there, dancin' on the roof. It didn't matter, he woulda been welcome: it was that out of control. Does that sound different? Well it was. We got lucky with a way out – all thanks to a bloke who's name I never even knew. Is that bad? The magical thing is, no – n nothin' was ever the same again.

We went back to the Chef. N we tried. But our professional standards must have started to drop a little. I think I accidentally missed a few days. N when I say missed, I mean, I missed 'em meself n all – I was a victim too. N then came the day I thought of nickin' me tea – schemes of petty fast-food crime which ultimately made me a better, more financially viable person. I needed an income source compatible with a new lifestyle to which we'd become deeply committed: so I found one, n we stopped botherin' to go in.

So. Chrissy had his secret obsession with his old man: with what he's lost. He's already – how'd yer say it? – interestin'. N then rave hits. It gives him back this feelin' he knows. But he's got no job, we're never at home with Mo, his structure's all gone, n he's packin' his head full of chemicals every single weekend. He was ready to blow. Anythin' could've happened. N it took a bit of time – but summink did. I'm just still not sure what.

• • •

'I'm seeing things.'

He's back. Back in the room. He's not though really. He's still back there. Miles away. Years away. 1992. With the bass n the beats. On rewind.

4

THEN, 1992

Chris

Fantazia.

I'm in The Main Room. Am I? It's bigger than a room. I don't hear anything. It lasts forever. I like to be in the middle so I can't see the sides: then there's nothing else, it's just us, in The Republic. Runcie says if you closed your eyes and never opened them again, this would never end.

'They tried to prove me wrong – they couldn't.'

I've taken my shirt off. Runcie's lost his spanner. Or hasn't brought a spanner. I can't remember. I feel a bit dizzy – sick. I can't feel my lips. I concentrate on my tummy, the outside of my tummy, the wobbly bit, and there's a rhythm: step left, watch my wobble, step right, watch my wobble, step left, watch my wobble. I'm "in a groove" but decide I should do something with my hands. I decide to be a marching soldier. Again. I'm not moving forwards or backwards. Just step left, watch my wobble, step right, watch my wobble, step left, watch my wobble, step right, watch my wobble. Eyes closed, rubbing myself on the chest. I lose a lot of time to hardcore. I wonder if it's possible to lose all your time to hardcore? It might be a bit much? I open my eyes again just in case.

'It's gonna be massive see Chris. Massive massive. Happy punters, everywhere you look, in a big black, spiritual love hole, all under one roof – it don't get more religious than that. Easter's come early.

Runcie said that, and then lost his pills on the way in. And then got them back again. But some were gone. Tax.

'I'm the Robin Hood of Rave – beatin' the system, helpin' the people party, lookin' after me crew. It's a film for our times that is. A shite film for our times, coz of Kevin Costcutter – but the fact it was like the biggest, box office, blockbuster ever or summink, n old Spotty Chops was number one in the hit parade for two hundred weeks, tells yer all yer need to know. This land is a-changin'. When that wally Kinnock gets in, he gets all the free pills he wants, this all gets legalised, I'll become an approved contractor, n I'll be happy as Larry Levan, payin' me tax, doin' the job I love. Coz not payin' tax is strictly for yer lispy Tory inbreds. I'd even get Joe Bloggs to make me an *I Heart Tax* T-shirt. Payin' tax now though? That's shite – but fook it, we're here to party. Where's Student? I need to give him a slap n a hug.'

Rooms, rooms, rooms. Easygroove, Mickey Finn, Ellis Dee, Bad Boy T, Slipmat, Lady J, Top Buzz, XTC, MC Conrad, Ratty, DJ Seduction. I copied the names out – on a piece of paper.

Searching The Republic.

A dragon breathes fire.
And then…something? Gone.
I can't see.

• • •

Everything drips. Again.

It's hot. I'm hot. Very, very hot. I know better than to just be in my pants though – last time it "caused an upset." The whiteness of the pants was part of the problem, which the adverts never tell you. A damp whiteness – a see-through whiteness. But a man came and hugged me and he wasn't even a clean, gentle gay – he smelt of crisps and showed me his girlfriend and a tattoo on his rude finger – so if it wasn't a problem to him, why was it a problem to the bouncers?

'They're on the outside Chris – *Your name's not down, you're not coming in* – they're peerin' inside, n they just don't get it. They wanna crush skulls, but there's no reason to, so they're totally brain-fooked. The best they can do is look for summink to stop: they're desperate. N that's where you n yer see-through pants come in. But to be clear: don't come in yer pants.'

There are so many people now. I get confused – I'm stuck on a thought. I'm looking for Runcie. Am I?

'Meet yer in Chill Out when I've concluded me business.'

He must have concluded his business by now. Although he did have a lot of business to conclude.

'More than ever before Chris. Huge.'

Somehow I find him, make it over. He doesn't come to the Chill Out to chill out because – well, he comes because this is where the girls sit and talk and dance. Julie's here. She has a cigarette, holding it out while she is tonguing a boy. There is always a male on Julie. I would find it really awful having someone on me like that, all the time.

'She looks bored Chris, but she's not. She's doin' what she loves.'

Runcie, proud of Julie, surrounded by "satisfied customers." I can't hear. I don't hear. I give him a hug and discover that I need a wee. I'll check the taps while I'm there.

'I'll check the taps.'

'Cool Bro, no need, but no problem – stay tuff yeah?'

I'm already moving.

● ● ●

The girls are in the Chill Out, the men are in the bogs. Maybe some girls are in the girl bogs? Maybe some men are in the girl bogs? But the main point I've been wanting to make to myself in this queue, is that I am in the bogs. There are lots and lots of men here, that was the point. And whilst that means I can't get to the loo because there seems to be no…system…it also means I can think.

When I think, I stop worrying. But I'm supposed to be remembering something. It's not that I need a wee, that's obvious: I'm in the bogs and I need a wee. It's not about the taps – on – Runcie always finds a way. But did you know, that if you can't remember something, you should wash your hands? Mum taught me. Runcie says she just told me that so I wash my hands. So it works, because here I am, washing my hands before my wee, which is a nice feeling and saves time, because after, I will just want to get on with my life. So I wash my hands. And I remember.

• • •

Blank space.

• • •

8 am.

• • •

Where is everybody?

• • •

Runcie

After Fantazia.

The venues are bigger. The line ups are bigger. The queues are bigger (mint). The meatheads on the door are bigger. N for those with stakes, the stakes are gettin' as high as we all wanna feel. So I pay me taxes, inside I'm careful – OK, I'm a bit careful – n the nights are still, really, gut-fookinly good, so good in fact, that this one's already a mornin'.

'Alright Mr Mornin'? Soz for keepin' yer waitin', we've been 'avin' a little party, but can I just say: top one, nice one, give us a hug.'

About 10,000 of me new pals are with us, breathin' happy clouds of warm air into the mist. Meadows. Horizons. Mud on the road. Proper. Spring has sprung, we're takin' what was in there, out here, n nothin' can touch us, as we stumble into the near future.

But there's a problem. Outside The Republic they're afraid – of who we are n what we want – so our journey into the near future, n whatever marvellous mayhem's on offer, is goin' nowhere. We found our cars n our mini-buses n our coaches, all of us, but now all the fearful fookers who didn't want us to arrive in the first place, are makin' it impossible for us to leave, with (fook da) police n daft Farmer Palmer types n all, blockin' up gates n lanes with tractors. *Red sky at night, get off my land – what were the skies like when you were young?* Forget yer livestock, feel the love, coz we don't want yer fields – we want yer souls, in that room with us. Oh, n then we want milkshake. Not from yer beautiful cows though, eyes like Flyin' Saucers – from the services.

The Runce. Chris. Stude. N Julie – dressed up, Cardiff-style. Why are we laughin'? Coz we don't need a reason, that's why. Remember that.

• • •

Back now – where it all started a million hours ago, with Julie n Student n Clockwork n Disco Sean n Crisp Wank n Clare, who's just Clare. 101 flyers on the walls.

Crashed out with Chris, to keep an eye. I worry about bein' crushed if he falls into the kind of deep slumber he should: for now though, on this luxuriant double mattress, elegantly slotted between the crap furniture in Julie's lounge, the curtains are closed, n the telly bathes us in the warm yellow light of The Hitman n Her. An old one. We salute the ravers who have slipped through the net; the wig dude in his Tarzan nappy; Strachan, lookin' hot, Michaela not Gordon. Delightful sights n sounds roll on, a cosy background rhythm to some epic pill(ow) talk.

'Ask 99% of the population what they want, they couldn't – wouldn't – tell yer. N it's crazy, coz as a human see Chris, yer really just a special kinda dog, that only wants to be happy, but also has this innate ability to express itself n connect. N that's all I am – a very sophisticated dog. Outside The Republic though, they don't understand, so they get served up shite: drinkin', fightin', Kylie n Jase…OK, I love Kylie…n I love Jase n all, I bet he's up for the party. But the world of Waterman there – that's bad. So: what I want is for them to be able to ask for what they want.'

Chris looks confused, which is not fookin' surprisin'. I try n reel him back in with some food talk.

'Baked Alaska. I could eat that right now. 1982, school trip to the Bayeux Tapestry. Paedo Perry, history teacher, took us off piste, n we went out for dinner in this haute cuisine – posh nosh – barn. Probably so he could get pissed n summon up the courage to do some paedo-in'. Anyways – Baked Alaska. It changed me life – it was the first time I understood yer could swallow summink n alter yer mood. It's got a lot to answer for. What'd yer eat right now Chris? If we could move?'

Pause.

'Bananas and custard.'

He has it every day.

'I have it every day.'

But what's he thinkin'? There are depths that remain unexplored by the masses, but at times like this, when his guard is down, yer get a peek into the abyss.

'More people are comin' to the raves now Runce?'

'They are.'

Pause. Pause. Another pause. Slowin' down.

'Is that bad?'

I've thought about this a lot. I give meself all week to get me noggin in order – work out what I want, think, believe. Everyone should do it.

'No. It could be good. Very good. Nothin's changed really. Yeah, there's a few more knobheads. But people can change.'

He stays lookin' at the telly, for a long, long time.

'But some people. I see them and…I wonder: why have you come here? What is it that you want?'

We're stuck between the light of day n the dark of sleep, makin' notes, before fractal oblivion descends. Half asleep, but searchin', thinkin' hard. I'm thinkin' hard about the secret.

N Chris? Feelin'. Thinkin'. But what?

Stuck on a thought.

5

NOW

Chris

I start with the facts. The main fact is that there's a light brown stain on the ceiling. It looks like the Isle of Wight.

I fell asleep in my recliner last night whilst making notes. It's all happening so fast. New things to see. New notes in my pad. But then rain happened. Cold rain. A lot. Not good. Because it created "The Case of the Leaky Roof." Which created a disaster. Which is making me fiddly diddly.

F (for Flack, Foyle and Frost etc.) all the way through to M (for Maigret, Marple, Mayo, up to Montalbano) have been leaked on. VHS tapes. I will try to count them. Now. Of all the times. Now. The case work of...several different detectives, possibly gone forever. Yet Morse walks away unhurt.

At least Columbo is safe.

F to M are placed across the lounge – which is also the Interview Room – floor. I have lined them up like dominoes. I'm Norris McWhirter. I don't think about A to E. I won't learn from N to Z today. I can't. I turn on the radio. I turn off the radio. I open the window to see if that will help. It doesn't.

I will never stop. I'm looking for the lessons you won't find in the rule book. Because there is no rule book. Apart from my rule book: My Detective Rule Book. Which is a collection of lessons that are not in the rule book – because there is no rule book. I find this hard to explain. I have tried explaining it to Runcie.

'A thousand times. You've tried explaining it, a thousand times,' he has said.

But he's not a detective. I'm not saying he couldn't be – we don't do that, and Hamish Macbeth was an OK detective and he smoked pot – but he might need to cut down.

I'm learning from the best – the rules of the people who break the rules.

'It would help if I could see this rule book of yours,' he has also said.

'You can when it's finished.'

'When will that be?'

'Never.'

You can even learn from Morse – what not to do – and the police too. Crimewatch. Not very realistic, but it reminds you, some crimes go unsolved – which is where us detectives come in.

I'm a very good detective. There are always cases. But there's only one that matters. And I have to be ready.

I'm going to have to leave my bungalow.

· · ·

The library. I wait for it to open.

And then it opens.

'Can you direct me to your Columbo section?'

I came here to see what Frosts they've got, in case I need to rebuild, but as soon as I arrived I just thought "Columbo." Because there are gaps.

I should have done this years ago.

'Columbo? How are you spelling that?'

'Columbo.'

'How are you spelling that?'

'I'm not. You'll have to though.'

'Pardon me?'

'I'm not spelling it – I'm saying it. I'm afraid I can't play... spelling. I'm a detective.'

I show him my note pad and what it looks like when I start making notes in it. He's nervous. He'd crumble in court. I show what I've written: "Would not be a reliable witness."

'Just a few more questions, nothing to worry about sir. I thought you were being...'

I consult my note pad again. I'd written this word down the other day. Just in case I needed it.

'..."ob-struct-ive," but I can see now that you just cannot spell, even though you work down the library.'

There's a long pause. Who will crack first?

'Right; could you show me how you're spelling that?'

'You've never heard of Columbo?'

'Well I've heard of Colombia obviously, and a long time ago there was a terrible thing called the Columbine–'

'No – Columbo.'

He laughs. At a time like this?

'Well, there's the detective Columbo, the daft fella with–'

I stop what I'm doing – which is making notes – and then start again. Faster and faster.

'Can I take your name please sir?'

'I'm Peter, but can I–'

'Peter. What do you see when you see Columbo? A fool with a funny eye?'

'Look, unless you can tell me a bit more about what you're looking for, there's a queue building up and…'

I do a "sweep of the room," taking in information "almost photo-graphically." There's one man standing behind me, poking a plastic bag into the top of a tartan shopping trolley.

'That's not a queue – that's a man. You can't have a queue of a man. You can't spell Columbo and you don't know what a queue is – either you are not cut out for your job, or you are being deliberately…obstructive. May I remind you that all this time, there's probably a body on a slab in a morgue.'

He looks concerned. He should do. Not because there's a body on a slab in a morgue. Although there probably is. And there definitely has been. He just looks concerned.

I close my eyes a little and "accept the things I cannot change."

'Are you after a Columbo DVD?'

Nearly.

'Got any videos?'

•   •   •

I'm back at home. Runcie is there. He has a key. Today he has Julie's hair dryer too. Because he tries to solve my problems.

'Always here Chrissy, coz once I was not.'

I feel fiddly diddly. He says that "actually we probably shouldn't use the hair dryer" – but he likes going to see Julie anyway because she tells him about sex.

I am holding onto a Marple, thinking about lost Frosts and the gaps in my Columbos.

'Yer alright Chrissy? Yer look down? Thought about 'avin' a wank?'

'That's not going to bring me back F to M.'

'Be good if it did though Aladdin.'

I get stuck thinking about this.

'I feel…fiddly diddly.'

'N yer've been to the library on the bus, already?'

I point very carefully, right into my eye.

'Always…looking.'

And when you look from the bus, you see. Things. For your files.

I look out of the kitchen window – the Incident Room is out there. Waiting for its incident. Soon.

'I mean. They've got a few of the other thing at the library, erm…?'

'DVD's? Definitely not worth making the move over Big Lad? I could even get yer a laptop – very reasonable price, as in, free. Digitise it all for yer. Create a central database. Give it a name, yer know, like C.H.R.I.S…central…home of recordins…interviews…n studies. A password only you know – n perhaps me for IT purposes. *Username n password please. Sorry, wrong password, yer locked out. Speak to the Head of IT. Who's that? Mr Runce – make an appointment arsehole.* I'm not talkin' to you there by the way Chrissy – just a bit a role play scenario. Imagine that though? Everythin' in one place. Stick it in a cloud. Detect on the go.'

I imagine it – for a long time. Then.

'No. I like videos.'

'Still collectin'?'

'You can't stop a collection. You have to keep going.'

Runcie shrugs and lies back down on my sofa, his head on a cushion.

And then he jumps up.

'Jesus! What the fook is that?!'

'That's my Town alarm clock. It's time.'

'Don't tell me? Shoestring's on ITV4?'

'It's time to solve a problem.'

Because practice, makes perfect.

• • •

Runcie

The Interview Room is about to have its first interview. All the action still seems to be based around me makin' brews though, while Chrissy sorta scurries about in slow chaos, settin' up, leavin' the room, n warnin' me to stay put, with a quick turn, a stop, a silent hand: like some sorta mute traffic warden.

There's a lotta waitin'. There's the bit where he had to find a table. The bit where he had to work out how to stick two chairs either side of it. The bit gettin' 'em round: Smith Versus Kapoor. The bit with them waitin' n all, sittin' not lookin' at each other, arms folded, while Chris waddled about turnin' lights on, off, on, offerin' brews, which again I made of course, n lightin' joss sticks – which the fat Brummie tutted about, coz joss sticks make this whole thing a stitch up, right? It all goes on for what feels like hours, meanin' I'm baked. Never knowinly under-baked though, so don't sweat it. N then finally, Chrissy is ready. *The Case of the Neighbours at War*, is about to be solved – maybe.

'I've got you some coffee Mr Smith, as I know you like coffee. As well as tea.'

It's a tin of coffee Julie took from her bank manager's office: he's put a tin of coffee in front of Mr Smith. He must have been worryin' about the implicit bias of them joss sticks n all – so he's evened things up a bit. With coffee.

'Right. Mr Smith. Mr Kapoor. Welcome. We are here to help you make friends. I am very experienced at making friends. For the tape, we have in the room–'

'Hold on – what fucking tape?'

I should intervene – but Chris can cope. He's right at home with this kind of madness. It's what he's been workin' towards – problem solvin' – so I leave him to it, content just to enjoy the proceedins horizontally from the saggy old couch I've made me stoned home.

'Now, Mr Smith. There's not actually a tape. That was just…words, so these proceedings will not erm…in any way be recorded, and "everything that takes place within this room will be confidential." Right. Erm, where was I? Runce?'

'Friends?'

'Yes. I am here so you can make friends. As, well, you see, I have been friends with people for…many years? Mr Runce here for example.'

Chris is doin' a TED Talk on friends.

'So using your socks, we're going to try and get you to be friends. Move past this business with the, erm, fence.'

We're gettin' down to the nitty-gritty now.

'Have you brought your sock puppets?'

Already it seems to be workin' a bit – they just shared a look, acknowledgin' their mutual shame at bein' involved in this whole fookin' farce.

'Mmm, yeah – are you taking the piss with this or what?'

Mr Kapoor looks doubtful too.

'I've asked both of you – and it's very important that it's both of you, for…erm…reasons – to make a sock puppet. Please can I see them.'

It's almost a stand-off. Who'll be the first to show they've fallen for the sock puppet gag? 'Cept of course, this is Chris. N it's problem-solvin'. So this is for real.

Mr Kapoor chances it.

'Ah – very nice. Sport socks Mr Kapoor. Do you play sport?'

'No.'

'Right. And Mr Smith? Hold yours up too please?'

He does it, reluctantly, flashin' me a look which confirms he'll kill me if this gets out. I flash him me winnin' smile.

'Good. So now we are going to see what your sock puppets have to say for themselves. Let them explain your feelings.'

He's now talkin' to their sock-puppeted hands.

'And don't be offended by what you hear. You're just a sock puppet and so are…you. OK – are we ready?'

'Not really.'

'Good. Mr Kapoor. What's your sock puppet called?'

'Sanjiv.'

'OK – the same as you. Good. Mr Smith?'

The fat, racist bastard looks away in shame.

'Socky.'

'OK Sanjiv: tell Socky what your complaint is.'

There's a pause. Chris looks-down-looks-left-looks-right-looks-down-looks-at Sock Puppet Sanjiv, who speaks.

'I like to be able to see across the neigbouring–'

'Sorry to interrupt. That's your voice Mr Kapoor. Sanjiv needs his own voice, or this can get personal – and we don't want it to be personal.'

Sock Puppet Sanjiv clears his throat. He's lookin' at the ground. He looks up at Socky n Mr Smith, n begins again. He has quite a high-pitched voice now, sorta like a shit tranny.

'I like to be able to see across the gardens towards the park. But Socky has added a fence topper, which blocks my view.' Sock Puppet Sanjiv pauses – then looks down n finishes. 'I'm very sad.'

I get me fancy phone out n carefully start filmin'.

Chris has a finger over his lip. He's lookin' as sensitive n thoughtful as it's possible for him to look – a heart attack candidate in tracky bottoms n a Ned's Atomic Dustbin T-shirt Julie nicked for him in 1990. We didn't even like Ned's Atomic Dustbin.

'Poor Sanjiv. He says he's sad. What do you think about that Socky?'

'Well'. Socky sounds like Ray Winstone. 'I'm sorry that Sanjiv is sad. But maybe Sanjiv needs to man up a bit. It's a fence – one that's been here a lot longer than he has.'

'Meaning what exactly?'

Sock Puppet Sanjiv is on edge, but Chris moves quite quickly – for him – to smooth shite along.

'Socky. If you were upset about something yourself…your socky self…what would you want Sanjiv to do?'

'I'd want him to ask me about–'

But Mr Smith has gone out of character.

'–I don't know how to do this. It's absolutely ridiculous!'

Chrissy though stands – to him, the solution is obvious.

'Show us. Just pretend you're Sanjiv, asking Socky if he is ok.'

He focuses. Deep breath. N now Mr Smith, aka Socky, is pretendin' to be Sock Puppet Sanjiv, askin' if Socky is OK.

'Are you OK Socky? I'm sorry if I have done something to–'

'Higher with the voice please Mr Smith – and slightly Indian.'

'I'm sorry if I've done something to hurt you.'

'And then how would you feel Mr Smith – as Socky – if you knew Sanjiv was so sensitive.'

Socky – Winstone style – can't escape from the truth.

'I'd feel…better about things.'

'Great. So let's try and see if Socky, can make Sanjiv feel better. Let's see if Socky and Sanjiv can make friends. Sanjiv is sad Socky – what do you say?'

'I'm sorry to hear that Sanjiv.'

Chrissy urges Socky on.

'How can I help?'

He's like a conductor – he's ownin' this madness.

'Sanjiv – how can Socky help? In your high voice remember?'

'Could Socky possibly put the fence topper a little lower, so that Sanjiv can still look out across the gardens?'

'Socky?'

Fatty Smith sighs.

'Yeah I suppose so.'

'And Socky. Is there anything you want from Sanjiv, to make you happy?'

'No. I just don't want to ever have to do this again.'

'Good, great great.'

Chris looks proudly at the two of 'em, a psycho Earth Mother who's taught her kids to ignore the playground taunts: *breastfeeding at eight is beautiful little warriors, I will protect you with the sacred sage.*

'And?'

'And what?'

'And if Sanjiv gets upset another time he can…?'

A bigger sigh.

'Yeah he can pick up the phone.'

'Or pop round?' says Sock Puppet Sanjiv hopefully, with his high voice.

'Phone's best.'

• • •

We're back out in the caravan. Lists everywhere. Steamy windows. I've made us a coupla brews n tried huntin' down some biscuits – actual ones, not photos – but they were all gobbled back inside the house by Chrissy n Captain Brexit.

Chrissy watches back the highlights, unemotional, n I let him bask in the professional glory of the moment, before askin' why he did it.

'How's this fit in with the bigger picture?'

'It's in my Detective Rule Book. People do things for a reason. You just have to find out…the reason.'

Right.

'And also, practice makes perfect. Then I will solve the case and everything will be…perfect.'

Mmm. Unlikely. He looks happy though – 'til he squints at his note pad, a problem emergin'.

'Oh.'

'What?'

'More jobs. There was a letter. Got to see a new head doctor. Julie's coming though. In case there's information.'

'Does she know this yet?'

Naughty Chrissy. We've had this conversation before – he knows he's supposed to try n respect that some of the grown-ups have commitments. But his mind's gone n his heart is true, so what can yer do? He shrugs, a busy four-year-old who's not even sure why he just poured a bucket of Transformers down the lav.

'OK Chrissy – I'll call her. Me Hilltop's outside. Drop you both off.'

'Yes. Then Job Club…Job Centre. With a plan.'

Uh-oh.

'Tell me more?'

'The final step in my mission to become….'

He's writin' his name in lights here…

'…a detective.'

'Mmm, right, OK. N that step is?'

'Telling them I want to sign off.'

Oh no.

'Why in Shaun Ryder's name would yer do that?'

•   •   •

Chris

Doctors always send you to see different doctors.

That's how it works.

Dr Watts has gone a long time without sending me to another doctor, so he's the doctoring champion. But now he has sent me to another doctor, "because of the employment people." He has sent me to a Dr Man. A head doctor. A head detective?

'Just act normal,' Runcie said.

I suck my pencil and watch Julie over by the lady at the desk. With the computer. With the information. You must always look for information.

I'm not sure I am normal. There's a problem with my head: remembering. But there might be problem with the whole of my head: they haven't decided. So they've sent me to Dr Man. Or a doctor who is a man? I'm not sure. And then he comes and says hello and we go in his office "for a nice chat."

•   •   •

He shuffles his papers a lot. His desk is very neat. Then he gets more papers out of some drawers, shuffles them, makes a small mess and then shuffles it tidy. He also squeezes his nose. I suck my pencil.

I haven't met a head detective yet who could be a real detective. They never seem to solve the problem they're so upset about (my head), and they always seem to want me to solve it for them.

'Have you ever wanted to start a family Chris?'

We're talking about childhood – apparently. About mums. And dads.

'Mmm. No. Well I like children – I'm just not always allowed near them.'

The doctor who is a man shuffles his papers again, quickly – searching perhaps for a clue he didn't spot the first time.

'Sorry, why are you not allowed near kids?'

'Oh, I sat on one once by mistake. I'm not very, erm…ballet. Like. But I do like…children – and they like me.'

The Dr Man man's papers are tidy. He squeezes his nose again and then looks at me. I make a note.

'I see you're making notes?'

'Mmm. Yes. If I don't make notes, I can't remember Dr Man.'

I've written "nose?". I change it to "nosey?" and then my pad is full. Oh.

'It's actually Dr Stone-man. You were saying that kids like you?'

Dr Stone Man.

'Yes. We're the same you see – me, kids – because we only think about things we like. Such as detectives.'

'But this detective idea? The idea of solving crimes and having problems to solve? Do you find that makes you anxious at all – or worried?'

'No. If I start remembering things, I start thinking, so I don't have time to be worried.'

He takes his glasses off. Puts them on again. Stares. Waits.

'Because the thing is…well, I know something. I'm just not totally sure…what?'

'Interesting–'

'It's like when you need a poo but you don't realise it yet.'

'Right. I understand that your own family life has had some…gaps. But you have good friends?'

'I have a lot of very good friends. Student. Julie. Runcie.'

'Ah, yes. A very special friend. Stephen is it? He's like a parent to you? In a way?'

'Yes, I think we are both sort of the parents. To each other. Because of the…gaps.'

'Right, so–'

'But everything I know, I learned from TV.'

Shuffle. Shuffle. Dr Stone Man can't find this on his papers either.

'Right. Documentaries, that kind of thing?'

'No – detectives. Erm. It's all in my book. And, well, I mean, look: I am 48, I am alive, I've got my own bungalow. The council gave it me. I'm "a success story." '

'I can't argue with that Chris. But happiness, and ultimately a sense of meaning – those are the accepted measurements for success in the long term. Some would say that getting out there – forming connections, exposing oneself to life's challenges – is pretty central to that kind of growth.'

I stare at him. I don't really know what he is talking about. I try to encourage him. I smile and pat his hand but he pulls it away.

'How about, I don't know – going to college? Or an evening course? How about getting qualified for a job, something that really interests you?'

Oh dear. Poor Dr Stone…Man.

'I wasn't good at…subjects. At school. I was only really a winner in PE – because of Kick Pringle.'

'What was that?'

'Well. I'd have the ball, in football, you see – and the game was that everyone else had to try and get it back, by kicking me.'

Dr Stone Man just took his glasses off again, very quickly.

'That's barbaric. Your PE teacher let this happen?'

'Mr Hinchcliffe? No, he always did cross country so he could go to the pub.'

'Hmmmph. That's terribly sad don't you think Chris – a gaggle of other children, kicking you?'

'Oh no – it was my idea.'

'Why? That's not the way to make friends Chris.'

'Really? I have lots of very good friends. Although I've mainly been watching telly anyway, so…'

'That sounds a little sad to me too Chris. Are you a member of any clubs?'

Am I? Mmm. Oh yes. I was.

'A.A.'

'Riiiight? Have you got a car?'

'No.'

'Then why would you need to be a member of the A.A. eh?'

'A.A.'

'Pardon me?'

'You said A.A.A. but it's not: it's just A.A.'

'Yes. So you like to drive?'

What an odd question. He must be playing good questioner, bad questioner. On his own.

'No – I don't have a car.'

'Then why are you a member of the A.A.?'

'Alcoholics Anonymous? Because I went along once.'

'Right, now I understand. And what prompted that? Would you say you have a problematic relationship with alcohol?'

He's shuffling papers again.

'No, I don't drink – and neither did anyone at the meeting actually. Even though drink is all they talked about.'

'So you're not an alcoholic?'

'No – I don't drink.'

'And you only went to A.A. just the once?'

'Yes.'

Dr Stone Man stares at me again.

'So you're not really a member of the club of A.A. as such?'

'No.'

'So when I asked you if you were a member of any clubs, you could have just said no, yes?'

This is really confusing.

• • •

The nice lady in the Job Centre looks at her computer screen – a big box.

'Still a couple of weeks until your review Chris but – ah yes, here it is, I see, they referred you for another medical advisory. Sorry about that. He's efficient though this Dr Stoneman, I'll give him that. It says you're "fit for work." But let me get this right, you're saying that's good, and you've popped in because you want to sign off? I know I should be pleased about this but…why Mr Pringle?'

'Just put "Wants to be the local Boon." '

'I'm not putting that Chris. What's a boon anyway?'

'It's a who. Not a what. Ken Boon. But call him Boon. Like: "Where's Boon? That sod owes me fifty nicker." '

'Does he? Or are you…no, he doesn't, does he? What's so special about this Ken Boon?'

'I won't say he was a detective. Because he wasn't. Mum's Brendan would say that "he's got absolutely no industry-recognised qualifications whatsoever." In Scottish.'

'So what is he then?'

'Was. A solver of...problems. And I like solving problems too. Like Boon. And now I need to be available to solve problems all the time, so coming here all the time is, in fact, a problem, which I am trying to solve, by saying...I will now do a job, as long as it has problems in it. Anything.'

'Okaaaay...this sounds promising...but—'

'I have experience. 1: Two neighbours, one fence, solved. 2: Fat Julie wants some cock, where's she going to get it from? Not me by the way, I just come up with suggestions based on my files, solved. 3: Who will bring me milk for my cup of tea if I run out and don't want to leave my bungalow? Runcie. Solved. All examples.'

'Right...'

'But then there's also a big problem. Which needs solving. And needs all of my...'

I point at my brain.

'...and that's the problem.'

I am examined closely, slowly and for quite a long period, over glasses. I decide this is better than through glasses or without glasses. It's a "tell me more" look. I need one. Because it works. Because now I am telling her more.

'See, Boon was, in actual fact, a fireman, but he gave it up, to solve problems full time. For money. And that's what I want to do. Give up being unemployed so I can solve problems. For money. Plus, solve a big one, because I have to.'

'Right, so what you're actually saying...again...is that you want to be a private investigator – sorry, detective.'

'No, what I'm saying is, I already am a detective, but now I want to get paid.'

I am happy. I have explained this really well. She has put her pen down. And we've reached the moment. The moment of...I wrote this down...I have a quick look at my pad..."destiny." She folds her arms, puts her head on one side and looks at me. I can't tell what her face means because there seems to be a smile, a frown, a sigh and something else. All of that, on one face. She picks up her pen again, leans towards me and whispers.

'So. Chris...if we could get you on a business support scheme, get you some mentoring, maybe some start-up support? Advice, that kind of thing? How would that sound?'

Oh dear. That sounds like a job – which wasn't what was meant to happen at all.

'Well I'm sorry Chris – you're flipping...dreaming.'

Oh thank goodness for that. She's angry – she might cry. She looks around. She leans in further.

'This isn't some, some sort of, er, utopia Chris...'

Flashback.

'...this is a flipping flip-storm – pardon my French, I'll keep my voice down – and I'm sure you're not into politics Chris, but it's upsetting. Things have come to a head, I'll tell you that. Something big is going to happen.'

How does she know?

'So I'm really sorry Chris, I can't help you. I'm not willing to tick a box that says, yes, I'll let you sign off because one day you might set yourself up as a problem solver, and earn a living doing what you love. Because they'll never have you back. So listen – let's stick to what we know. Six more months I'll give you before we have to revisit this again. I'll just confirm here that you've continued to look for work, and we'll see you in a fortnight. Take some government issue pens as a bonus. Walk away with some-thing, please – as well as your self-respect.'

I pat her shoulder. She's a very good friend of mine. She shakes her head: at the state of things. I make a head note: "<u>Would</u> be a reliable witness." I won't remember it though.

'Got any pads?'

•   •   •

Ready.

Columbo. Frost. Bergerac. Holmes. Watson. Foyle. Vera. Marple. Magnum. Maigret. Frank Burnside. Wycliffe. Stella Gibson. Jim Carver. Rosemary. Thyme. DCI Barnaby. DCI Banks. Inspector Lynley. Dennis Booker. McCallum. Strike. Shoestring. Commissioner Gordon. Wexford. Hetty Wainthrop. Michael Knight. Poirot. Petrocelli. Pete Ritter. George Gently. Jack Regan. George Carter. Rebus. The other Rebus. Ironside. Jessica Fletcher. Starsky. Hutch. Chief Inspector Jane Tennison. Bosley. Poncherello. Erick Estrada. Rick Hunter. Monk. Brian Lane. Jack Halford. Jimmy Perez. David Addison. Maddy Hayes. Steve Arnott. Kate Fleming. Dangerous Davies. Inspector Jean Darbley. Kojak. Miss Fisher. Scott. Bailey. Fitz. Mrs Bradley. Dale Cooper. Sarah Lund. Inspector Sledge Hammer. Jonathan Creek. Mayo. Pembleton. Leroy Jethro Gibbs. T.J. Hooker. Montalbano. Chambers. Keating. Brother Cadfael. Father Brown. Remington Steele. Laura Holt. Quincy M.E. Hardcastle. McCormick. Grissom. Lewis. Jim Rockford. Luther. Saga Noren. Richard Poole. Lacey. Cagney. Tubbs. Crockett. Pascoe. Dalziel. Boon. Dr Mark Sloan. Gene Hunt. Sipowicz. Kelly. Campion. Hamish

Macbeth. Inspector Goole. Jonathan Hart. Jennifer Hart. Columbo. Columbo. Columbo. Pringle. Detective Chris Pringle.

Everything is happening. Everything is ready. The clues are reminding me: the case needs solving. The memories need remembering. And I remember: that after, after Fantazia…I remembered.

6

THEN, 1992

Chris

Runcie sleeps and I don't sleep.

Still in Fantazia, spinning. Spinning, and then I walked. I was walking. It was quiet. I was looking for Runcie. Around the room, around the rooms. I found Runcie – the Chill Out – but I was still stuck on a thought. So he wasn't the thought.

The water was on – in the bogs. Why did I go to the bogs? I went to the bogs because I needed the wee. So that wasn't the thought.

I looked at my hands under the taps. I turned them round. It was a feeling. I put my head down. Into the sink. I splashed water on my face, again, and again, and again. People patted me on the back. They didn't say "hurry up you freak, stop fackin' blah blah," it was "lemme get in there geezer, phwooaaar, need a wee, where's me, oh no, eee's gone." We're very good friends.

I washed my face.

I turned my head, my body, to the right.

And I remember what I'm supposed to be remembering – who I was supposed to be remembering.

The face wasn't in the crowd now – it was against the wall. I'd seen it before, but here it was, here he was…against the wall. Next to me. Holding the wall – his head against it. Looking down, mouth open.

He was trying to get something out of his mouth: a long… spit. He couldn't. It was hanging down from his lips. His tongue chased after it, trying to…I don't know. In. Out. One or the other – he was trying to do one or the other, but he couldn't do either. He banged – on the wall, with the side of his fist, as if it was the wall's fault, and then he put out a straight arm, to balance himself – his legs were wide apart, really wide apart – and he used the back of his arm, his shirt, to wipe away the problem. A bit of the spit hit his shoe, and he put his hands on his knees to balance and take a look. He banged his head, on the wall.

I kept on watching. And he turned, eyes closed, and he was mumbling. I couldn't hear. And he wasn't alone: they were coming. I didn't want to see. I didn't want to feel.

It wasn't what I wanted and I didn't like it – because it was exactly what I wanted.

7

NOW

Runcie

It's nearly dark outside, n Chrissy's flickin' through the property pages of The Chronicle, talkin' at me. It's the weekend. A time to rest his weary mind? No.

'As I prepare to "roll out my services" beyond…erm…'

'Yer imagination?'

'…to a wider erm "client base," well the only rule, because there are no rules, is if it isn't a problem, I won't try and fix it.'

'Yer sound like Batman. *Makin' Shit Town a better place for one n all.*'

'Batman's not real.'

'N Boon is?'

'Yes.'

'But Batman's not?'

'He's a man, who is also a bat.'

'Well, yer've got me there – all that hangin' round with some teenage lad's a bit suss n all: *Come with me, stick these pants on, yer'll look like a Robin.* Get out there with someone yer own age yer wally. Like Boon. Batman n Boon – awesome. Where did Boon work?'

'Birmingham.'

'Right – well he'd be happy enough to move to Gotham then, even if Shermans are all fookin' mental.'

'Batman doesn't exist.'

'Nor does Boon.'

Silence.

The week was long. He's not built for action-packed schedules this lad, n he's away with the detective fairies right now, that's for sure – but still, a lot happened.

First he created harmony in the hood.

Then he met his latest state-sponsored shrink. There's always summink round the corner for him like that – social worker, noggin appointment – coz they wanna give what he's got a name, it's a developmental disorder, an intellectual disability, Asperger's, OCD, mutism for fook's sake. There's never been a diagnosis, but they don't like missin' out on prescribin' the treatment: they want him in a lifelong straightjacket of copin' skills, workshops n medication. But really, what's crazier: Chrissy thinkin' he's a detective, or this desperation to tell him that he isn't? N if they ever get him off benefits? That would be bad. A man has to eat: n if that man is Chrissy, he has to eat a lot, mainly premium brand snacks. So when he says this latest fella indicated he'll be leavin' him alone – n bonus, Julie did some diggin', n now he's got a file on him into the bargain – what I don't get is, if he's fit for work, n sayin' he wants to work, how come they aren't makin' him do any?

'I can't – I'm nearly ready.'

Mmm. There's stuff still buried – but yer can't get it out for him. I babble on a bit more, but note pad poised, he's readin' his usual Chronicle tales of hilarious road spillages, burst pipes, n vandalised lavs. Shit Town.

But now he's got a peculiar look on his face. His eyes are rotatin', flickin' from paper to ceilin', to window, to paper. He's absorbin', absorbin', absorbin' summink. Could be nothin'. Usually is.

But this dark winter evenin' it isn't. Lookin' up, he says the words I suspect he's dreamed of sayin' a thousand n one times – in the way he's dreamed of sayin' 'em. He's neutral but smilin', excited but scared, amazed but focused, calm but fiddly diddly. His time, has finally come.

'I'm nearly ready because…there's been a murder.'

PART TWO

THE LAST

AND EVERLASTING

RAVE

8

NOW

Detective Inspector Graham Kaye

'What are we doing about lunch?'

That seems to be how it started – the beginning of the end.

'We, Graham, aren't doing anything about lunch – because what you mean is, what's Sandra going to do about lunch? I'm not one of your team you know – if you've still got one.'

I didn't mean what was she going to do about lunch. I meant, what are we going to do about lunch: as in, a futile attempt to do something together?

'So I'm off to meet the girls instead. You don't try and make me happy, do you Graham?'

Well I do – did.

Weekends are the worst: face-to-face with the consequences of Sandra's life not having turned out exactly as she wanted it. She's changed. Have I? Probably.

And now this: a room full of people looking at me, and a murder case – just when I was starting to think I'd got away with it. Not the murder – ironically, I lack the conviction – the ever having to deal with one. Sentenced to two more years of trying to motivate fuckwits, fend off fuckwits, arrest fuckwits, and then inevitably release fuckwits, I beg daily for peace and free shit coffee at my desk, and to not be confronted with the kind of case I actually thought I was signing up for 30 years ago. So all I can think now is: run, back to that desk and drink – swig – from a vodka bottle wedged inside a blank note book.

I let go a deliberately long and extravagant sigh – just to remind this depthless pond of plankton that I hate them – clear my throat – a last request for the respect my position and this situation is supposed to accord, although fat chance of that – and begin.

'Right. Listen carefully to what I'm about to say.'

They are, at least, all staring at me. And it's quiet now. Just the water pipes churning away at maximum output – the only noise. I see 30% boredom, 30% loathing, 30% rank stupidity, with the odd attentive face in there. Maybe they take it in turns to look like they give a shit? Or are the young, bright-eyed, bushy-tailed ones like Trim really yet to comprehend that the journey they've embarked upon will be re-routed via a twenty-year drip feed of systematic failure? Hold that thought.

'So: 7 Brunswick Villas. What do we already know? Seems pretty clear that this fire was started deliberately or through gross negligence. But at this stage we can't rule anything in or out. It spread fast, largely – but not necessarily entirely – due to the presence of a significant amount of petrol. Obviously that suggests arson – doesn't prove it. There was also evidence of some kind of corrosive acid at the scene, which probably won't have slowed the fire down – severe damage to an area of the floor, and some sort of bucket or container which may have been used to carry or store that material. We await Forensics' report.'

There's some note-taking, some murmuring. Looks of concern on some faces – that an actual crime is not going away – sheer, hard-earned disinterest on others.

'So what's new?'

A pause to allow them to wake up – some shifting in seats.

'There were also two handguns. No sign – yet – of either weapon being discharged. Ballistics are examining both, so too early to say definitively – but the SOCOs are saying no bullet cavities have been found, there was no obvious sign of forced entry to the property either, and as yet no witness reports of gunfire or any significant kind of disturbance. Absorb all this: but let's not be leaping to any conclusions. Investigate. Regional's eyes will be on us throughout – do not fuck this up.'

Why always PC Paphaedes? Catching my eye at times like these – lower lip hanging down, brows furrowed in confusion, arm ready to go up, the general public's safety resting in this man's hands. I'm ignoring you Paphaedes. Ignoring you.

'So who's the deceased? The short answer is we don't know. Property is owned by a Daniel Scott – local landlord, several flats and maisonettes at the bottom end of the market. No suggestion he's implicated in any way, but he's not done his job and doesn't seem bothered – zero paperwork and he can't even remember the tenant's name. He's looking. Paid up front month-on-month, no ID or deposit, had been there six weeks. Thanks for nothing.'

I look up, to see Paphaedes examining a pen he's been sucking, which has left a bubble of blue ink on his lips. He wrinkles his nose and wipes his mouth on the arm of his uniform. Idiot.

'No news yet on DNA. We await the full report, but the body was badly disfigured. It looks like a male in his sixties or seventies, white, 5 foot 10, medium build. The flat itself was pretty bare. A few possessions are being logged, a phone melted to a crisp, so we'll probably get nothing from that. No word on prints throughout and I'm not hopeful. The lack of lifestyle evidence is unusual – so think. Was this a bolt hole? County lines?'

Write it down – they should all be writing it down. Everything.

'So. We've got a body burned to a crisp, guns, acid, petrol. There's no reason for us to believe at this stage that anyone else in the community is at risk, but it needs to be handled sensitively. I'll be putting out an appeal – "We believe there was a witness to this fire, we'd like to speak to that person" – let's not say any more than that. But someone must know something. Start ticking boxes: get your Long Johns on, get out there, and knock on doors. Spiral out from Brunswick Villas after Forensics, until I say stop. Highest priority.'

I surprise myself with how convincing I sound. Not because I don't know what I'm talking about: because I hate what I'm talking about.

'Any thoughts or questions?'

Give me strength. Paphaedes has his hand up.

'Seems very complicated sir – are you sure there's no evidence?'

Great.

• • •

Runcie

'What we doin'?'

Chrissy answers with the faintest squint towards the screen. His eyes never leave it.

First there's Marple.

He's in his recliner, with the crumbs of a bumper packet of crisps all over him, n a massive jug of squash on his little built-in table. I can tell the crazy fool's been up all night. Note pad on lap, he's starin', bleary-eyed at the action, of which there isn't that much, coz it's Marple innit: Werther's Originals for the eyes. I'm not against that, mind – n I like Marple. She knows every fooker – she's always in so-n-so's house, talkin' over the garden wall about such-n-such, hoppin' on the bus to go here, attendin' a function there. It's always the busy ones who fly under the radar, so it wouldn't surprise me one bit if Marple was doin' a spot on the side to be honest, yer know, cookies for arthritic friends, that kinda thing. Everythin's a bit too easy for her. She's connected – like the Runce Dog. I pretty much am Miss Marple, but with less of a focus on unlikely murderers. I keep this thought to meself though – I'm not sure Chris would appreciate it.

• • •

Next it's Rebus.

'He's tired of life Runce.'

'He should try n have a bit of fun along the way then?'

He has a think about this.

'He's always in the pub?'

'That pub there? There's not even a pool table.'

'Rebus wouldn't play pool. He likes curry though.'

'Not fun though is it, curry? Where's he based?'

'Scotland.'

'Mmm, yeah, I got that, but–'

'There's always someone behind the scenes in Scotland…in crimes…pulling the strings. Rebus is after the, erm…big guys.'

'The puppet masters.'

He's lost, n I choose the quickest way possible of gettin' him back on track.

'The big guys.'

• • •

N then he's suddenly all action, his way – a whizzed-up sloth, who's moved us to the Incident Room aka caravan. Hands on hips, white cap with sun visor over the top of his Town bobble hat, he's shufflin' slowly from side to side, scannin' a loada back-to-front wrappin' paper he's gaffa-taped to the window over his sink. The Chronicle headline is stuck to the top: *Mystery death in flat blaze.*

'What yer got here then Chrissy?'

He stops suddenly, realisin' I've spoken. He's not a nimble man – it's a five-point turn, tryin' to work out where the sound came from. Spots me.

'Murder Wall.'

He's been to Staples, n points a chubby finger at his brand new display area, hoverin' about in front of it, like this is Minority Report. It lacks summink though without all that futuristic floatin' technology – or indeed anythin' else to look at, apart from a newspaper headline and a piece of string connecting it to a picture of a banana. In his hand though, is the outline of a body with a question mark on it, cut out from one of his crime magazines. He finally decides where to put it – right next to the newspaper headline. Workin' at this rate, solvin' crimes may take some time.

'Banana?'

'Banana skins. Watch out for those.'

Will do.

'That's it then, is it?"

He considers. Looks-down-looks-left-looks-right-looks-down-looks-at his Murder Wall.

'Yes. That's…it.'

The simplest minds sometimes have the biggest dreams, n all Chrissy's ever wanted is to make everyone happy again. N I don't know how, n I don't know why, but he's decided this is it, this is his chance: his case.

'Training is never over. But now…I have to…'

There's a pause. Again.

'Have to…'

More pausin', then he slowly punches his fist in the air, kinda like a half-arsed fascist.

'Launch?'

'Mmm. I've been getting ready these past few, erm…'

'Decades?'

'…weeks…'

Nitpickin'.

'…and now, well…'

He proudly shows me his wrappin' paper Murder Wall, like it explains everythin'.

'I've got a map of town too – see? With routes in and out?'

'Great, are we leavin'?'

I let him get on with it, n peruse the top of his shiny red table.

'*DON'T GET MAD GET CHRIS.* What's this?'

He takes the piece of paper from me n looks down his nose at it, squintin'. I've noticed this new concentration face he's been workin' on. It would look better if he wore glasses, but I won't mention it – life's too short for that kind of conversation with Chrissy.

'Detective…business…thoughts?'

'Pity yer name's not Stephen.'

He crosses out Chris on the piece of paper n writes in Stephen – sees how it feels.

'I could change it?'

'I wouldn't. Chris is kinda yer, whassit, USP?'

'What about Kris with a K? Mum had a cousin in Taunton. His name was Norman. Changed it to Kris. With a K.'

'Why?'

'He thought Norman was square'.

'Kris with a K makes me think of Kris Akabusi.'

'Well that's good – he's a very fast runner.'

'Yeah, but would yer want him on a stakeout? Out in the car, pissin' himself laughin' at fookin' anythin'?'

He seems upset – like this matters.

•   •   •

Julie's here, readin' magazines, sprawled on Chrissy's sofa like the hot mess that she is. David Bowie eyes, tattoo of a rat on her left ankle, Flock of Seagulls fringe over the right eye, whole bodily regions which move in mysterious ways: she's a buzzin' vision of asymmetrical beauty. Cute as razor blades, n still amazin' me after all these years. Her n Angela Rippon.

All this activity of Chrissy's is distractin' me though. See, what it is right, normally he's absolutely catatonic, so yer really notice when he's not. N right now, he's sat across the table, tongue between teeth, workin', it seems, on the next stage of his plan: puttin' himself out there.

'Chris. Yer think maybe sendin' the police a message usin' cut up bits of newspaper, makes you look like the murderer?'

'They aren't bits of newspaper. They're bits of the Cooper's catalogue. Cooper's of Stortford.'

'Does yer message contain the phrase *cat scarer*? Why Cooper's of Stortford? Won't they think it's a clue to do with Cooper's of Stortford? Like, it's a serial killer – who offs people with really unlikely household gadgets?'

'One murder does not a serial killer make.'

'Calm down Yoda. It might be a serial killer though – could just be gettin' started. It's unlike you not to give someone a chance Chrissy.'

'The police aren't going to solve this crime. I need them to not solve it faster, so they'll invite me in to do it for them.'

'Okaaaaay, good. N yer poison pen letter helps coz...?'

'They will be really confused, which as a police man or lady or detective you should never be, so they will be forced to ask for my help.'

'*The case is a ladder. One step at a time. The killer is old. He is not a bird feeder.*'

'Feeder is coming off. I've put the scissors down somewhere.'

He scowls n looks around.

'N what does all that…mean?'

'The killer's a man. Probably.'

Mmm. I've forgotten how easy it is to get lost in a Cooper's.

'Sweet – an omelette maker!'

Julie's ears have pricked up – she's always hungry in one way or another.

'Student makes a good omelette.'

'Yeah, but I can't wipe him down n put him straight back in the cupboard afterwards can I?'

'Let's go for chips then. Chris?'

'Battered sausage please – jumbo. And some extra newspaper.'

Knowin' that fish n chip satisfaction awaits, Julie slaps down her magazine, stands n gives Chris's work the once over, deliverin' her verdict in wildest Welsh.

'OK big man. Letter's tidy. It'll freak them right out. But if it's business time? Get a business card. One big sausage, coming right up.'

Julie. Straight to the heart of the matter. Yer've gotta take care of business: and we've gotta be there to help Chrissy. Coz once, when I was takin' care of business, I wasn't.

9

THEN, 1992

Runcie

The week begins when we wake up on Tuesdays.

There's usually a hole in me head where Monday should've been, containin' a loada details from Sunday, Saturday n probably even Friday. I've got sensations – stuff that might've happened – but it's a shit jigsaw. I'm happy though.

'It should be free this feelin' – so my job is to make it free, for us anyway. While it lasts.'

They look up.

'What do you mean, while it lasts?'

It's Student who voices the fear – *Please don't take this away from us* – but Chris who feels it most. I can tell.

• • •

It's Friday before we really wake up again. We used to head off Fridays. An adventure. Magical. But now there's always summink on yer doorstep. N that's how easily yer surrender the greatest things in yer life, without even realisin' it – just like that.

We still meet Fridays though. Tradition. Every Friday: Acorn Records at high noon. Before that though, jobs to do.

First: the bakery, for two cheese rolls n a cream slice. Safeway's for liquids n kiwis next, me pre-match secret: confuse the body with the Vitamin C it'll be cravin' for the next three days. Throw it off the scent. Plus the kiwi also looks like a bollock, so I get to openly massage it at my next stop, readin' the grot mags at Smiths. I do this purely to see how many granny tuts I can get. Always lookin' for free entertainment. N then it's off to Acorn to sit in the arcade outside, waitin' for Chris, on a little buzz, spreadin' the good word amongst those joinin' us for the forthcomin' festivities.

Acorn is enjoyin' what Student calls *a renaissance*. 'Cept the appallinly-dressed n not-nice smellin' owner Simon, preferred it when it was dead. Now yer've got kids comin' in demandin' mixtapes n white labels from faceless superheroes, it's a whole new world, n he can't – won't – get his noggin round it. Bored of waitin', I go in n discover Chris, sittin' behind the counter on a Val Doonican chair – he does generally like to sit – safe n wide-eyed in a cosy, meticulously organised, A-Z world of choons. They're both starin' at an old flyer for Rat Pack Utopia – yeah, went to that – n Acorn, as literally everyone calls him, is bothered.

'I mean, what is a Rat Pack Utopia? There's always been something in a scene I've liked. The hippy thing. Rock. Country. Prog. Reggae. Punk. Disco. New Romantic. Indie. Electro. Hip

Hop. Christ – don't tell the indie kids – I even used to love that American Heartbeat album. Soft metal ballads. But this is just garbage isn't it? Am I wrong?'

He's gutted: one more person, on the outside, whose world's been turned upside down by The Republic.

'Yer gotta get involved Acorn. *Just get on your feet n dance,* yeah? The summer of love, the wall, the Roses on Top of the Pops: it was all part of it, seismic this is!'

'Mmm. Well. The Field Mice won't even come in here anymore. It's too busy.'

'Who? What is this? Beatrix Potter?'

'Sarah Records? Saviours of the scene, they were supposed to be. It's dead in the water now though – no-one cares.'

He's makin' money. He'd never have been in it for the money though – a businessman after me own heart.

'But who are all these people?'

It's Chris who says it. He's been doin' this: fine one minute, dippin' the next. He's lookin' at the crowded windows. School kids. College kids. Doleys. Olders. All sorts.

'Friends? Ravers? Republicans? Who knows. Fancy a bucket?'

For someone who spends his weekends smashed together with thousands of loons, he's not great with crowds – or loons. N it's gettin' worse.

'But why are they suddenly…here? I mean, I'm not saying they shouldn't…be. I…erm…don't tell people what to…do.'

He does leave long gaps though.

'It's just…well, some people…'

We don't get to hear about *some people*. But I know what he means. Coz there are some people. A crucial part of welcomin' nearly everyone, is wantin' to shield yerself from the few who can never qualify: the arseholes. Trouble is? Yer can't.

We check the phone box on the way out the arcade – the list of dates n numbers a work of art, n oh the tales they could tell – n then I steer Chris home. Time to meet the arseholes central to our own weekend n beyond – n that's a job for me alone.

● ● ●

The First & Last. The worst boozer in town. Or the best. S'all about perspective. Every Shit Town has one – pool table, hooky juke box, sticky floor, stench of stale baccy with a hint of piss n B.O., n a scatterin' of mumbly old cider heads, ignorin' the scaffolders who drink here coz they like chemicals as much as fightin'.

N if yer don't fit in? Walk straight out. Me though, I know how to fit in just fine. Just make sure they know yer not afraid, don't want trouble, n are happy to turn a blind eye. Coz these places are all about two things: 1) gettin' slowly, massively pissed, n 2) bein' open to business 24/7. N all of that business is dodgy.

Today that means a drink with a paira knuckle-nogs called the Maskells – psychos from builder stock who've embraced the rave scene without takin' on board any of its more community-minded messages – they love takin' their shirts off, but they might just slice yer if yer don't stick on some hardcore. A coupla right charmers – but it just so happens they can get me as many great big bags of the best pills around as money can buy.

N it's a ridiculously fookin' good arrangement. The thicky Maskells know some proper hard bastards who bring 'em over from Rotterdam. They like bein' all Billy Big Balls n hangin' with the tough nuts, so I'm not allowed near 'em – what a shame – but they don't wanna do any sales work coz – well, they just like to get monged, get sweaty, take their shirts off, n slice yer. Basically they're really fookin' angry, n love takin' their shirts off. Together.

The less psychotic Maskell – Karl – once told me that they'd always shared a room growin' up, n when they were 13, their ma sat 'em down n said: *Boys will be boys, but I don't like washing crispy sheets, so I'll pop a clean hanky under your mattresses each week, and mum's the word.* Proud of his wanky hanky he was – but all I'm thinkin' is, did you weirdy inbreds enjoy this mummy-approved masturbation…together? I never asked.

Anyway, deal is, they hand it all over cost price to Runcie of the Republic, in return for a 10% cash skim-off at the end of the weekend. I kindly do the maths for 'em – coz even tryin' to work out 10% would twist their tiny brother-fookin' melons – n they walk away happy.

Rip 'em off? Not interested. All I'm doin is payin' for the party – for me n Chrissy n Student n Julie n whoever else. Petrol, a bit of rent, threads, kiwis, n Bob's yer uncle, the weekend's ours – *Yahtzee!*

'Half a Gold n a packet of cheese n onion please landlord – n whatever yer 'avin' yerself Squire.'

A coupla the older soaks are sat over on the little tables against the back wall, Racin' Posts out as they shout garbage to each other. N that's it, apart from Sue, who's cleanin' the bogs, badly. I build one up ready to smoke out the back in case the Shit Town Mitchell Brothers keep me waitin' – but then in walks Karl.

Karl is slightly less likely than his brother to attract unwanted attention by stampin' on someone's head, which is why he's the one I perform the business aspects of our business arrangement with. Darren is absent. There'll be a reason for this, n it won't be life-affirmin'. I give it full throttle cheeky chap – always best to ramp it up for the spuds.

'Alright Boss Man, where's the bro?'

'Yeah, well, classic.'

'What's he done now?'

'A fucking shitload of acid. In me old man's car. We was going up to Corby to see family, n he does like four purples before we set off, and he's sitting in the back reading a porno, and that pissed me mum off for starters. And then when we get to the services, he starts getting para. First he starts wiping his knob on the McDonald's window...'

Mmm. That won't work – try deep breaths n huggin' a tree.

'...then he goes in the bogs, and 20 minutes later he's not come out. So I go in there and he's standing at the piss-wall, and he's shaking his knob like mad.'

He stands up n shows me what a man shakin' his knob looks like. He's laughin', loudly – a challenge to everyone else in the pub (me, the knows-better gaffer Keith, n two half-dead old alchies) to tell him to be quiet.

'So I says, "What you doing you nutter?" and he says, there's a sound stuck in his foreskin that he can't get out. He's really upset by now, the big poof. Takes his trousers off, runs out and climbs up a tree. Police get called, he gets arrested, spends the night at the station. Back home last night. Me old man gave him a kicking which was pretty funny, and he's sleeping it off.'

'Stay away from the brown acid. Why bother when there's pills? Talkin' of which?'

He dumps a placcy bag on the table – no standin' on ceremony here – n looks over at Keith, beggin' him to say summink, but he just looks away nervously n starts buffin' a tankard.

'I'll smash that cunt if he looks at me again.'

'Yeah no worries – I wouldn't bother though.'

I pocket the pills – prayin' we've not reached the day he's diddled me – n move on to the real reason I'm here: the future.

'Heard about this biggie then – comin' up?'

'Nope.'

A slightly aggressive response, like I personally have been keepin' him in the dark. Then I start thinkin' maybe this isn't a good idea, but I've started, so I'll have to finish.

'The Avon Free: every year up Bristol way? Used to all be shrooms n Hawkwind, course, it's all changed now – we all wanna go.'

'Fuck that. Find something decent. I'm not going anywhere with a load of stinking hippy scum.'

The Maskells don't like crusties. Karl told me that after the Battle of the Beanfield they considered signin' up for the cops – so I tend to play down me contact with our more van-oriented pals from The Republic…like the fact I go to the Free every year, n love it. But this is our future. N it's gonna be the real deal: amazin'. Chrissy's birthday weekend n all.

'Don't panic, yer don't have to. Know what this is Karl? An opportunity – that's all. Coz this is gonna be huge – like, biggest-thing-ever huge, n no-one runnin' the show. Which all means… I can sell us a lotta pills.'

'How many pills?'

'Five times as many. Ten times. Easy.'

'That's a lot of pills Runcie. You get nicked, you're screwed, I get nicked, you're screweder. And dead.'

I give him a bit of Runcie Fonze.

'Heeeey?!'

He glares at me, searchin' out any chance I'm somehow takin' the piss in a way he's too stupid to understand. But no. I'm dead straight – so I send it back on him.

'Can yer do it though? Can yer get hold of say…6000?'

'Course I can. If I want to.'

He's thinkin' about it. The old Maskell cogs haven't been properly Hofmeistered yet though, so they're grindin' even slower than usual.

'6,000?'

I give him a wink.

'All the cash up front. Do that, it's happening.'

It's happenin' alright.

What he don't realise of course is, once this is done? I'm done. Shuttin' up shop – party time – n I won't ever need to see Bros on Steroids again. So I follow him out into Friday afternoon with a jaunty spring in me permanently stoned step.

It's on.

10

NOW

Detective Inspector Graham Kaye

I have no power over my own life. None.

Exhibit A: my own house is for sale. Apparently. All part of Sandra's grounds for divorce agenda.

'I didn't agree to be slumming my way through my fifties Graham'.

Sort my act out, or I'll be slumming my way to a single plot in the cemetery, that's the message. She's put in what she says is a "ridiculous offer" – was this supposed to be some kind of concession? – on a "nice, clean, new balcony apartment" on Bristol docks, which she clearly wants to live in alone, and I've been put on a fucking timeline. I've got until she has an offer accepted to prove we should buy a penthouse together instead, although presumably I'd be confined to the guest room, where I could have a long hard think about paying the bills in peace.

It's not doing much for my grasp of reality all this – I always quite liked our house.

'You're not engaging. Graham. You don't seem to want anything. Well I want a better life – in a smarter place, a nicer house, not the one we've been stuck in for 20 years.'

'14 years actually.'

'Oh shut up Graham.'

Maybe I'll move into a barge; call it Shut Up Graham; ruin her view, piss off the foredeck and raise a can of Special Brew.

'It was in your marriage vows Graham.'

What was?

But how did I find out my house was for sale? This morning I left, huddled up round the corner, waiting for Sandra to leave, and then went back, just to use the loo in peace. Have a read. Take my unbalanced mind off things, before dragging it into the station to oversee a murder case and focus, focus, focus.

No sooner have I settled down into reading the paint colours Sandra's circled on a chart – Sunset in Shangri La? – and inspected the bath for the spare hairs she finds so offensive, then I notice there's no loo roll. Because apparently Sandra uses up loo roll like we're living in some sort of 24/7 fiesta, and if there isn't any left for me, well then I only have myself to blame. Normally, there would be great wads of the stuff shoved barely-used into that irritating little bin, but today there's just clumps of discoloured cotton wool, a leaking, supposedly empty plastic bottle of Argan Oil, a large hair ball, and the plastic packaging that used to contain all the loo rolls. The moment is ruined. Just like that, gone – tarnished. It doesn't just end badly though: it gets worse.

I have no choice, so I grab the cotton wool, hold it against my arse, and waddle down the stairs towards the downstairs loo, which Sandra calls the cloakroom, trousers round my ankles, shoes still on. I'm only halfway down when the front door key grinds in the lock, the familiar sound of Sandra slagging off my inability to mend things peaks my blood pressure, and makes me think of my constant emasculation at the hands of the fucking father-in-law, and in she comes with a shiny-suited, smart-arse estate agent, who's flaunting an expensive-looking coffee and smirking. Beneath contempt, Sandra just gives me a pitying look and invites him through to the kitchen, where she apologises that he must suffer "frankly the most embarrassing social space," which will soon be lining his pockets with a cool 2.5% – easier money than I'll ever make in my life. And guess what? No loo roll downstairs. I gently headbutt the wall.

'I took the loo roll to Alison's. I'm not using our bathroom until you fix the light.'

• • •

One catastrophically expensive trip to Waitrose later and here I am: keeping up the pretence that this is just another day in a life I long-since mastered – because at 58, in charge of a major police operation, I surely must have done?

'OK, pens down, phones off, eyes forward. Two things to report. Firstly PC Paphaedes and his team have now spoken to all other occupants of Brunswick Villas. I'll let him take you through his findings.'

I decided to let him enjoy his big moment – teach him not to stick his hand up and ask stupid questions when I ask for them. I hate myself for wishing ill on the dimwit, but I hate myself anyway, so in terms of Karma, it probably doesn't count. He gets up, concentrating as only he can, but, it has to be said, not looking at all nervous. A distant part of me is pleased for him – the barely present me hates him more.

'Er right, well, we've spoken to all the other tenants in the block, apart from one old dear, er, lady, who was, and still is, in hospital. Nothing fatal – bit of smoke inhalation. I expect she's just on the dodge – enjoying the free food and lodging over at the General for a few days!'

Paphaedes gets a modest sprinkle of titters for his light-hearted joke. They're just words, unfunny words, but I don't know how the human race can on the one hand demand so much, whilst on the other, accept so little. I scowl so aggressively he can feel my jaundiced hate, boring into him. He snaps to the point.

'So. A lot of people were tucked up indoors, but pretty consistent reports on the occupier. Moved in five or six weeks prior – as confirmed by the landlord. Kept himself to himself round the Villas, no known friends or family, although apparently he was always off to the pub. A bit of late night shouting reported with some some fellow unsavouries on a couple of occasions at kicking out time. No real trouble though, or suggestions of any criminal activity. As for the night itself? We know the fire was called in at 8:24 pm, so we're working back from there. We have two leads, though not from entirely reliable sources. One witness says he saw the occupier leaving the property in the afternoon. Doesn't remember the time, didn't chat to him. A second witness statement, from a smoker, says he saw two different individuals separately entering the flat, maybe an hour apart, between 6 pm and 7 pm.'

The bastards actually seem quite impressed with what the dozy twonk has had to say. He even gets a pat on the shoulder when he sits down. At least Sgt. Trim – my one and only hope – has the intelligence to look unhappy, like she has a heap of unanswered questions. I do.

'Thank you Paphaedes. These accounts may be patchy, but we have to assume there's something in them. We have at least two men – or women – to identify. The deceased – who may or may not be the tenant? Someone out there must know they're missing, so let's circulate. But who was this other individual and what they were doing there? We've no leads, so focus on the tenant, and maybe the other fellow will fall into line.'

Right. I flick a switch, look at the projector screen.

'So the second development could be interesting. Or a total waste of time. Either way, it demands investigation. An anonymous letter, sent to the DCI's office, redirected to us – offering help in solving the crime. Take copies, discuss, think. Be a hero. What does this mean? Who's it from?'

Oh yes – some murmurs and seat shuffling now. And that, Paphaedes, is how you hold a crowd.

'Anyone want to start me off?'

Trim.

'It looks like some of the words have been cut out of the Innovations Catalogue sir?'

She actually seems to care; to think. And as a woman in policing, the shit she has to put up with on a daily basis means she has my sympathy.

'Good, yes–'

'Actually sir, it's Cooper's of Stortford?'

Guess who? Bloody Paphaedes. I look to Trim. She hasn't kept her eyes off the screen – always thinking, good – sensitive to my desperation.

'He could be right sir.'

Now all the chimps have woken up.

'I fucking love Cooper's of Stortford. Classic shitter material. Them white oven gloves are the absolute dogs.' Platt, the longest-serving, laziest, least inquisitive moron of the lot – all donut, no detective.

'I'm more of a Lakeland man myself – better gadgets. Cooper's is all for–'

'Shut up Paphaedes. Or carry on – but without being a dickhead. Cooper's of Stortford then. What do we know? What's this telling us?'

'Maybe the murderer is from Bishop's Stortford sir?'

Chapman. The dolt to end all dolts, but fuck me, is that really the best he's got to offer? He even looks proud of himself, like he's found a smoking gun. Now Paphaedes – thick-skinned, no idea how much I resent him – wants to get involved again.

'Whoever authored the note isn't saying he's the murderer though, is he sir?'

'No PC Paphaedes, he quite clearly isn't saying that.'

'So surely that's quite suspicious sir? The crime scene hasn't got any evidence, yet someone tells us they can solve the crime for us, but doesn't just come in and tell us how?'

'So?'

'So maybe he's saying he's not the murderer, because he is the murderer.'

'Well go and find out who wrote it then. And if you think he's the murderer, you can arrest him yourself Paphaedes. You can go on News at Ten. Or Points West at least. And get me Cooper's of Stortford.'

'On the phone sir?'

Dear God...

· · ·

Runcie

Student is here – a rare visit – readin' on a tablet. While Chrissy gawps at Midsomer Murders – no blinkin', not a move, clutchin' his note pad like a favourite teddy, insights still bein' taken on board – Stude thinks he'll get some peace n quiet.

'Whatcha readin' Stude?'

He flips me a quick glance of a title – no eye contact.

Archetypes in Bram Stoker's Dracula. Oooh – yikes. Here – I've always wondered? Does Dracula only drink blood? Does he ever just have toast? Does he like strawberries dipped in chocolate?'

He's ignorin' me – I need to be more annoyin'.

'Not that I do. But it don't change me question: does Dracula eat normal food? Or exclusively blood? I don't remember Christopher Lee sittin' down for his tea – but blood must get borin' after a while? What d'yer think Stude? What d'yer think Chrissy?'

Chris goes rigid – a sudden break from the highly informative work of DCI Tom Barnaby. Yer can see his strange brain whirrin': this is a mystery, so he simply has to get involved.

'Draculas only eat blood. Not boring though. Erm. Tonight they might get it from a horse, tomorrow from a hen, or...'

Student's given up in a strop, forced to join the debate – so I kill the whole convo for me own amusement.

'I could never shack up with a Dracula then – can't stand fussy eaters. Right then Chrissy, what we doin'?'

Suckin' a pen is what he's doin'. It's been quite therapeutic watchin' him tappin' the ballpoint on n off on his pad n then jammin' it in his never-shut gob. He's stuck in a cycle…suck, mutter, tap, repeat. Now he's frozen again – it's what always happens before some kind of action.

N here we go…

'I always wanted to make Chris my middle name.'

OK. Good. Back to the great mystery of what Chrissy should call himself. Again.

'Why? D'yer want it out the way or summink?'

'No. I like it. Chris. I just think it might be better in the middle – on my business card. Which will say Detective.'

He points his pen at Julie to acknowledge the debt he owes her – for helpin' him reach this momentous decision – before discoverin' she's not here yet.

'Ok, so middle name Chris. What's yer first name gonna be?'

'Chris.'

'Chris Chris Pringle? Why would yer do that?'

'Well. Erm. I think things would be easier, filling in forms, on the phone and…that.'

'How?'

'Well I wouldn't have to remember that extra detail – of what my middle name is. The great detective "eliminates the unnecessary." So, like, all of your brain is available for what matters. Like dusting for prints. And organising your …disguises. Old man in the park, fat tourist, lurker, brown cow.'

'What's yer actual middle name – remind me?'

'Gary.'

'Oh yeah. What was the issue with that again?'

'There hasn't been a new Gary in Britain since 1989.'

'Right, right. But then wouldn't yer effectively be killin' off Garys altogether by becomin' Chris Chris Pringle?'

Pause.

'Mmm. Yes. I should probably have kids. But...'

But don't tell me – yer haven't got time...or a wife...n there was that community picnic where yer squashed one that was hidin' under an inflatable armchair.

'So yer'd call yer own son Gary? If yer gonna save an entire species, why not go the whole hog. Gary Gary. Son of Chris Chris.'

'Trouble is, costs £36 to change your name.'

'Mmm. Pricey. D'yer not think anyway though, that bein' called Chris Chris Pringle on a professional business card might make yer look a bit...unprofessional?'

Pause.

'Lots of people have two first names. Elton John. Ricky Martin.'

'But d'yer notice how it's two different first names?'

He leafs nervously through his note pad before landin' on whatever it is he wants to say.

'I must never be predictable.'

'Well, Chris Chris Pringle Detectives is certainly unexpected.'

'The point is, I erm...need to...do it. I need to, erm...get it...done. Soon really, because...'

I swear he does this deliberately sometimes – these pauses – 'til he gets everyone's attention.

'I've had..."the call." '

'Explain Chrissy?'

'My letter. I've had "the call." To go and help the police. Solve the case.'

'Already?! And actually?! How?'

'Oh. Well. I sent it to the man at the top, see? "DCI Mogford." '

'Right? But how does he know that?'

'Ah, well. I wanted to get started. So I called him up and told him. And I told him all about my Rule Book. And I said I would be very good at solving this case. And he was very happy. And he put me in touch with my new colleague erm let's see…"Police Constable Paphaedes," who asked me to come in and help them with their enquiries. Tomorrow.'

Shite.

'Riiight. That's probably not what yer think it is?'

Student is lookin' panicky.

'Look guys – I will do anything to help you Chris. But there's a point at which, well, I can't be getting involved. They are going to take a pretty dim view of wasting police time – not that I'm saying you are Chris, I just…I know what you think this makes me Runcie, but I have a job, mouths to feed.'

'A comrade in need gets no help when yer've moved to the dark side, eh Student?'

'Selling stair lifts is hardly the dark side. We're salting drive-ways for free at the moment – it's a very ethical company.'

Chris has stood up. He's hoverin'. Waitin' for silence. We all notice at the same time.

'Don't worry Student. I made notes in my note pad. They really want me to be there. And they said I could bring someone with me. So I chose.'

'Who?'

'Runce.'

'Me? The best dealer they've never nicked?'

'Yes, but you're not a dealer, are you Runce?'

'Well, actually, I am.'

'Yes. But only pot. And you're probably not going to tell them, are you?'

'Probably not, no. See Student? Everythin's been thought of. Best you stay out of it anyway – police hate students, coz of all yer traffic cone antics.'

'You can't let him do this Runcie? Chris, you've got to be careful mate. I really think you might need a solicitor.'

Chris has his head in his hands – like a bear who can't understand where all his honey has gone.

'Detectives don't have…solicitors.'

I actually agree with Student – n that never happens. Whilst I can foresee chucklesome times ahead, what we can't have is our Chrissy thrustin' his magnifyin' glass into a police investigation without some serious thought goin' into it. I mean, he'll say he has a plan, but when that plan's insane, it does tend to put yer at a disadvantage. N trouble for him means trouble for me means more trouble for him. So a bit of heavyweight help? It's a thought.

But not yet.

'It's too on the radar – too para. We'll stay cool, DIY it n stick with the plan: makin' sure you Chrissy, look like the real deal. N who is that can always find us some little advantage in the market place – whatever that may be – just coz she feels like it?'

Together, we've reached an understandin'.

'Julie.'

Julie. Always delivers – always did…

11

THEN, 1992

The Message: *'Right, listen up revellers. It's happening now and for the rest of the weekend, so get yourself out of the house and on to Castlemorton Common. Be there, all weekend, hardcore.'*

Runcie

The Courgette is finished. Student forgot to put oil in, n it burnt itself out when he was off with his right-on student girlfriend Tasty for a spin n a failed fumble. She's given him the heave n all – his relationship's as dead as his wheels. But yer can always rely on The Fat White Duke. She's drivin', deliverin' us unto Eden, savin' our future. Even the way she motors is filthy – brilliant.

We meet Melancholy Stu, as I decide I'll now call him, up at the hospital roundabout. Now that he's a man makin' his own way in the world, he's got a canvas rucksack, he's smokin' a rolly I can tell from half a mile away is a disastrous comin'-apart attempt

at a cone, n when we pull up, me eyes don't deceive me, he really
has got a book stuffed in his back pocket. Student labours under
the carefully-cultivated (by me) impression that I'm a fookin'
uncultured spazmo, so this is pure unadulterated studentin'. But
I stash that surprise for another day n look forward to playin' me
part, while he lobs his crap fag – tryin' to make it look like he's
flicked it, with a little flourish – steps in, n we're off.

'What yer readin' Melancholy?'

'Beat poetry – Ginsberg.'

'Ooh, I love him – especially his pasties. Give us a goosie.
I like to memorise poems me, recite 'em to meself when I can't
get to sleep.'

'Really?'

'Nah man, I just heard someone say it on Radio 4 when I was
round at yours, shaggin' yer mum.'

'Funny.'

'Yep. Just a little joke. I was actually bummin' yer dad. In
fact, question for yer – would yer rather shag yer mum or bum
yer dad?'

I toss the book out of the window n shout *Hardcore, you know
the score* at some kidders with sports bags, waitin' for a bus.

I can see where Student's comin' from though. We've got
wheels, we're off in search of spiritual enlightenment, n we've
got no idea how we're gonna find it: this is a road trip. But the
way to get over heartbreak is to eat a loada psychedelics, not read
about 'em, so I need to focus our studenty friend on the plan:
free entertainment.

'Where is Tasty anyway? How can she miss this?!'

'She's gone to see some political pottery.'

Hold on, hold on, it's comin' – got it.

'Sounds like it's for mugs.'

Boom-boom. We, are, free.

'Breakin' the law, breakin' the law, breakin' the law, breakin' the law.'

• • •

The Avon Free: a top buzz. Every year it's got a bit more men-tal, n a bit more annoyin' for the residents of Chippin' Sodbury, who've got their house prices n what they think down the Conservative Club to worry about. They don't like the open air toilet vibe, they don't like the feral dogs worryin' their sheep, they don't like the devil's music, n they don't like the all-round lawlessness of it – which is a shame, coz that's the best bit. So they've laid it on thick with Avon n Somerset's finest, n with rumours growin' that this thing's about to get ten times big-ger, they've done what every self-respectin' NIMBY police force would do n shut up shop, shuntin' the problem next door for the neighbours to deal with.

Handily for the one billion nutters n crusties who've picked up the party message n joined the convoy, the neighbours are away, n they've left the back door wide open. So we're gonna break into Worcestershire, hold the biggest party yer've ever seen, n we promise to clean up after. We'll even call the Yellow Pages if we have to, we're feelin' that co-operative.

The illegals. That's where it all began for us – that's where the force runs deepest. I remember one party under the Horseshoe Bridge, sound system the loudest thing yer've ever heard. I was bouncin' away quite happily for hours, n then at some point long into the misty mornin', I noticed the sound quality had dropped off a fookin' cliff. Which was when I realised I was dancin' to the sound of the generator. What a time to be alive. We're free to feel good, but I'll say it again n I'll say it always: freedom's never free if yer have to pay for it. So right now – coz this is big n free n huge n free n massive – I'm so excited, I'm havin' to smoke block continuously, just to stop meself from hangin' out the car window like a happy Labrador, n yeeee-haaaaaa-in' me way to our destination. Hangin' out the car window is more Chris's thing anyway, the wind on his big, round, confused face. Chris though, is quiet.

Too quiet.

Quiet like when life's dealt yer a bum hand. Like when he missed seven days in Amnesia coz he realised he didn't have a passport. Mind you, I was there, n it was clearly mega, but I don't remember a second. Yer can't do 'em on trade descriptions.

Today? Well, he looks happy enough, rockin' in his seat to the choons, playin' his spottin' game, where he gets a car of every reg, then every colour, then every make, like meditation - but there's a faraway look n all, deep thoughts brewin'. Julie's got the Duke eyes on the road, Student's in Melancholy Studentland – but I see it.

• • •

Probably the Best Services in the World.

Rammed with party people lookin' for action it is, n I'm happy to oblige, with the best four hours of their lives, guaranteed.

It's mostly ravers. Inside, a few hundred over-excited, hat wearin' loons are causin' lovable chaos, skinnin' up in the food hall, nickin' chewy in Smiths, dancin' to the bangers in their heads. Some have dropped already, everyone is lookin' to get sorted, n there's no corporate Rave Droids to spoil me fun. Some of the cider-punks have had a few too many tins of noisy, n they ain't keepin' it on the QT – but it's all sweet, n before yer can say *Toponeniceonegetsorted*, the whole weekend is paid for, there's still more than 5000 pills stuffed in Julie's borrowed wheels – the pills that will pay for a party for life – n we celebrate with an all-day breakfast. The Last Supper.

After, with Julie off somewhere – she really could be doin' anythin' or anyone – n Melancholy no doubt practisin' his rollies while no-one's lookin', or feedin' coins into a phone box to see who picks up at Tasty's, it's me n Chris left behind.

'What's a-foot Chris? Little Runce, that's what.'

Nothin'.

'Yer mighty quiet Chris?'

A longer-than-usual pause.

'Do you miss having a job Runce?'

'I've got a job. Salesman of the Month me – again!'

Pause.

'What do you think it's like to be normal Runce?'

'Well if by normal yer mean borin', I wouldn't know, n I'm never lettin' yer find out. What's all this about then Chris?'

He stares out the window n lets out what is, considerin' the size of him, an exceedinly modest little squeak of a fart.

'Can yer tell me any more than that?'

'I'm just thinking about…"the mysteries of the universe." '

Uh-oh.

'Yer didn't have any of the cake I left in the car did yer? In the tin foil?'

'Cake? No. There's cake?'

'It's special cake. Not to be eaten in cars Chris. What yer on about then?'

'Mysteries of the universe. We've all got them. I've got this...'

He pulls a long slow face which goes from neutral to vaguely constipated in the space of an eternity-like ten seconds.

'...mystery...'

He holds his hand out in front of himself. Raises a finger. Looks at it. Fook knows where this is goin'.

'...of who's here and ...why?'

Oh. We're back to this again. The world is comin' to Chris, n I forget, he's never left Shit Town really – just raves, n before that, Radio 1 Roadshows.

'Ravin'?'

He nods a Marlon Brando nod, small, certain. I hope I never wake up with a horse's head. I know I'm one step away from some horse's head types out there – I try not to think about it.

'Look Chris, it's us that make a rave. All we gotta do? Party like there's no tomorrow – so, just take enough of these n there might not be! Only jokin', cool as milk these.'

I mentally tap the pockets of me Diadora n get lost in a dozy daydream of the carnage to come. But I get the nervousness.

'It's gonna be OK. The bad punters won't win Chris. Not this time.'

'Who will win Runce?'

'You will Chris. *Best in Show, 1992*. I'll get you a rosette: Champion Raver.'

He thinks about this for a long, long time.

'I saw him Runce. You see.'

'Who?'

'At Ottery.'

'Right. Who?'

'In the bogs, propped up against...with his head kinda... he was...'

It really could be anyone. But it isn't.

'I saw Dad.'

•   •   •

I won't tell him he's imaginin' it. If yer rule is yer don't tell each other what to think? Well, yer can't be picky about it. N we've all seen 'em before – the unlikely sorts, with a pint in their hands, lookin' mad out of place. His dad though? Who walked out to spend the rest of his days forgettin' everythin' in a boozer? His dad?

So, there's nothin' I can say, not right now. I pat him on the back, give his massive shoulder a squeeze n look deep into his eyes, which don't look back.

'Yer see him again? Tell me Chris. Tell me.'

•   •   •

We've left the convoy to avoid unwanted dibbo attention – rule numero uno when yer don't wanna be diverted into a layby by a sniffer dog with a truncheon – n I have a dab of speed to celebrate. Rank. N talk, talk, talk, keepin' Chris on it.

'All this Ravers v Crusties bullshit – I don't get it. It's like, *look at that, so yer not lookin' at this.* At the money thing. Coz money just turns wankers into bigger, more aggressive wankers. N that's been there, from the moment they put in a door n said *yer in or yer out.* Coz wankers don't treasure freedom like we do. All yer need is a field full of anarchists, lazy bastards n heads, even the scallies – coz fookin' believe me, I understand the scallies more than any other type of human bein' – even the scallies know a gift horse when they see one. It's when yer get some prick whose ambition isn't to feel good forever, but to be Mr Hollywood-Yacht-Big-Balls – that's when the trouble starts. So the question is: can this, the real Republic, survive?

'This, what we're goin' to now? This is the biggie. If this goes off like it can, the party to end all parties – it goes global. Either way though, we're sorted. For life. After this, business is closed, n I'm strictly a customer. Anyway. I'm droppin' now – take the edge off. By the way, when I say sorted for life, I mean three years. That's our party sentence. I'm sendin' y'all down to Party Town, for three years. Sorted. Now – skin one up Student. Actually forget it, I'll do it.'

Chris stays silent. Student takes over the talk.

'Who's making the money then – who has all the pills? Organised crime – or just psychos?'

'Neither. Both. I dunno. But anywhere there's a door, there's a gun. There's no bar spend – no-one's downin' eight pints of Skol or gettin' a burger from the food hatch – the money's up for grabs.'

'And who do you…talk to Runce?'

'For yer own good n mine, I never disclose me sources – but let's just say I like to keep me psychos stupid n local. If they're in a suit, they're above me pay grade.'

'Like the Heavy Boys?'

N Chris misses a beat. It's the little things yer notice about someone yer love – n I notice it alright. He's still lookin' out the window, still hummin' – but he's listenin' now too.

I gotta be careful here. The Heavy Boys. Yer see 'em around: cold-eyed, leathery robots with a kind of a mythical status. Not-nice people. Proper, Marlboro Red-smokin' Euro-nutters, they say. Leg breakers, they say. Not the kind of spooky goons I wanna spend me days with. So I don't. But am I already indirectly in business with 'em? I don't know. They're Dutch, so, tick. N the word is they shop a lotta pills. But all along, have I been in bed with this paira rubber-faced, shiny slip-on n jacket-wearin', awful-haired, scary bastards? I don't ever wanna know. The secret to bein' a chancer is to stay well out the way of real trouble. N that's the truth.

'The Heavy Boys are out of sight Student. But there's one thing I would like to give 'em.'

'What's that?'

'Jeff Banks's phone number.'

Chris. Eyes on me, still, watchin' – n I know not why.

'Right you'se lot. Take one with water every four hours. Orders of Dr Runce. Coz that traffic jam there: know what that means? This is it. A brighter future awaits – but I'm warnin' yer, it could get messy. In a good way. So. Citizens of The Republic of Julie's Motor – a moment's respectful hush please, if yer will.'

With an empty Filofax, a full heart, n bulgin' pockets, I've cleared me schedule n consumed me pre-match meal. Castlemorton, here we come, n we're not alone: we've got pills.

'Ravers n Chemical Men, for the deep, deep love yer about to receive, may the Lord make yer truly thankful.'

12

NOW

Detective Inspector Graham Kaye

A late night – avoiding home, avoiding sleep. An early morning. Aching, queasy and off-centre from paperwork, a hangover, instant coffee and beta blockers, two of which I popped to get me through this ordeal: the Briefing Room. Upping the dose. Drowning the panic.

I clear my throat and seek out Paphaedes' face in the crowd, in the hope that his look of baffled uselessness will be somehow reassuring. He gestures frantically to me. I have no idea why, but remember he called last night and again this morning. Calls that I haven't returned. Because I couldn't face it.

'Ahem. Right all. Victim DNA was successfully retrieved. We've run it through: six million profiles, no matches. And still no-one coming forward. The few, melted bits and bobs we were able to rescue have now been logged and fobbed and there's a two-page summary. PC Paphaedes? Stick it on HOLMES and then, I know how inquisitive you are – organise a sit round, go through it all, take notes, come back to me later with thoughts. Now though. A little more on cause of death. Yes, a massive fire roasted this person into a charred stump, the photos of which some of you have had the guts and misfortune to take a look at already. If not – here you go.'

The screen is filled with the stuff of nightmares. Nightmares I stayed awake all night to escape. I don't look. The message? I don't have to, I'm ruthlessly professional and see this kind of shit every day. The reality? I'd puke, right now, if I had to look at all that again. Once was more than enough.

'Report confirms the victim was drenched in petrol. The burning was fast and severe – it would have been over quickly. But. We can now confirm that the victim had ingested a significant amount of alcohol as indicated, and he wasn't well: chronically reduced liver function, and bone cancer. And. Eyes on, everyone, now. Note that the fire didn't reach one arm as severely as the other arm, the torso, or the legs. This may just have been to do with the distribution of the petrol. But it may also have been because of the way it had been tied. Because that's right. Please note, this is particularly sensitive, but obviously key information – the victim had apparently been restrained in situ. Leaving you in no doubt I hope, as to the seriousness of this incident, and how seriously we need to take it.'

It does, indeed, seem to be sinking in.

'A few more details from the scene. Batteries had been removed from the smoke detectors, or at least they were empty. One set of prints on the outside of the front door. No prints collectable throughout the interior, mainly because of the fire –

but was there a clean-up? Few possessions, as noted, but there's a suggestion that the property had been extensively – perhaps even systematically – searched prior to the incident. All the drawers were a half inch open. Thoughts?'

Murmuring. And some pretend murmuring. Trim's hand goes up again and I waste no time in giving her the nod – I need her on this.

'Someone with knowledge of police protocol sir?'

Paphaedes likes the sound of this – wants to get involved.

'A professional job sir?'

'Anything's possible.'

I nod forcefully – who am I kidding?

'But call up any previous arson attacks again too. And double check logs for recurring names in case we've missed a fall-out.'

I leave, walking swiftly to the loo to hide, exhausted.

• • •

Back at my desk. Paphaedes – looking fidgety.

'Have you got a minute sir? It's about our tip-off.'

Shit.

'Yes? Hold on – why have you got your arm in a sling?'

'Slipped on a bit of lettuce last night sir.'

'Is it broken?'

'Sir?'

'Is your arm broken?'

'I don't think so sir.'

'Well take it off then man. You can't write or drive with a sling on, and you're not having time off during a murder enquiry.'

It's all too much for Paphaedes. Should he remove the sling – or talk?

'Er. Right. So this tip-off sir? It's not anonymous any more. I managed to find out it's from one Chris Pringle: aged 48, lives on the Corsham, the old bungalow estate – Phillips Farm Road. Probably a timewaster. We've lined him up for interview.'

Am I hearing things? Paphaedes has done this? Is this the world, finally passing me on the way up, as I drift helplessly in the other direction, plummeting slowly but surely to the very bottom?

'How on earth did you track him down?'

It takes so little for him to revert to his default expression of confusion and bewilderment.

'Sir? Oh. I see. He got in touch with DCI Mogford sir. And DCI Mogford passed him on to us. Again.'

The true extent of Paphaedes' achievement has become clear: it doesn't exist.

'And why does Mogford want us to see him?'

'I think it's a scheme sir: something about wanting us to "reach out to the people who trust us the least"?'

'Why would we do that?'

'Because apparently they're also the people who know what's going on.'

'Because they're usually the people responsible for what's going on!'

And the law of the scumbag means they won't dob anyone else in either.

'There's a piece of paper sir. They're sending a copy through now. Apparently it was in the newsletter.'

A scheme. A bloody scheme.

'Who's this poison penner again?'

'Name's Chris Pringle sir. By all accounts a bit of a numpty – er, I mean, not considered that bright sir. Long term on benefits, council bungalow, spends a lot of time with various dubious characters.'

'And when's this piece of paper getting here?'

'I'll go and check now. OK if I grab a sandwich while I pop off sir?'

I glare at him with real hatred. He hesitates – but not for long.

'Back in a minute sir.'

'And bring Trim with you.'

Because in a crisis situation, there really might be something about her. Anything would be good. Something would be unprecedented with this shower.

Has Paphaedes gone to the fax machine? Is there a fax machine? Promoted off the shop floor a decade ago, I don't know how to do anything. Maybe some old school muscle memory might kick in? Short-term hospitalisation would be better though - something minor to keep me out of the way, walking out in front of a bike perhaps…just for the peace and general anaesthetic that would follow.

Paphaedes re-enters with – Chapman? Wonderful. Dumb and Older and Dumber.

'Where's Trim?'

'The DCI's called her over on secondment sir.'

'Secondment? Since when?'

'Just now – there was a memo sir.'

Letters, memos – but not it seems, faxes.

'Why? Why?'

'The DCI seems to like her sir.'

I like her! The one brain in the office, swapped for a piece of paper.

'That it then?'

He hands me a print out of an email from the Chief Super and I take a deep breath.

Jesus Christ.

Conscious of the need to brush off this latest humiliation, I muster up what I hope sounds like a rum old chuckle.

' "C.L.E.A.R., a new community liaison and transparency drive, standing for Community, Liaison…EAR?" '

'As in, we're going to listen, I think sir.'

Yep – that's a migraine coming my way, right now.

'We're going to listen? To every fucking criminal, scrounger and timewaster out there who's heard we've got a scheme? "C.L.E.A.R. offers an amnesty on minor unconnected issues. Full details to follow." Oh, I can't wait for those. Hand me your firearm Paphaedes – I'm going to shoot myself.'

Paphaedes looks nervously to Chapman. They're all trained to look for the tiniest cry for help the younger ones – so no more suicide jokes, or I'll find myself on a mindfulness course in Didcot.

'I don't have a fire–'

'Yes, I know. So we get to interview a, a…'

'Nutter sir?'

'A crank, we get to interview a crank, with a penchant for poison pen letters, from the Lakeland bloody catalogue–'

'Cooper's of Stortford sir.'

'We've got you your copy, like you asked sir.'

'Whatever.'

'Oh, and actually, we're not allowed to call it an interview sir – so his aid said. Says it's a meeting. And Pringle says "he can identify the killer, if we can identify the victim." '

'Oh that's brilliant! Brilliant! I could fly...if you gave me wings and some flying lessons.'

'I hate Paul McCartney.'

Chapman has finally been able to come up with what he believes is a useful contribution. Paphaedes is hooked though.

'Everyone hates Paul McCartney. Especially his ex, that, what was she...Heather Mills? I always thought she'd have been good in that house in Geordie Shore, remember that? She'd be all like–'

'Please, please – please! Whatever you're going on about, shut up. This aid of his – DSCC is it?'

'No. Pringle says Mogford told him his friends could come too. He's a Mr Stephen Runce?'

'Runcie?! The bloody pot dealer and smart-arse?!'

'I hate Runcie – he's a bloody...hippie.'

'Yes, thank you Chapman. What about Pringle – he got a record?'

Paphaedes scratches his head and looks at a print out.

'A bit of a basic-case as I said sir, but no convictions, although he is on file, dating back to 1992.'

'What for?'

'Cautioned for possession of a large cake.'

I close my eyes. I need headache pills – capsules, tablets, anything.

'Explain yourself. Immediately.'

'Well, the records don't say much. Seems he was involved in the illegal rave scene in the early '90s – bit of a mascot for some of the crews who ran around together at the time, again

Stephen Runce, a pair called the Maskells, one of whom's doing time, various others. Anyway, there was this one huge event up Castlemorton way apparently, illegal party, 20,000 people or more, came from all over, seems they used to–'

'Get to the point Paphaedes – I don't need a history lesson, I was already on the force.'

He looks at me as if I'm claiming I lived through the Blitz, or saw the Beatles at the Cavern Club.

'Er, so, he was caught in possession of a large cake, assumed to be laced with cannabis or some kind of psychotropic drug. Turns out it wasn't. It was just a cake.'

'What?'

'It was his birthday.'

'Dear God. So he's got a grievance?'

'Hasn't mentioned it. Just says it's a "whydunnit-howdunnit-whodunnit," and he has some useful information on "how we are going about our enquiries all wrong." '

Paphaedes actually looks quite put out.

'OK, OK, for fuck's sake – get him in tomorrow.'

'He's already here sir – been here for two hours. Sorry – I tried to…wave.'

'C.L.E.A.R. stands for clear your diaries does it? Right. This is great. And Somerset's No. 1 Teflon dope dealer is with him too is he?'

'And he's also brought Julie Duke.'

'Fat Julie?'

He nods.

'Fat Julie with the reputation?'

Paphaedes looks appalled.

'I wouldn't.'

Chapman has woken up again.

'I would. Well I wouldn't sir, because I'm engaged sir – I'm just saying that my missus is pretty hefty and I like it.'

'I will do you the courtesy of not repeating that description when I see her at the Family Day Chapman. Right. Let them stew for a bit – Duke can wait out front full stop, then get the other two through. Might as well get this freak show on the road.'

• • •

Runcie

The cop shop.

We're bein' kept waitin'. But like I say, I can wait. N Chrissy's waited years.

If this gaff was a commercial enterprise, the shutters would be well up. No professional pride. There should be pictures of bunglin' burglars bein' led off to the nick – or silverware from cop shop contests. But no – just crap office seatin' that drunks have leaked on, some posters about not abusin' staff, a camera watchin' our every move, n the loudest radiators I've ever heard in me life. Depressin'. Totally Shit Town.

I soak up the sight of Julie n why she's here. Julie out-earns every fooker I know, coz she can sell anythin' to any man, n then, when their heart's beatin' too fast to cope, she takes a little bit of whatever she fancies or one of us needs. Today the brief is really fookin' vague: *When we're in there, n you're out here? Do what yer can.*

Meanwhile the small talk, as always, is on me.

'When yer a detective Chrissy, get a horse. I mean, Shit Town's like the Wild West anyway – but authority figures deliverin' justice on horseback? Nice one. I might get one meself.'

Julie looks at me witherinly.

'You're not an authority figure Runcie.'

'The revolution's comin' Julie. Everythin's changin'.'

'No Runcie, we've been through this.'

'I'd still like a horse. Fill me saddle bags n just trot around. We're gettin' off the point though – d'yer want a horse or not Chrissy?'

He's drawin' a horse – badly – on his pad.

'McCloud had a horse.'

The door through to the inner sanctum opens up, n the glarin' bloke behind the thickened glass waves Chrissy n I through. Julie's left behind to work her magic – the fools! For us, it's the firm hand of the law.

• • •

If yer took each individual sale as a single felony, I've probably committed more crimes than the rest of Shit Town put together. Victimless crimes of course, nothin' but the finest pollen since 1992, for the dreamers, the self-medicators, the agein' rebels, friends one n all. But the dibsies of course don't see it that way or care. They see a skanky Northern gobshite gettin' away with it, n it drives 'em fookin' loco. So as we enter Interview Room 2 – but not for an interview, obviously, *suckstobeyou* – I have a little nosey around, just to annoy 'em a bit more.

'Bit bare in here? What no dart board? Austerity hit yer hard did it? Also – me n me client love a brew? *Lubricates the vocal chords* – that's the kinda thing cops say innit Chrissy?'

There's Angry Middle Aged Monkey cop, who I've seen about – looks like he wants to kick the shit out of me; n Teenager cop, who we met earlier, who looks like he's pretendin' to understand a joke that's gone over his head. We'll all be confused soon though – once Chrissy starts talkin'.

'Just–'

Angry Middle Aged Monkey is about to tell me to shut the fook up, when what's clearly the Boss Man walks in. Chris stops dead, points a finger at him. Gives me the look.

I was expectin' a bit of sportin' action, but this geezer looks disappointinly broken. Another morbid drinker – the Runcie Radar can spot 'em a murder-mile off. Why oh why do they not come to me for help sooner?

Chrissy's starin' at him good n proper – his first actual, real detective – mouth even more ajar than usual. He sniffs. Boss Man eyes him back suspiciously. But Chrissy's not bothered. He's got an agenda in his head so far out of this fella's sphere of normal, it's gonna give him nightmares. Chrissy breaks the silence.

'You should have a moustache. Like Magnum's. He was a "private detective" like…erm…me. But as the top police… detective…man…or lady…you should still have a moustache.'

Boss Man tries not to look disorientated.

'Right. Chapman. Have we asked our guests if they'd like a cup of tea? Sort that out and then you can leave PC Paphaedes and I to crack on.'

I give Angry Middle Aged Monkey a double thumbs up.

'Two brews please Fella, plus some biccies for the big man. Oh, n if yer've got Chocolate Digestives n think that means yer treatin' him? Welcome to the land of no goin' back.'

This should be a dream come true for Chrissy – seein' where the magic happens. But he's had a long look around n he's disappointed. Too polite to put it impolitely of course – but his innermost thoughts won't stay that way. When it comes to detective work, they never do.

Boss Man attempts to warm things up with some general chit-chat.

'So, Mr Pringle. May I call you Chris? I'm Detective Inspector Graham Kaye, I'm the senior investigating officer overseeing the Brunswick Villas enquiry. But for today–'

Chris is ready.

'Babababababa – hold on…Inspector…erm…Graham… Detective. Now – do you know why you're here today, Inspector…Graham…Kaye?'

Boss Man looks from Chris to me – am I insane too? – but sees I'm just happily watchin' a good friend at work.

'Rule 1: whydunnit? You have to find out why they…done it…did it…would do it.'

'Motive,' I add just to get involved, clickin' me fingers and pointin' at Boss Man.

Boss Man's not sure about Rule 1 though, n he's heard enough: time to try n impose himself on the proceedins.

'We're here today Chris, because that's the way I wanted it.'

Angry Middle Aged Monkey has walked in again. He plonks our brews down n stands, smirkin' aggressively at us – before a dirty look from Boss Man sends him lopin' back out the door in search of bananas. A brew should never be plonked – I shake me noggin sadly at the state of things.

'OK, so – I think we're ready to begin. PC Paphaedes, please start the tape…thank you…this is Interview Room 2 at Poll's Hall station, in attendance we have PC Paphaedes and myself, Inspector Kaye. For the benefit of the tape please confirm that we also have here Mr Chris Pringle of 45 Phillips Farm Road?'

Chris gawps enviously at the tape machine – makes a note, slowly. I lean over n it says: "Tape."

'Mr Pringle, just confirm please that you're here.'

He nods.

'Right. For the benefit of the tape, Mr Pringle has nodded his head. Mr Runce–'

But unfortunately for Boss Man, here endeth his sermon, which was shite anyway.

'Look, for the benefit of the rest of the day not bein' wasted sat in here, turn the fookin' tape off n we can crack on. This isn't an interview – if it was, he'd be interviewin' you lot, askin' why yer wastin' time interviewin' him.'

I'm lovin' this. 30 years of hurt – OK, 30 years of mild concern about gettin' nicked – n it all seems worth it now I'm some sorta legal eagle for the day.

Poor old, broken Boss Man, with his Exhausted Civil Servant looks, sighs n rubs his forehead with his knuckles. Man needs a hug. I decide to talk a bit of mainstream to him instead, put him at ease, as if everythin's gonna be alright.

'Go easy Champ – might never happen.'

Yer know – sentences like that, which mean absolutely fook all? *Be lucky Fella. Happy days Blue. Safe home Pal.*

He sighs.

'Right. Stop the tape.'

Teenager is milkin' his role.

'For the benefit of–'

'Just stop the bloody tape Paphaedes. Thank you! OK Gents. Right. A chat then. An off-the-record chat. Are you going to waste my time though? Because this is a murder case. So I promise you: wasting my time will be looked upon very dimly indeed. However, if you're here to help – really here to help – then I will ignore the means through which you've come by any information. And any other…minor infringements. OK? Deal?'

I put me hands into a prayin' position n tap 'em against me lips, eyein' him as if in deep consideration, but really of course, just keepin' the Boss Man danglin'.

'Let's crack on then Chief.'

PC Paphaedes, who's clearly hard of thinkin', has spotted another way in which he can be helpful.

'You shouldn't call DI Kaye Chief, because the Chief Super's known as the Chief, and DI Kaye is only–'

Boss Man's gonna have an eppy in a minute.

'Shut up Paphaedes!'

Boss Man folds his arms, sits back, n then, realisin' it sends out the wrong message, makes a big show of puttin' his pencil down n offerin' Chris a biscuit.

'Mr Pringle?'

He takes four, has a slow chew, n a long, last look at his note pad, before slowly closin' it. Looks-down-looks-left-looks-right-looks-down-looks-at Boss Man's chest. Stands up, hands behind back, walks to the window, peers out n then turns, sharpish, on his heels. Loses his balance just a tiny bit. Then settles.

'You are familiar, I am sure, with the Columbo case, Any Old Port in a Storm…?'

• • •

Detective Inspector Graham Kaye

The odd couple have shuffled off. Time to think. But about what? Pringle? I've seen him around – he's unmistakable to be fair. Never assumed he'd be that far off the scale though. Never assumed he'd have…specialist interests. In being a detective.

After marching around the room, blethering on about Columbo and some woman called Vera, and repeatedly reading out the word "whydunnit" – which he'd written in a book – he then said "it's always the rich bloke" and asked when he could get started as the detective. When I pointed out that he couldn't, he stood by the door and said he wasn't ready yet anyway.

'But I will be. And then we will get started – on the case.'

He's a fantasist. And then he was gone.

Paphaedes has returned with Runcie's record sheet.

'Cautions. Possession of a spanner at a rave event in Taunton, February 1991.'

'A spanner? Not a knife…or some pills? What are these idiots doing at raves with cakes and spanners?'

'You could give someone a good clout with a spanner sir?'

'He didn't though, did he? And, irritatingly enough, I suspect he's not the type – so why's he got a spanner?'

'Maybe he's just very practical.'

'What?'

'I keep a spanner in the glove compartment of my Berlingo sir – and an instant camera. In case I get into an accident.'

'Yes, but if you took your poor long-suffering girlfriend out for a nice meal at…?'

'Nandos?'

'Yes, would you take your spanner in with you?'

He thinks I'm really asking him this.

'Sir?'

'Just give me the sheet. "Possession of a spanner and a skeleton key at a rave event in Shepton Mallet, October 1991. Possession of a spanner at a rave event in Bridgewater, December 1991. Court appearance for non-payment of poll tax and a warning for contempt of court." '

'There's some cuttings on that last one sir – see there, he told the judge, "I'm exempt from the Community Charge, because I'm not from your community, I'm from Uranus." '

'Christ – a Poll Tax martyr.'

A blank look from Paphaedes.

'Then he's gone off the radar a bit see sir, apart from being banned from Nike stores – some suspected scam to do with buying hooky trainers online and then returning them. And finally, a caution in 2011 for giving away Ecstasy at a church fete. Turns out they were just Smints. Claims he wanted to see how many OAPs would "get involved." Basically, he's got away with murder.'

'No PC Paphaedes – you've just been through what he's got away with and it's important, Policing 101 in fact, especially in these circumstances, that you can tell what is and isn't murder. We're simply dealing with an aggravating little chancer, who isn't stupid, but thinks he can do whatever the hell he likes – and what he likes today, is watching his mental-case mate winding us up. But – panic ye not – it's not happening while I'm still in charge.'

'You don't think they'll be back sir?'

'Put it this way, I won't be extending an invitation. Scheme or no scheme, this is a murder enquiry. If they don't belong here, they can't be here. Return no calls.'

• • •

Runcie

It was a classic Chrissy smash n grab. Go in, empty the contents of some painstakingly over-organised brains onto the floor like a hoodie with a handbag, then waddle off lookin' happy, with no-one else understandin' why. N if yer lucky, that's the end of it for a while.

'Mission accomplished then yeah? Nice one. Let's never go back.'

'No. Not until I'm ready.'

Oh.

'Julie?'

By the time we left, she had a new piggy pal eatin' out of her well-manicured hands. Which means results. Coz handily for Chris Inc. – of which I am, of course, CEO – not only is Julie the world's Welshest sixteen stone honey trap, but even though she's now legit – saved herself, sorted her own agenda, became the Gordon Gekko of telesales or summink – she'll always be a fookin' relentless klepto. Give her a sniff n she's at it like a rat up a drainpipe – just coz she wants to. N I just knew that in a cop shop, she'd want to.

First she got Mr Front Desk Man to let her back where she shouldn't be, to have a swing on his chair n a play at answerin' the phones, like a kid in a cockpit. Big mistake. Coz whilst she's cloudin' his head with innuendo, n he's wonderin' why he's allowin' an unforgivable breach of security, she's slidin' any old knick-knacks that take her fancy straight into her giant, posh Tardis bag of magic.

Now we're off back to Chrissy's, havin' headed round the corner n jumped in Student's corporate wheels. Efficient as ever, she keeps her steals in a separate compartment, which she empties out onto his back seat.

'Julie! This is a company car.'

I'll always step in for Julie – not that she needs me help.

'Company shmumpany Student – this is a fookin' murder case. Apparently. Plus yer should indulge yer good pal Julie – she's doin' what she loves. To help Chrissy n all. *Don't be a bystander, be an upstander.* I saw that on a poster inside. We're all takin' summink away from this experience. What yer got Julie?'

Glowin', she silently examines her finds. Handcuffs – intriguin'. A mobile – interestin'. Some paperwork – official lookin'. I go to grab it, but she cuts me off at the pass, foldin' it into her bra.

'All in good time Runcie. Let collectors collect – I'll share when I'm ready.'

N she's also got a – really?!

'Chronicle? Where's the fun in that?'

'It's this I wanted you toss pot.'

She rips, n rips again: a voucher.

• • •

If the cops ever raided Chris's flat – soz Big Lad, bungalow – he could easily be mistaken for a serial killer.

First there's his general weirdness, which I find comfortin' after all these decades, like a hug n some cocoa, but which yer first-timer might find unsettlin'. His collection of Yellow Pages n his ear wax jar – stuff like that.

Then there's his case studies. Shelves of videos of his detectives, recorded over a period of 20 years. Organised by detective, n then, in Chris's words, *as they happened*. I heard that autistic kids like collectin' video tapes, so maybe he's autistic, with all his loggin' n note-takin'. Like I say though, no-one's ever managed to pin any labels on him despite tryin' really fookin' hard – but it don't change the fact that it's all kooky.

But most worryin' of all for the stranger would be his files – coz they might just find they've got their own starrin' role. See, Chrissy keeps files on everyone in Shit Town, stacked up along his shelves in his punchiest attempt at alphabetical order. Inside, there'll be a photo or crayon picture from Chrissy maybe, n then a little form for details, where they work, any aliases… not sure he's ever filled that line out, mind…n usually, a mystery: summink for Chrissy to solve. Then, if he ever meets yer, even though yer won't have a Scooby who he is, I'll get a look which means he knows yer, just like I did with our clinically depressed new pal, Inspector Graham Kaye. Maybe we'll come back to him another time, but we're enterin' new territory here, so best we proceed with caution.

Coz he's never done anythin' with these files Chrissy – they've just sat there gettin' fatter n more ridiculous, like him really. But Julie knows: information is beautiful. N even though she's got a half-price voucher for the Print Shop, it turns out 50% off business cards is, well, not enough. She's goin' all the way to make sure Chrissy gets treated like a detective, not a care-in-the-community job, so she wants leverage on the fella that runs it, who goes by the name of Digby Crown.

'You're not a charity case Chrissy, I'm not bailing you out like some kid – just helping you, help yourself'.

Chris opens a file with a big purple D on the side, n concentratin' like a beast, thumbs his way to Digby Crown. Out comes a piece of paper with scribbled notes on, a leaflet for Crown Prints, a drawin' of a shop, n a coupla photos. Of complete strangers. Chrissy, Chrissy, Chrissy. I shudder at how bad it looks.

'Oh yeah.'

Chris is slowly – very slowly – reviewin' his notes from *The Case of Digby Crown.*

Julie puts down her magazines, lets out an earthquake of a burp, sniffs her hand, n gets up. Chrissy senses movement around him n eventually spots the change in the room.

'Right boys, I'm off. People to see, people to do. We'll say hello to Digby Crown tomorrow. Runcie: sort me some wheels – butts don't get this big from walking.'

'Cars,' says Chrissy coz, as usual, what's in his head bears no fookin' relation to the moment we are in. 'There's always a problem with cars.'

He's driftin' away – an aimless driftin' yer'd think, peaceful. But it won't be. Never is. Not where he's goin'.

13

THEN, 1992

Chris

The Castle.

'This is yer treasure map Chris. Car: here. A little map home –
x marks the spot. Stick with us though – try. But also, see yer
in two days. It's on. This is the one. N remember: everythin's
gonna be amazin'.'

I have a map. X marks the spot.

'Everythin' yer could ever want mate – 'cept showers.'

I don't know where to look. I don't normally have to, because
I look at my feet and they take me where they want to go, which
is nowhere. Marching nowhere. We're in The Republic. But it's
The Castle, and there are too many things to see.

'The bass n the beats Chris, the bass n the beats, that's all
yer need.'

That's what Runcie says. Because the music keeps me still, marching but still, and I can stay with the feet, the gaps between the feet. But the music in The Castle comes and goes, and when it goes I look up, because there are so many things you have to see.

'Don't wander off Chris, don't wander off.'

And then I'm lost. In a long night. A long night with days in it.

•   •   •

I stop counting the days in the night. It's dark. I can taste the ground. I wait for the next day, so I can find everyone. I wake up, but I can't find everyone.

Then it's two days, but it's really a very long night with days in. There was a night where elevenses should be and a night at lunch. But it could all just mean I'm hungry. And lost. And... damp.

I hear my name.

'Chris.'

Again and again.

'Chris.'

People are saying my name.

'Chris.'

Runcie says The Republic is a place in your head you can walk in and out of.

'It's the past n the future.'

But I can't get out – I don't want to get out.

More people.

I'm afraid of what I might see – or what I might not see.

'Runce?'

X marks the spot, but I can't understand the map…and it's gone.

Lost.

• • •

I had a cake.

A police man. Notes in a note pad.

Happy birthday.

• • •

I had a chili dog. I fell asleep and woke up on a car. In a car. I had to touch my face, because the order of things got muddled. My new friends gave me tea and then things weren't OK. Runcie wasn't there.

'Are you alright mate?' they said.

And I was alright. But I'm not alright.

'Mum?'

I am scared I will never be able to talk to my mum again.

'Can you see inside my head? Can you see me Mum? Can you see me? I'm pretending.'

Mum's got the National Geographic. I've eaten bark. The breasts are melting. The ground is like making a cake in a bowl.

The light's coming. I want Runcie. I want Julie.

I'm asleep. In a dream. I am walking. I have the map again – x marks the spot. I am looking for something and I'm happy, because I finally remember what it is, although I don't remember what it is. We are all walking to the top of a hill, and when we get there a man is talking, everyone is listening, everyone is happy again. I wave, so we can talk, so he can see me. But he can't see me. Can't hear me. Can't talk to me. Because it's not real. And the map has gone. But there's still a school trip to go on. It's a history trip. We're going to Europe to look at graves. We're going on a coach. We're going on a ferry. Runcie's going.

'It's a Grave Weekender!'

Mum's going too.

But they won't let me go. I'm not allowed to go. It's too late. I'm the only one at home. I shut the door.

● ● ●

It's dark again when I wake up – in a car again – not Julie's car, but Julie is there. There's banging on the window. I can't hear what they are saying.

Julie is with a new friend.

'Speak Chris. You have to talk. If you're lost, you have to tell people what you want.'

And then Julie is gone and she has left me a note saying "Bedlam."

I keep the note. I look at it a lot of times.

Looking.

We are all in a cloud together, so I know that the bits of my head floating around me are not going to be left behind. The noise feels biggest here. I won't let anyone give me things to eat, just because they like it when I dance. I will dance though. I am happy. But I need to find Runcie. Or Bedlam. Is Bedlam bedtime?

I meet an old man. He has a long piece of string and a wolf. I ask him to take me to Bedlam please. He laughs and takes me for a cup of tea inside a caravan instead. I give him some money. It's "a nice thing to do." He gives me the money back – it's "a nice thing to do." And then we're right in the middle of everything and everyone and I march. And he points to a sign which says "Bedlam." I can't feel anything. I can't hear anything. And I can only see with my eyes closed. But the one thing I keep seeing is my dad.

When Dad left, I was quiet. So when I see him now, I'm quiet.

He stops.

His mouth is moving. His mouth is moving – but there's no sound coming out. I count things, when there is a reason to count things. How many times have I seen my dad? I told Runcie once.

But he hasn't come back.

And then…

Bang.

And I can hear, suddenly I can hear, everything. It's too loud. It's not what I want. It's not what I want. It's not what I want. All we can see is ourselves, and he looks scared and I think…

"Why is my dad scared?"

He's with the Heavy Boys.

I know that they are the Heavy Boys and you "mustn't be seen laughing." And I know now, that the sees – the five, six sees – they've been there too. The Heavy Boys. I remember. And this time, they see me too. I'm not laughing. They are shouting. The ground is cracking open and everything is so loud and they're screaming – one is screaming and my dad is in the middle.

'Fucking watcher. Always watching. Watching too much, the motherfucker! So I'll fucking kill you if you want? I'll fucking kill you!'

And they see me. My dad really sees me. He saw me before. But we all see each other now.

And there is nothing I can say, so I have to leave and never look back.

I close my eyes.

I hold my head.

I cover my ears.

I turn round.

I can't move.

I look down.

I try to walk.

I try to run.

14

NOW

Runcie

Welcome to Crown Prints.

'Julie, is it?'

'That's right Petal. Haven't seen you around before Sweet Cheeks. Digby isn't it, is it?'

She pokes him with an elbow n giggles – he giggles n all, but nervously. Digby Crown doesn't really know what he's lettin' himself in for. I don't really know what he's lettin' himself in for either: this shit's organic. He's obviously a nice fella – a bit Chinny Hill, picture of the wife framed there on the counter, happy with a simple life in Shit Town – just a poor unfortunate geezer whose 50% off voucher was in the wrong place at the wrong time. Julie places it into his hand, before squeezin' his wrist.

'OK, ahem, Julie, so you've got the voucher. Done really well we have with those – a good promotion. So that's 50% off your total order, so if you want…how many was it?'

'500.'

'Yes, 500 cards, that'll take you down from….'

He does some very clear typin' on his calculator, tongue just pokin' out from between his sensible teeth, just an Honest John, makin' an honest reduction.

'£104 to £52 – and we can call that £50.'

It feels like a proper sting this – layin' the groundwork with some everyday chat – n The Runce Dog can't help gettin' involved.

'D'yer find yer competin' with the service stations these days Digby? Yer know, for them weirdos who decide on a career change halfway through their Greggs?'

'Oh, you know, I always say "live and let live." Those machines and the online trade don't affect what we do too much. We can't compete on price, but what we offer is very much a more bespoke service for gentlemen – or ladies, forgive me – who perhaps don't want something off the shelf, so to speak. Plus of course we use minimum 540gsm stock – much less flimsy. The 50% off is a great offer though.'

'Mmm.' 'Terrific.' 'Lovely'…we all say at the same time.

'Now. Design. What's the nature of your business then Julie?'

'Oh it's not mine Lover-Lumps, it's Chris's – detective agency.'

'Gosh – exciting. So what are you Chris: ex cop?'

Julie's outraged, givin' it the full Valleys.

'Fuck off Digby – cops are wankers.'

Digby decides it's best to ignore this glimpse into the Twilight Zone n press on.

'Ok, so – let's get an idea of what you're looking for. Business name Chris?'

Looks-down-looks-at pad, looks-at Digby Crown's shoes, looks-at Digby Crown.

'I don't really…erm…"Chris's Crimes"…"I Solve Any Crime Dot Com"?'

Ambitious – but Digby Crown is a consummate, customer-oriented printing professional.

'Maybe just a job description? Can I just say, if you need some flexible funding – and every new business does, especially in these challenging times – my bank were more helpful than I thought they'd be. Do you know much about business models?'

Chris scratches his head. Julie's away though.

'Like Sam Fairs eh Digby?' she says, jabbin' him in the ribs.

Digby winces and opts for the safe route.

'Oh – no, what I actually mean is, Chris's bank could help with what's called a "business plan," check he's got the money to cover his set-up costs, that kind of thing. Like his cards here?'

N so, me time has come.

'Yep, about that Digb–'

But Chris beats me to it. He's on his feet doin' his Columbo/ Poirot, hands-behind-the-back thing, clutchin' his paperwork, walkin' slowly around the shop floor.

'Last year. June. The Midsummer Fayre. Sunny. Wonderful. "A family day." '

He's crackin' on, n we've not even finished settin' the scene. Digby is foxed – looks to us for clues.

'Er?'

It's like in Total Recall, where the old lady starts goin' a bit funny, n then, next thing yer know, Arnie pops out of her. Digby Crown is startin' to look worried – like that's about to happen with an overweight man he thinks he's never met, who he's just discovered wants to be a detective. If he's got any sense he'd go back in time, get a panic button installed, n start pressin' it right now – coz shit's about to get unexpected.

'Do you remember what you were doing that day Mr...Mr Digby Crown?'

He's really thinkin' about it.

'Working on a Coconut Shy?'

'Yes. 3 Shots for £2.'

I have a sudden urge to get involved again, play the Good Cop or the Bad Cop or summink. I go for Irrelevant Cop.

'Not exactly cheap, is it Mr Crown?'

Maybe too irrelevant?

Weird Cop Chrissy picks up the reins again.

'Bad things happen don't they Mr Digby? Crown? Do you remember the bad thing that happened to you...that day?'

'Er...well there was a drop of rain I seem to remember, early doors...?'

'Your car?'

'Er...oh. Oh! Someone, someone scratched my car!'

'Ever find out who?'

'Well, er, no. I mean, I have to say, it's an A to B thing for me – I'm not actually that into cars?'

Irrelevant Cop strikes again.

'Yer dead right Diggers – car fans are usually right dollops.'

'Yes, mmm, yes, that annoyed me that did though. Oooh! You're going to tell me who did it now, aren't you?!'

Silence. Excitement turns to worry.

'Not…you?'

More silence. But when a business negotiation stalls, that's when yer need a Julie.

'Now Digby – a new business needs paying for its work – right?'

This could be Chrissy's first ever official client. There have been loads of unofficial clients, who never realised it, with no money or intel changin' hands. It's a big moment, n Digby sorta understands. It's like some kids have offered to wash his car – the scratched one – n he's decided he's game.

'Er, right, OK. Yes. Very good. OK, what say I give you £5 for a name and £10 for proof!'

Julie is straight in there. Bosh: deal time!

'Free business cards for Chris, Digby. That's what we've come for.'

'Oh.'

Digby Crown suddenly looks tired, disappointed – so this is what it's all been about.

'Oh, I see. OK then.'

Chris gets a photo out n places it on the counter, face down, milkin' the moment.

Pause.

'Digby Crown. It was…'

He turns it over.

'Your son. And here's a picture of your son…doing it.'

'How did you…how were you?'

Julie keeps things focused.

'You get the dish, not the recipe.'

Digby Crown is not a happy print shop guvnor.

'So I have to, effectively, give you £100, on top of having had to fix my car – and now I'll have to punish my son too? He's a good boy – he's just gone off the rails a bit.'

Chris nods seriously.

'I know – I saw him urinating in the Safeway Car Park. Want to see a pic–'

'No!'

I attempt to outline the positives.

'Cheer up Mr Crown. Yer payin' for a mystery solved. Isn't he Chrissy?'

'You're paying for this,' he taps his head, 'and this,' he taps his file, 'and that.'

'Not that – my name is Julie.'

He stands corrected.

'And Fat Julie.'

Julie's not bothered – she owns it – but I wag me finger at Chrissy on her behalf anyway. He's not 'avin' it though.

'There's nothing wrong with being fat. Look at Poirot. And me.'

Julie's moved on anyway.

'I'll need a card too love, just in case. Bookings Manager.'

Digby still has a bit of fight left in him.

'Don't detectives have customers – rather than just stalking innocent locals and harvesting pointless details about their daily routine?'

Julie massages his shoulders and he's obedient once more. Lucky fooker.

'Just think of it as a service to society Big Bear. And practice for the main man here. Coz what does practice make Chris?'

'Prizes?'

'Perfect Chris. It's your own motto. Remember?'

Digby's perusin' the text again, thoughts perhaps now movin' to layouts. Or maybe not.

'Pringle. Mmm. Did I used to know your mum? Lovely lady? Down at church?'

Julie answers coz Chrissy's not interested.

'See? Family friends.'

Chrissy's thinkin'. Everyone knows it coz there's a long pause. We allow his pauses. They're Chrissy's. He needs 'em, to get his noggin in order. He looks around in wonder at the inside workins of Digby Crown's reassurinly well-ordered print shop, then pats him robotically on the shoulder with a meaty Pringle paw.

'I see you do mugs?'

· · ·

We drop Julie off.

'Alright Chris? Happy?'

'Yes. No. I need to get home. To my bungalow. Inspector Kaye will probably be worried. About the case?'

Mmm.

'Possibly not Chrissy?'

Julie gives me a look – me lack of belief deemed staggerin'.

'Don't worry chick. I got us another bone – from the cop shop, right? Just need to go stick some flesh on it.'

· · ·

Back at the bungalow.

Chrissy has no messages. Not from the dibsies. Not from his ma.

'How is yer ma?'

'She's not responding to my requests for…enquiries.'

She's not returnin' his calls. But Chrissy wants to talk about a case well solved.

'Boy – we really helped that guy out.'

Mmm. Kinda.

The kid's a saint – a Shit Town saint – n I don't like to see him doin' his own dirty work.

'Yer files are a weapon, n we've just fired off a few rounds. Exploitin' knowledge for the greater good: for the community. For the kid. For Digby.'

'He's a very good friend of mine.'

'I expect he will be dude – I expect he will be. But anyway: how's about next time – yer know, to save yer energy – I'll be the leverage delivery system? Via the medium of rap – n you can just watch? I've already been practisin'. Checkit: *Spittin' out rhymes at the speed of the chimes on a clock, Times a million, coz that is a billion of O's in me bank, So I'll buy me a tank, To blow up this place like a boot in yer face, Coz I ain't some soft lad from Alty, I'm Basil Fawlty, I'm angry n kickin' me wheels* – n that's me done, coz rhymin' with wheels ain't easy man.'

Chris is lookin' at me through a magnifyin' glass.

'You need a dictionary, Runce. An A-Z of…erm…?'

'Mad sick rhymes. Good idea Chrissy. The Runce Dictionary of Rap. As used by everyone from me to…MC Tunes.'

'What's it about then, that rap?'

'Lee who runs Lee Stores. I asked him to get Vegan Tikka pies in – refused. Whatever happened to customer comes first?'

• • •

Chrissy's told me to take him for a brew in Starbucks. I couldn't be fooked arguin'. He got given cake, but he'd brought his own biscuits. He's eatin' them first, with his eyes closed.

'Why Chrissy? Why?'

'I want to get better at touching.'

'Said the priest to his legal counsel.'

'So sometimes I eat biscuits with my eyes closed.'

'Yer gettin' better at tastin' innit?'

'Oh no. I'm already very good at tasting. I'm identifying these biscuits by hand – then eating them. With my eyes closed.'

Right.

'Think of the biscuit as a witness.'

'To what?'

'Not all mysteries start with a crime Runce. Sometimes the detective has to begin by discovering some evidence.'

'Of what?'

'Anything.'

'OK, settin' the bar low there Chrissy – sounds like there'll be plenty of work for yer.'

'Practice makes perfect. Rosemary and Thyme. They're good detectives.'

'Good, we've changed the subject then have we? Rosemary n Thyme. Well – I wouldn't want 'em pokin' round me greenhouse, that's for sure.'

'They're always where the murders are – if the murders are in gardens. The lady who works here? She's a very good friend of mine. I get free cake.'

'I noticed.'

'Because ladies, you see, "know what's what." They're good detectives. Which is why I'm…"a hit with the ladies." '

Shudder.

'They know when things don't…add up? And they need to add up, see? When you're a detective? So you keep asking more questions and then you get…'

Even more insane?

'…answers, and then everyone gets happy. But the best detectives, well, the answers, erm, annoy them, because they just show up the gaps where the answers are…not. And right now I'm annoyed.'

He stops to eat cake. I've never seen anyone look less annoyed to be fair. The silent stare is his signature look though. I'm still not sure if he's workin' out simple things very slowly, or really complicated things with a stupid expression on his face.

'It's when you keep asking questions…'

Sponge is flyin' everywhere. Old people in massive brown coats gawp at him.

'…and keep looking, you see something's not right and that's when…well, erm. Cormoran Strike is a new detective, a man, but he's got it too and he's only got one leg.'

He stops – thinks about a one-legged man I've never heard of. Pats a coat pocket, packed with free business cards.

'I'm a detective. With one case.'

But two legs.

'I've learnt from the best Runce. And I've got the answers. Now I just need to get them in the right order. So things add up Runce – for Inspector Kaye? Mmm. So I better go home. He's probably called.'

• • •

Detective Inspector Graham Kaye

The sea of robotic faces in front of me is programmed to deliver paperwork and avoid independent thought: to do no harm. Because this is policing, and it's as broken as I am. But they can't know that – I have to keep going.

'Ballistics. And I'll spell it out for you again – read this stuff yourself, absorb it, come up with some ideas perhaps? Because that's our job? So. Two identical 9mm Makarovs, and we can confirm now that neither were fired in the property, nor indeed had been fired recently.'

The picture is up. Oooh, guns, actual guns, from a murder site: now I have their attention.

'One wasn't loaded, but had been cleaned: completely rinsed, consistent with the acidic traces found on site – which also showed up in notable levels on a front door key and a phone, so again, suggestion of a wider clean-up – but that's not a proven link. For posterity's sake, that's the weapon on the left.'

Paphaedes is scowling – trying to remember his left and right perhaps.

'The other was loaded, but hadn't been cleaned. What does that mean? What can these guns tell us? Think. You'll need to, because no prints were salvageable from either.'

They stare not at me, but at the screen – it's a relief.

'We have, however, got something: confirmation that the one set of prints we do have – from the exterior of the front door – are not consistent with the DNA of the victim. Backing up the theory that we have a victim and a clear main suspect. Two separate DNA collections, both identities remain unknown. OK?'

Our failings, there for all to see.

'The victim: who was he? To recap: suggestions of a toxic lifestyle having put his system under the cosh, certainly there's evidence of heavy alcohol use in the hours up to his death, and protein levels indicating an advanced bone cancer he probably would have known about. We need more. There are persons out there who must know that this individual has disappeared off the face of the earth, not come home, gone AWOL from work, missed an appointment – but they are conspicuous by their absence. Still no grieving relatives, friends, acquaintances, business partners, debtors. No-one's coming forward at all – why not? Do they not care? Are they afraid? Of someone? Or something? We need to find out more as soon as we possibly can. The public is waiting. Top brass are waiting.'

Top brass. Christ. What have I become?

• • •

Thinking, processing, analysing, it makes me feel better – but isn't it all really just cowardice? Door closed, phone off the hook, I'm stuck – paralysed – staring at a mug. But not just any mug. A mug that makes a mug of me. A mug, sent by the simpleton sleuth Pringle, gift-wrapped. It says: "The best damn detective in this station." Mad – or messing with my head, aided by

Runcie and his chimps? Secretly, I like this mug, because I am the best damn detective in this station, on this case – the only detective. I place it in my middle draw and consider the note it came with: "Why haven't you called? See you soon – Detective Chris Pringle (very good detective)."

A moron, inveigling his way into a murder investigation. Or wanting to. Wanting us out there – wanting to be out there with us. Why?

I need to think, but of course I can never think, and then the phone rings: Mogford. And he just starts talking, talking. Julie Duke's been on the phone. Making sure Pringle gets started. Very persuasive. Had a copy of the C.L.E.A.R. memo. How? Wanted the details. Very persuasive. So he sent her the details. Sent it to all the leads too, so it should be in my inbox. And he, DCI Mogford, just wants to make sure that I, DI Kaye, understand that scheme or no scheme, n'er-do-wells or no n'er-do-wells, the Chief Super's will is not to be questioned, and I need to play the game. Is that C.L.E.A.R.? (Likes everyone to play the game of course does Mogford – keep things ticking over with some bullshit here, a few easy wins there, and if you can quietly tuck the rest out of sight, all the better, so he can glide towards retirement, honours, the Rotary Club – but most importantly right now, he needs me to play the game). It's just a scheme, we set the parameters, they think they're getting what they want, they're mistaken, simple, so play the game, the man sounds practically care-in-the-community, we'll look like we're really trying and then I, DI Kaye, can get on with the real job in hand, a rudimentary-looking murder case from which he, DCI Mogford, expects results.

'Yes sir. Yes, sir. No, nope, perfectly clear sir. If I can just say…no, no you're right sir, we were going to get him in again, but… absolutely sir, we will get him involved right away sir, that was always the plan, I just thought we ought to agree with you a basis for…right sir – I'll read it right away sir.'

I put the phone down, because, well, there's no-one there any more.

I take another big, imaginary lug from my top drawer, and then press the intercom, get Paphaedes in. Not only are we now officially lumbered with Pringle, but the Chief knows I've been trying to shirk it. Awful.

'Paphaedes. We need to get Pringle in. To…'

I can barely unpucker my lips enough to say it.

'…to…help.'

He nods – no reaction. Jesus.

'When do you want him in sir?'

I'm determined to cope with this – determined to get through without the anxiety taking over. Keep Pringle and Runcie in their box. Keep the DCI off my back. Get Trim back and going up in the world, Paphaedes staying where he is until he grows a new lobe. Restore order and solve this case. Maybe make it the pinnacle of my career – not the death knell.

'I'll call him myself. By the way – anything turn up on the logs? Arson? Run-ins? Any patterns? Anything suspicious?'

'Nothing sir. Three different people on the Paddy Ashdown Estate have complained about a guy who keeps a very loud goat – but I doubt it's connected.'

I take my unreasonable but not inconsiderable rage out on Paphaedes with a glare, and he looks stung.

'We need a break. Mogford's on my back and The Chronicle don't like bad news stories – but all it takes is a few "concerned citizens" pointing out that we're getting fucking nowhere, and this will kick off.'

I point him out of the room, pick up the phone and dial. A landline for fuck's sake. Even I've moved on from landlines. It picks up first time.

'Yes?'

'Is that Mr Pringle?'

'Well that depends who's asking. Who's asking? Wait there.'

Jesus.

'Got to get my pad.'

Christ.

'Right. So who's asking? If it's Mr Pringle?'

'Inspector Kaye.'

'Oh yes – the sad old police man. No then.'

'What?'

'Detective Pringle is here.'

'Can I call you Chris?'

There's a pause.

'Well – we've had a lot of chats about that here, and I'm not sure.'

I'm not calling this buffoon Detective Pringle – but I don't have time for this.

'How about we just see how it goes?'

'OK.'

It's a moral victory.

'So, Chris.'

'Yes Graham?'

Focus. Stay focused.

'I'd like to invite you to, well, come in and try out some police work. Maybe sit in on a few things, go out on the beat? We thought maybe you'd like that?'

'Mmm. Yes, I'll be setting up my agency soon. It's a detective agency.'

'Right?'

'There's a "gap in the market." '

'What's the gap?'

'Victims of crime who want their cases to be solved.'

'Right. OK.'

'Do you know Ironside?'

'I know who he is. Detective in a wheelchair, right?'

'No. Consultant Detective in a wheelchair. He was a very good police detective – the Chief of all police detectives, San Francisco Police Department. But then he was injured in the line of…job. Very sad. Wheelchair. He had to stop. But he became a…you see?'

I massage my temples. Migraine, migraine, go away, come again another day.

'There are one or two small differences between you and Ironside Chris.'

'Mmm. So I will be the "Consultant Detective." On the case.'

Those pictures. The blackened bone and sinew. I can't get away from them. But over my dead body is he getting near the sharp end of this whole sorry business.

'I'm already busy with my enquiries. So I won't have time to…help out Internal Affairs or…hand out parking tickets.'

'Well obviously Chris, any information you can give us will be gratefully received. And you can sit alongside us – when I say so, until I say so. Because you are here to help us Chris – not the other way round. Do you understand?'

'Yes. I'm not stupid.'

You are.

'I'm not.'

This guy freaks me out.

'Look. Murder enquiries can take a long time Chris.'

'Oh – I know.'

'Right. They're complex. We're always juggling layers, personnel. The procedurals – on TV? They actually bear some resemblance to real police work. And I get it, you like your TV detectives, they're the mavericks, they're fun – but they're not real.'

'Are.'

'No they're not.'

'Then why do they show their cases on the telly?'

Really?

'What I'm saying is: detective work isn't just staring at a wall, looking at pictures and drawing lines from A to B. It's boring processes: ticking boxes.'

All I can hear is his breathing. Slow – an effort.

'OK. You can do that bit. Do I get a gun?'

'No. Come in Thursday.'

'Erm...no. I'm planning to watch Shoestring on Thursday: "A Dangerous Game." Very tricky case. And I have a meeting.'

'Really?'

'Yes – a meeting. With Peron at Purvis Cuts.'

'A hair cut?'

'He'll cut my hair, and I'll tell him who's been spraying "Bell-End" on his shutters.'

'That's police work Chris – and we do not encourage vigilantes.'

'Peron Purvis is not a vigilante. He's 63 and he just tells their mums. I think. How about...now?'

'Tomorrow Chris – let's make it tomorrow. Oh, and you'll be with the police – so try and look neat.'

'10-4. Oh and Inspector Graham Kaye?'

'What?'

'There's been a murder.'

Gone.

Alone again.

Playing the game – it works for millions apparently. So why can't I make it work for me? Because…what's the endgame?

I push open my laptop, launch email and force myself to hunt down Mogford's precious "details."

15

THEN, 1992

Runcie

It's toodle-pip to The Castle. Lord of the Rings Land. The Republic.

Awake for a night? Yer lips are rubber, the top of yer head does its tinglin', yer brain's jelly, it's all a mess. Awake for half a week though, n yer on a roll. Fit as a fiddle me. SAS fit. I mean, OK, proper holy visions n that, from three days n nights spent out on the moors, yer get me – but I will not falter. Game on. Ready to go. Ready for home.

But there's summink else. I've seen a few crash landins in me time – where the mix in yer noggin just goes, n yer question everythin', yer know, Jimmy in Quadrophenia? N it's not that. It's that me feelins aren't clear, n they should be. So I try to find a reason.

It's true that The Republic started to look a bit tired these last coupla days. Perhaps it grew too fast – like one of them Chinese cities Student bangs on about. Or maybe it was just the mornin' – the final dawn – when a four-day refusal to drop the kids off at the pool gave way to a squat in the far corner of some farmer's field. The problem? I was not alone. Cider loons, wantin' to chat me through me special moment. Two little crusty kids called Tusk n Warrior with the same dodgy barnets, tryin' to sell me king size. It was all too much. But no, that's not it.

A bit of me will always be in that field. No, not just that bit – a bit of me soul. The secret can never be taken away. Inducted into The Republic for life now we are. When I'm 80 n lookin' back, me skin will prickle, thinkin' of all me fellow ravers, takin' their sunburn home with 'em. N wads of cash mean I did what I came to do. I partied hard, I sold everythin', n I will only have to see me wonderful, skull-crushin' pals the Maskells once more, ever again: to give 'em their 10% n say goodbye. *Hasta la vista thickos: one day I might make a comeback, but yer'll be in prison or dead from summink daft by then, so laters: it's not been a pleasure.*

I'll make that call as soon as I get back. Hit the F&L for a ta-ra, then go home n sleep for a week or two. But…

Maybe it's the lack of kip?

Maybe it's me kiwis wearin' off?

Maybe me mind's feelin' fine, but me body's got a cob on, n it's tryin' to get me attention?

It could be all of 'em – but it isn't. Summink's actually botherin' me. N that summink is Chris.

Me beautiful mad lad is gone gone – n it's dullin' me afterglow. Coz this future stuff: it was all about him. He's all I care about. Really. But he's not just lost-days-of-fun-in-a-field quiet, catapulted back from medieval mayhem: there's more. A thousand-yard raver stare, then sleep, but then shoutin' out lines of blether now n again, as he sweats n snores away next to me in the back of Julie's wheels, barkin' nonsense at trucks n cars n locals, a vivisection dog havin' nightmares.

I close me eyes, nice n easy, n soak up the rhythm of the road. Naughty cats need cat naps – n maybe when I wake up, everythin' will be amazin'.

• • •

When I do wake up we're home. Shit Town. Maureen's. But the rhythm of the road keeps tickin' on, coz the engine's still runnin'. We're not movin' though, n the not-movin' has hooked me out of me dozy-do. Rude.

Me face is in Chris's upper arm, a soft squishy pillow made from a man I love, asleep, his legs jigglin' little jelly quivers. I stretch like only a cool cat can n check out me driver, who sits at the wheel, smokin' her billionth fag, Student next to her. I squint from me back seat slouch n I can see he's pullin' himself together for summink, a bit too quickly.

I follow Julie n Student's look, an odd, flat look, n then see why the air's gone funny – coz the real world has cast a nasty spell on us, suckin' the magic right out of Julie's motor, n whiskin' not just the whole fookin' weekend away from under our feet, but maybe everythin'. Just like that.

Coz there's a cop car on the front drive. N in a bag stuffed under the seat, sits that future of ours, n some personal. N how I might pay for that personal now. So the Runce needs a plan, fast. Which should involve us drivin' off, quickly, quietly, right now.

'Why the fook aren't we leavin'?'

Julie – she doesn't turn.

'It's too late Runce. There's one in the front seat there – clocked us n radioed in straight away. The rest must be in the house.'

In the house. Fook. I sit up. What's in the house? Is there anythin' in the house?

Chris's eyes are open now. He's the last person they need to see right now, which is why there is immediately a problem when he clocks what's goin' on n starts gettin' out the car. Before I can hold him back, he's gone, n I'm tellin' Julie n Student to wait, n followin' him past the lady copper sittin' there, who looks at us n nods, radio in hand, n we're at the front door, n Chris is through it, n I'm after him, n he's movin' forward, on a mission. N we're into the lounge, n two police are there, n they turn, like they've been expectin' us.

'Mr Runce?' one of 'em asks, like he's waitin' to tell me what to do. What a waste of life.

'At yer service?'

I give Maureen a wink but she's not smilin'. I don't know what she is – but she's not smilin', frettin', cryin'. Just…nothin'.

'Would you mind stepping outside?'

So that's a fooker innit? Stephen Patrick Runce. Manchester's mightiest Stephen Patrick, two rozzers n a Maureen, lookin' at me. Our whole world, outside, with Student shittin' himself, Julie smokin', n a rozzette watchin' on. There for the takin' it was – so near, yet so far.

'He can stay,' says Maureen.

Eh? It all moves on though. The lady one. Not fast – but definite.

'Chris, would you sit down please?'

'No thanks.'

N I finally get it – this isn't about me.

Maureen still stares. She speaks too though.

'Just say it.'

'Chris, it might be better to have a seat. No? OK.'

She's in charge – n she's been through the formalities. Slow. Clear.

'Mr Pringle. Chris. There's been an incident this morning with a car. We understand it had been travelling from up near Pendock – where you've been yourself I believe. At 07:51 it came off the road on the B3130. No other vehicles were involved. The driver was Frank Christopher Pringle: your father. I'm very sorry to say that he died at the scene.'

I can hear the telly in the neighbour's gaff.

I told Chris it was all gonna be OK. I said that. I promised him.

He just stands.

Scannin'.

For summink…summink to confirm all this stuff…a newspaper maybe, that says yeah, today is today, to confirm he's awake, that it's all real, horribly, horribly real. But the only one who can offer him anythin' – of course – is Maureen. Not me. Not these rozzers in his lounge, lyin', talkin' shite.

He looks at her. She looks back – gives him the tiniest of nods. Without emotion. He waits 2, 3, 4, 5, 10 seconds. He looks at me quickly. Back at Maureen. N then very slowly, he lowers himself down, right where he is, onto the floor.

N suddenly it's like, this is what I never knew I've always been afraid of: Chris, on a floor, surrounded by strangers, n we don't know what to do. Maureen is frozen, n just like that, she's one of them little old ladies they take yer to for carols as a kid, dead but alive, n when yer look in their eyes, it's just regret, n there's nothin' yer can say.

So Chris is alone.

I get down on the floor with him, put me hand round his shoulder. I've never seen him cry. He's tough, or empty, or summink. I dunno. But he's cryin' now. Little sobs. Little sobs from a big lad.

'What d'yer wanna do Chris?'

What a question. It just came out. N he looks. N for one moment I think he's gonna suggest a trip to the swings, forget all about this nonsense. But no.

'I want to remember. I just want to remember.'

PART THREE

PLEASE DO NOT THROW ME IN THE BIN

16

THE FUTURE

Police Testimony:
Stephen Patrick Runce

DIGK   'Police testimony of Stephen Patrick Runce. Those
        also present are: on behalf of Mr Runce, Ms Patricia
        Liversedge; myself, Detective Inspector Graham
        Kaye; and PC Tim Paphaedes. Please confirm your
        name for the tape Mr Runce and then we'll begin. Mr
        Runce?'

SR   'Mmm?'

DIGK   'Name?'

SR   'Oh. Right. Sweet – an easy one. So: Stephen Patrick
        Runce, just like yer probably said Boss Man, but
        call me Runcie, or MC Chester, or President of the
        Republic of–'

DIGK   'Date of birth?'

SR   'Well, it was one of them years...yer know – back a bit?'

DIGK 'Fine – have it your way. So, to confirm. Mr Runce: ahead of the inquest and any subsequent prosecution, you're here to tell us what you know about Chris Pringle, and events leading up to the fatal fire which occurred at No.7 Brunswick Villas. We know the basics. But there's a lot still missing. And for a number of reasons, Mr Pringle's accounts are...compromised. So that's where you come in: help us fill in the gaps. Take your time. There's no hurry. And please – let's start at the beginning.'

SR   'Right Boss. Fillin' the gaps. Takin' me time. Tellin' the tale. Got it. It's a journey mind, so clunk click: there's a bit of now, a bit of then, now-then, now-then – but yer'd like that, right? See – he had to make a choice: between keepin' things buried, n diggin' 'em up? He didn't have the answers – course he didn't. But he did have a plan, a crazy, stupid, ridiculous plan: to get involved. The trouble was, yer let him – n we all know how that turned out.

      The beginnin' though, right? OK, let's go. I'm not as baked as I like to be for deep thinkin', yer get me, but that's probably a good thing, coz I might well start off on a philosophical debate – which yer'd lose – about what that means. Coz yer want me to talk about the crash right? 1992? Coz that was the beginnin'? But maybe it wasn't? Maybe it was the beginnin' of the end – or the end of the beginnin'?

I mean, as far as the rest of the world was concerned – you'se lot – it was more like the end full stop. As in, end of. His dad dies – one more no-mark comin' to his own natural conclusion – forget about it; wife's not really his wife any more, son's a weirdo, move on.

N I mean, someone else's grief? It's hard to understand innit? Yer know it's there, but it's only an idea – a concept. If yer see someone's head split open, 'Bena spurtin' everywhere, yer think: *Oooh, bet that hurt*. Grief though? Even though it's worse? Nah – it's only a theory. Yer don't wince the same way. Or maybe it's coz if yer went round feelin' everyone's pain, yer'd never make it through the day? I dunno – but anyway, no-one stepped up, n I get it.

I'm there of course: just coz I didn't want a mortgage n a subscription to Saloon Car magazine, don't mean I have – had – no fookin' understandin' of the fundamentals of human love n emotion. Far from it Blue – I'd fooked up. Let him down.

It was a communion to me see, rave, a moment where a higher collective purpose might reveal itself. But I could handle the truth that really, it wouldn't – that there's no such thing. That the quest continues, always – and it's all on you. But while I'd just been playin' with questions in me noggin, Chris had been lookin' for answers. Already. I shoulda realised – but I hadn't been payin' attention. Not hard enough. So now I owed him – after?

But picture it...me back then? I weren't exactly *counsel yer through the trial of yer life* material, yer get me? Yeah, I was there for him: I've never made that mistake again. Trust me. N Student could probably come up with a quote from one of his great philosophers. N Julie helped him – she's always been better at stuff. But grief wants answers, n when it all quietened down, the only person who could give him any was Maureen.

N her reaction? Well her reaction, from the moment we heard the news – well really, it was no reaction. A one-woman emotional lockdown. She said nothin', like she felt nothin'. She'd always been chatty Maureen, always...we'd thought...open? But yer'd see her now, n all she'd talk about – apart from normal stuff, shoppin', tidyin' – all she'd talk about when it came to that? Just the facts. That's all she would deal in, in the months after – facts, facts, repeatin' the facts.

They took DNA from the body n matched it up to Chrissy – fact, so she didn't wanna see it. The car was registered to his old man as a rental, fact, the booze in his blood, all facts. Death by misadventure. No proper grievin': she was just...numb. She'd lost a husband who hadn't been there anyway I guess? She didn't want to get sucked in. I remember her sayin': *something like this was always going to happen.* No questions. It was over.

The horror of it all did summink to her. She quietly threw away Frank's stuff – there weren't much, but it was too soon, n then there was nothin' left for Chrissy to hold. She pulled the phone out the wall. She surrendered herself to the Church, n then, that was all she'd talk about – work or church. I don't really remember her goin' to church before, she probably did. But this was different. Different level church-goin'. I'm not sure what she did with all the hours – printin' orders of service, flowers, summink to do with candles? Lists of jobs to be ticked off. But she was at work, or at the church – n everythin' was dictated by the parish calendar, her church routine. We'd never go n see her at church of course. We'd have Saturdays. N that was it. Yer could see she was just copin'. I'm not blamin' her. Yer can't forget all she'd given Chrissy? Chrissy hadn't. Chrissy never would. Still though. It was hard for Mo – but it was harder for him. Brutal.

Coz OK, he looks simple? N coz he was closed up – coz Mo was – never more simple than then. Fine. But did that mean he couldn't feel – that he didn't notice that no-one was askin' questions? That no-one cared? I don't think blame's a thing in all this – for what happened then, for what it did to Chrissy, or for what's happened now. But it got to him: everythin' bein' just…forgotten. His pain weren't on any radars – not at all. It was like his dad didn't…count: coz he'd half shuffled off already? He'd stare out the front window, left, right, but no-one came. He tried speakin' with the rozzers, the fella in charge. But when yer just crossin' t's, a lad like him's easy to ignore innit? He just wanted to talk I suppose – someone in yer life goes, n yer not there to hold their hand, to know they went peacefully, to stop it? I guess yer always gonna try n pull summink from the scene, some kinda reassurance. But the truth is: they blanked him.

Chrissy'd lost his dad – n messed up as he already was, he was just left to float. No-one was sayin' anythin', askin' any questions at all. He only ever saw people as good people, n it didn't change him – but it knocked him down. He was out for the count.

He moves out. Julie sets him up – got him his bungalow. He sorta drifts. For the '90s – the rest of the '90s. I mean, he didn't miss much. It was good times in Uncool Britannia – happy apathy makes for shite music see, fake vibes, Loaded Lads everywhere. But, OK, right, I can tell – that's not important to you squares right now is it? So we'll crack on Chief. Coz yeah, he watched telly. That's about all. He stayed at home – in his bungalow? He signed on. He didn't talk to anyone. We as good as lost him – as much as we tried. He went madder. And then the Millennium came, n it went...

N he sorta decides...realises. No-one had asked any questions: but he still had some questions, all of his own.'

17

NOW

Maureen

Dear Lord:

Thank you for the rain. It's a pest to most folk Lord, and they'll be looking at me funny thinking "Who wants rain?" – but it droughts in winter as well doesn't it Lord, even when it's chilly? I expect not everyone likes to bother you as much as me, but – Lord? The gardeners, the farmers, the folk down the allotments over at Barton's Marsh – they'll all be chuffed. That's all I'm saying. And thems who are used to rain – they aren't bothered either, so that's a bonus, like Brendan for example, because you know where he's from of course Lord? Or maybe it's nice to be reminded of some of the details, you know, what with your workload? He's from Scotland.

Not much has happened since we spoke this morning Lord. Do you see more of me now I'm not at church all day? Or less?

Who do you focus on? Thems who turn up? Or the ones who don't? Anyway, you can set your best watch by me I'm that boring.

I pray for the poor souls suffering in pain Lord: the homeless out there freezing alone, the folk with the real blues, or with physical sort of, difficulties, the unhappy spastics, "gender warriors," all sorts Lord, the "trans community" even, I read about them. And the folk who block it all out.

Erm.

Sorry Lord. I was drifting. I'd say "Look at the time," but you don't need to, do you? Because here I am again? I don't know where it goes, the time, but anyway, point is, I expect lots of folk are grateful Lord and I just thought I'd say "Thank you." On their behalf? It's too bloody cold mind, black ice, and I don't like Brendan out on his chuffing moped. He's home now.

I often wonder who you talk to yourself Lord? I was reading the other day in BBC History Magazine that in the olden days, before alarm clocks, they used to have "knocker-uppers," who would come round and give you a knock, wake you up? But the knocker-upper needed a knocker-upper too, and what happens if the knocker-upper's knocker-upper wasn't knocked up themselves? We all need help from time to time. Though I probably wouldn't be much use to you mind, haven't done half the things some folk have.

Erm.

I do a good cup of tea – if you ever fancy a natter?

What am I going on about?

So. Bless Stephen, Lord. He's a good boy. And Julie – wiser than me, much, much wiser than me, that's the truth of it Lord. The truth of it. And bless Brendan. And I pray for Christopher as my own son Lord, but you know all about sons of course, though you were probably a bit firmer with yours?

Be quiet Maureen.

Thank you for Christopher. He's a special boy Lord. He never complained. He's always tried to do things. But I worry where he's going Lord – where he's got to. I pray for him to go steady Lord.

It's my fault Lord.

Night night Lord.

● ● ●

Chris

'Yer alright Chrissy?'

My home – my bungalow. No. 45 Phillips Farm Road. Details.

I am very good at being in my bungalow. I have an Interview Room which is also a lounge. But it's day one as a Consultant Detective. With the police. Inspector Kaye invited me and we will probably be partners. I told him he was pleased and he said "Is that a question?" so I said "Good idea yes," and he said "Ever-so-pleased."

Runcie has come to wish me luck, with a big box.

I look in the mirror. In my Interview Room. I get stuck. I remember that I try not to look in mirrors because: is it me looking in the mirror, or me in the mirror looking at me?

Down, right, left, down. Look at Runcie.

'It's cold Runce.'

Runcie forgets things – "short-term memory loss Boss, occupational hazard." So it's my job to remember – because I can never forget again.

'They don't let me have gas Runce.'

'No.'

And then I remember that Runcie has brought a box.

'What's in the box?'

'Got yer a pressie Chrissy.'

'Oh. Is it a sandwich?'

'Er, no.'

'Did you steal it?'

'No. Look, this isn't 20 questions – just wait n see.'

'Everything is 20 questions to the detective Runce. Sometimes more.'

'Right. Well, yer about to find out if that's true. Spotted this down the station, thought it might be useful, so I got a set borrowed from the library – with whom you by the way, before yer start, are the one with the problem relationship. I just skip the whole library card side of it that's all coz, well, yer know – *Super Catchphrase* - you ain't seen me right? Anyway, I sent Disco Sean along n…ta da!'

Oh dear.

'That's a very big…book.'

'Correctamondo Chrissy. That's two very big books. *Blackstone's Police Operational Handbook: Practice and Procedure* and… *The Law.* 2015 edition. Sweet.'

Oh dear. A handbook. A rule book?

'Listen – the cops are chumps right, but if yer wanna play their game – n Frankly Mr Shankly, I'm a bit wonked out you ever heard from 'em again – yer gotta know the rules. N I know what yer thinkin' – lots of words, not many pictures…but we can do a bit together every day, just us. I'll build one up, read some stuff out, it'll be boss. Julie – you in?'

Julie is examining her claws.

'Oh yeah – sounds amazing, I'd much rather do that than, say, something better.'

• • •

'Let's go to work.'

I say it in my head. I will help the police, in my best tracksuit, which says "DETECTIVE" on it.

I turn around to show Runcie the big white letters that Mrs Winstanley from No.37 stuck on the back. Runcie puts a hand on my shoulder – he's proud of me.

'How many fookin' layers yer got under that – yer look like yer gonna float off? Just be careful yeah Chrissy? Boss Man cop, Teenager cop – they're rozzers remember, innit? N generally speakin', when rozzers don't have answers, they have a habit of makin' 'em up. I mean, it's a miracle they're gettin' you in, but it's one of the *Top Ten Miracles of All Time Ever* that they're leavin' me alone.'

'No.'

'What d'yer mean – no?'

'Well it's the whole imm, imm, imm…'

I pick up the piece of paper, carefully. I point to Julie, but she's not going to help me. I show it to Runcie.

'Julie borrows stuff too. She borrowed a piece of paper from the station and then she spoke to…someone…and then she got a better piece of paper, and this is the better piece of paper.'

Runcie reads it.

'C.L.E.A.R. – new Witness Immunity Scheme.'

Runcie reads all of it. Runcie is laughing. Runcie has to sit down.

'An immunity scheme! That's fookin' mint Chrissy! Mint! C.L.E.A.R.! That changes everythin'. *Gettin' away with it, all me life!* I'm in the clear! Again! As always! N so are you Chrissy – in the fookin' clear. So what's yer strategy? Yer in now, right? Yer've got threads that literally say *DETECTIVE*, n a free pass to Cop Land, thanks to the daftest fookin' idea I've ever heard in me life. Yer livin' the Chrissy dream: it's happenin'! So go on: who yer gonna base yerself on, really?'

Who's the killer? I have thought about that, a lot. And which detective am I? I have thought about that too...a lotter.

'I am all of them Runce. But also none of them. Because I am only me: Chris.'

It looks like Runcie is finding this hard to...erm...so...

'I am not Inspector Morse.'

He looks happy.

'Phew – glad we both still agree he's a prick.'

The doorbell rings.

'Right – that'll be me man from Hilltop's. I'll drop yer off at the station. Need to do a coupla business transactions en route though Chrissy, know what I'm sayin'? All adds to the irony of the situation.'

Yes. Probably.

'Let's go to work.'

• • •

The station. I am a detective. I am a real detective. A Consultant Detective. Detective Chris Pringle.

'Come through Chris, come through.'

PC Paphaedes has given me a quick tour of the station and told me his name is Tim. But PC Paphaedes can't answer any questions and always seems like he's unsure that the next thing he is doing is a good idea – whether it's opening a door, taking off a coat or putting on a kettle – so he has taken me through to see Inspector Kaye.

Inspector Kaye has a desk with a picture on it, of his wife Sandra. I pick Sandra up, but he grabs her back and puts her in his top draw. I look at Inspector Kaye again and make a note on my pad: I write "sad" because I know that he is.

'What are you wearing? You can't sit in on police business with a tracksuit on'.

'I bet lots of suspects do.'

'Yes, well, you're not a suspect here are you, you're with the police.'

I make a note.

'In an unofficial capacity I might add,' he does add.

'It's a Sergio someone tracksuit. Runcie got several and I looked after them for a bit and got to keep my favourite.'

'OK. Well at least take the VW badge off. I was half expecting you to dress like Columbo, or Poirot, you know, the hat, the gloves.'

Mmm. I better tell him.

'Britain is afraid of men who wear hats. If you wear the wrong kind to a disco you may get punched. Although, not if you are a detective at a disco. Which is unlikely. Poirot never went to discos as far as I know. It would have been sweaty with his gloves on. So that's erm case…solved. You could be like Frost though Inspector Kaye. To be more like Frost, pick up and drink your boss's cup of tea – on purpose! You may not have gone to the right school, or play golf, and you might be an alcoholic, and eat all the best sandwiches and then leave during the speeches at regional get-togethers...and your wife is leaving you – actually...some of that is you, some of it's Frost... but anyway, if you take a slurp of your boss's – DCI Mogford's – tea, it shows him that you are the boss. That's why you need your own mug. That I got you. Where is it? You can put your vodka in it.'

I look around. When my looking means I see Inspector Kaye's face again, I notice it's looking back at me.

'Inspector Kaye? Where's your caravan?'

'My what?'

'Where's your Incident Room?'

'That's it Chris – out there. Not much to see is there? Very little to get us started on this case Chris. Very few facts.'

But Inspector Kaye is wrong. I don't remember all the facts, but I know they're there. I say what Runcie told me to say.

'You need to help me, help you.'

I ask Inspector Kaye – with my hand – if he wants to do a high five, but he just looks a bit ill and sad.

'Also...'

I look at my pad and take my time...

' "Immunity," yes?'

'Apparently.'

Oh dear.

'Not "apparently" Inspector Kaye – "yes." You need to say yes more, like, all the time – that's what Julie says. Say yes?'

'Yes.'

'Good. So now that you have said yes, you have to let me do my job – which, not sure if I said, is to help you do yours, by being a very good detective.'

'Great. PC Paphaedes: get a car ready, take Chris for a drive. You do understand, again Chris, that you are not here to solve this crime for us?'

What a silly thing to say! Of course I am. I ignore it.

'You're here in very unusual circumstances Chris, and not as a part of my—'

I stand up, shush him with a lip finger, show him the back of my tracksuit, and then hand him a business card, to show him how ready I am. My friend Digby has been very helpful.

'This has our insignia on it? Which implies you are a police officer?'

'Does my business card say police man on it?'

'No, but—'

'I'm a Consultant Detective. On a major case. I really don't have time to keep telling you – amongst other things I keep telling you – that I am not a police man.'

'Then why have you got our badge on your card?'

I look at one of my cards.

'When you nearly run a detective agency, it helps if suspects know you're a police man.'

'But you're not a policeman – you just said that.'

'Yes, but they don't need to know that, do they?'

I tap my head to show that this is a clever plan. Inspector Kaye puts his head in his hands and then starts arranging things on his desk. I don't think he likes change. He looks tired.

'Right. Question 1. Will we be working together like two top detectives, or will you just report back at the end of the day, or wait for me to solve the case?'

'You'll be accompanying PC Paphaedes.'

'Right. Let me make a note of…that. Question 2 then: when can I go to the lab?'

'Some information can't be shared with a civilian Chris, and even if I could–'

'Would you like me to have a word with path…patha… patho–'

'Pathology? No thanks.'

Inspector Kaye doesn't look at me. He presses a button – it makes PC Paphaedes' voice come out of a box.

'Sir?'

'He's all yours.'

• • •

Detective Inspector Graham Kaye

I wake up choking every night. It's been two years like that. Suppressed anxiety apparently. Best put me in charge of a murder case then. A peculiar, insidious murder case, with an unnamed victim. And an unknown perpetrator. And an overweight special needs child who thinks he's a detective, cluttering things up.

Before they headed off – delayed while Pringle took a ten-minute break in the staff loos – I tried to explain things to Paphaedes.

'Keep an eye on him – while making him feel like he's involved. Just make sure he's not wandering around getting up to God knows what. Because I don't want anyone, including God, to hear he's been up to anything – I myself just want to know that he's been up to nothing, but neither him nor his mates will be phoning bloody Mogford again to complain about it. Got it? That's what this scheme is about. I think.'

And then I got Chapman to take some bullshit shots – Pringle and I having a co-operative chinwag next to the community messages board.

'Make sure they're good enough to send to DCI Mogford, but not good enough to go in a newsletter.'

All I want to do is sleep. And then I need to focus. Everything else – Sandra, the wreckage of home, the indulgence of mental disintegration, the booze, the never-ending questions, sitting there unanswered, about why I can't just hold it together like everyone else, and play along, before I drop down dead? Everything else has to wait. For this case. But is it a case – or a PR exercise? And how is it a PR exercise?

But the thing that keeps me awake? Still? Those pictures. And this. We're enabling a benefits cheat. And Runcie with him – word is he's just flogging dope to a few regular customers, but not even he would deny that he used to sell pills. And Julie Duke, who it seems holds down some sales gig, raking it in apparently. And then there's Stuart Taylor on the fringes too: proper job, wife, kids, no dirt at all, plenty to lose. All of them have got every reason to keep their heads down – yet instead they're letting their special friend waste police time in the middle of a murder enquiry. So what the hell are they playing at? And why am I still thinking about it?

18

THE FUTURE

Police Testimony:
Stephen Patrick Runce

SR   'Now you'se lot – *Mainstream posse in the area!* – yer not familiar with Daytimeland are yer? A nation of placcy bag millions, livin' to the tick of stopped clock.

    What it is right, out there in Broken Britain, there's
countries within countries: different kinds of normal. The
Republic – our republic, back in the day – was a state of mind
yer committed to forever, of hopes n dreams. Daytimeland
is just a state of low expectations. Bit of free advice though:
get to know it. A bit like yer scheme intended, yeah? I
mean, yer'll see the ones who get out n about: the specials
stayin' warm down Maccy Dees, the not-so-yummy mum-
mies smokin' fags with their kids, the old soaks headin'
from bookie to boozer n back again – still though, that's

only a few of its fine citizens, the ones who can be arsed to squeeze out the front door. So let me explain about the ones who can't.

When I say Chrissy'd just stayed at home n watched telly for a few years – for the '90s – I mean, really, that's all he did? Watched telly. For the '90s. N telly's different in Daytimeland: methadone for the eyes. But it does offer ways out.

First of all, there's the quiz shows – easy money, buy all the Stella yer've ever dreamed of. Then there's the racin' – bit of a flutter, same deal. There's yer antiques – yer sittin' on a goldmine. N then there's yer detectives: so the citizens of Daytimeland can overlook their own criminal tendencies by focusin' on murder – nice one – plus they also get to think they're fookin' geniuses, by pretendin' they've solved those murders.

So. When Chrissy's old fella carked it, he went proper wonky – like I said. Stopped goin' out, didn't go back to work: Daytimeland. Didn't speak to anyone apart from his ma, me, Julie, Student occasionally, n then just the odd word like *yes, no, biscuit.* Just stayed in with his headphones on. Or watched telly. Sat in front of a screen, watchin' anythin.'

Then, some time, not long after the Millennium, 2000, I walk in one day, n he's in front of Columbo. Now, we used to watch Columbo all the time when we were kids, when I came to stay with him – a jug of squash n a bag of mini cookies from Maureen, proper happy memories Blue, yer get me? So I thought: this is good, we can have a chinwag about this. So I sit down n go, *Oh, this is the one where Dog*

– that's his dog see, Dog? – *where Dog's the fookin' hero.* N he just stops n looks at me, like he don't know what I'm talkin' about, but with a strange look in his eye. Then the next day, he's at it again, with a pad out. New episode, but again I go *Yeah, seen this one too, eh?* N he stops writin', n just stares again.

After that, he's a Columbo machine. At first I thought maybe it was just soothin' for him – repetitive. He'd always been a bit like that, even as a kid – lists, tapes, the way he would do things over n over. N now he's recordin' all these Columbos – but he's also makin' notes. Stops the tape, rewinds, works things out. N at first, Maureen says nothin', but I'm happy, coz at least it's given him summink to think about, yer get me? But after seven, eight years of him bein' Mr Silent Sausagemeat I'm bored, so yer know, now there's a chance to chew it, after a while I just come out n ask him: *Why?* N this is what he says: *I've forgotten my Columbos.*

He says it's like life's wiped out part of his noggin. But Columbo gives him back this feelin': it's like through those stories, he's wakin' up to who he was before it all. But there's more – coz with Columbo, yer know from the start who the murderer is. So he's watchin', he knows the solution, he can see whatever Columbo sees, n he can work out how Columbo works it out. It's fookin' boss, it's genius, it's Dictionary Corner. N then he thinks *All these learnings, might just make me a detective…*n that look on yer grill there Inspector Kaye? That means yer still tryin' to work out if they did or they didn't. Right?

Anyway. After Columbo, he's like, what's next? He starts on Bergeracs then Lovejoys n Shoestrings n Minders n The Saint. He's a livin', breathin', detective-bingein' animal. He signs on, eats, sleeps a bit, watches his detectives. N Julie sorta encouraged it. She'd always made sure he was good to go, forms all signed, money comin' in. When he was down down though, he'd said there was voices in his head. *We all have voices Chris – the trick is not to ignore them.* That's what she said. N the detectives – that meant he was listenin'. Actin'. He had a focus. He was movin' forwards, n Julie helped make it happen.

Made it a bit hard between her n Maureen of course, coz Mo was...failin'? But she knew, Mo did. She couldn't face anythin', Chris needed to be out there, Julie was helpin'. She tried with Mo n all Julie did – tried to get her to move on or talk – we both did. But she had her church routine – that was it. Draw a line.

Meanwhile, we'd all thought maybe Chrissy was just gettin' summink out of his system – coz one day, it's like he just clicks...starts goin' back out into the world, starts talkin' to punters again. But no. Did he stop with his detectives? Nah man. Far from it. In fact, so into his detectives is he, that he tries to start it all up again with the rozzers – like I said, he had questions. But, well, it was the Nice Clean Results Brigade right? Case still closed Pal.

But he didn't take that. He didn't stop with his detectives. No. He'd just started workin' on a case of his own, that was all: *The Case of His Old Man.* Case, not, closed. N I'm secretly thinkin', s'all well n good: but to be a detective, yer need a crime? N yer know that feelin' yerselves now fellas, when he turns to yer, n it's like he can read yer mind. Coz right there, right then, he goes: *I have a crime Runce. It's the crash. The crash is the crime.'*

19

NOW

Chris

We're in PC Paphaedes' car again.

Police work is boring.

I do some staring.

'Why are you staring at me?'

'I'm not staring at you. I'm staring at your head. The side of your head.'

We're just going round and round and round. It made me feel sick, so I stared at something that never moves – that's the trick.

'Have you got a dad PC Paphaedes?'

'Manny. Well, Manos actually. Retired now. What about you? What's yours called?'

'My dad...died.'

'Oh. Sorry to hear that.'

Yes.

'How, er, how did he die?'

I don't know.

'I don't know. I'll find out.'

'Er, right. Er. Shall we go and have a hot drink at yours Chris – warm up a bit?'

Police men are always hungry.

'I don't have any doughnuts.'

I stare out of the car window (cold) and think about "the scene of the crime" (hot). Detecting. I think about what the crime might actually have been. When you stare for ages, you get a sucking feeling in your head, which is everything emptying out, like in the bath when the water goes down the hole – and then all you are left with is yourself and any facts or ideas that are too big or important to go down the hole.

• • •

When we get to my bungalow, Julie is reading magazines. Runcie is lying on my sofa, cuddling his big police books. PC Tim Paphaedes stops – it's quite sudden – sniffs the air, looks at the coffee table. He takes his police man hat off and then puts it on again. Looks at the door. Runcie is sleepy, but wide awake.

'Chill yer chops, cop-padre. I've just been makin' up some J's is all. Help yerself, I won't tell anyone yer inhaled. Anyways. What've I missed? Where've yer been?'

I explain.

'Detecting.'

PC Paphaedes nods.

'Fook me – yer really are lettin' the kid drive the bus then Papha? What could possibly go wrong? Meanwhile, checkit.'

Runcie shows PC Paphaedes his big books.

'Yer'll be pleased to know I've been *bridging the gap between the practical and theoretical worlds of policing.* It's heavy. I feel for yer Papha.'

I do my pondering face – Runcie taught me it – and make sure PC Paphaedes knows I'm pondering him.

'Don't worry PC Paphaedes. There are no rules to being a detective.'

'There are – loads.'

'No – no rules. Except in my Rule Book. So, forget about rules, and how about we…erm…expand your mind?'

I start doing big-fish, little-fish, but then remember to focus. PC Paphaedes looks nervous.

'I expanded my mind at college and that was enough thanks.'

Runcie is chuckling.

'You smoked pot at college? Yer dirty dog!'

'No! I went to a police training college, so I didn't smoke pot at college. I expanded my mind by filling it with training. I'm not – Inspector Kaye wouldn't be – in favour of further expansion.'

'Let's play,' I say.

Runcie rubs his eyes, puts his cap back on and examines PC Paphaedes closely.

'I think what Chrissy's tryin' to say is, let's open up yer mental chakras, with a board game.'

'Yes. That is what I am trying to say. Yes. And then thoughts will come and you can just grab at them – or look out of the window at a tree.'

PC Paphaedes still looks nervous.

'Bloody hell. What's the game?'

I'm looking for it.

'Actually, if it's chess, I'm pretty good.'

Runcie knows it's not chess.

'Nah man – chess is the Daily Mail reader of board games. Thinks it's way fookin' better than it is.'

'I will give you a clue PC Paphaedes. It will "boggle" your brain.'

'Is it Boggle?'

I am so happy for PC Paphaedes!

'Yes! It is Boggle! You actually could be a detective! Maybe.'

'Not really.'

PC Paphaedes seems quite down.

'I know – but we're going to change that. With Boggle.'

Runcie is rubbing his hands together.

'It's the crack cocaine version of Scrabble innit Chris?'

PC Paphaedes looks like he's trapped.

'Easy Sailor. He's touched nothin' for a lifetime, n I only smoke dat. Open like yer Razzle on a stakeout we are Papha. Don't be afraid of knowledge – it's all there is.'

• • •

I am sitting in my special detective chair watching case studies – detecting. With my pad.

PC Paphaedes still looks sad – even after coming an impressive second in Boggle. He's looking around at everything, like he's never been in a bungalow that's also the office of a Consultant Detective.

'Is that a caravan out there?'

Runcie's reading one of his big books.

'Did yer know – yer probably didn't – that crimes aren't actually crimes unless they're accompanied by a guilty mind? That's mint – I've never felt guilty about anythin'. It's coz I'm not British. Republican, see? Where's your name from anyway Papha?'

'My dad was from Cyprus. Mum says she was a "regular Shirley Valentine" – I've not watched the film in case that's bad.'

'Right. Names aren't important anyway. Unless yer givin' 'em to other people of course. Like, if I think someone's a big-shot bellend, I always call 'em Chief. Or Fella. Or Blue. It's a win-win: I'm happy, n it's probably what they wanna hear. Psychically, I'm all square.'

Runcie has made cups of tea.

'A nice brew – help yerself to a biccy Papha.'

'Not that tin!!!'

Runcie sees the problem.

'Yeah, not that tin Papha, that's actually a collection of – whatever, just have one of these, own-brand Garibaldis innit? Any good Chrissy?'

I shake my head. PC Paphaedes looks at the fly biscuits.

After a while he manages to think of a question.

'Who's your favourite villain then Chris?'

I look at PC Paphaedes for a while. Then I shrug. I'm not keen on villains.

PC Paphaedes looks out of the window again.

'What's in that caravan?'

Now that I'm a Consultant Detective with the police, I need to keep being a Consultant Detective with the police. What's in your files…doesn't solve cases for you…but it can keep you going…so you can think. Detect.

'Runce?'

'Chrissy?'

'Why don't you show PC Paphaedes about…"information"?'

Runcie looks at his big book, looks at me, shuts his big book, stands.

Julie is still reading her magazines. But she will help too.

'Give me a second boys. Just reading about stalkers. Ironic really.'

• • •

Detective Inspector Graham Kaye

Paphaedes has plonked himself down on the seat in front of my desk to blow on a mug of hot tea, without even a knock on the door, or a "May I come in sir?" and yes, "I'd love one, thanks for asking." I want to drink, drink, drink and drink some more until I feel weightless – like I did in my poor mother's womb. Christ man, get a grip.

'We went back to his house sir. Took us ten minutes to get to the front door. Had two neighbours come out and tell me how wonderful he was – and Runce too because he'd "prescribed cake as part of the solution." Got past eventually.'

'And?'

'First we played Boggle sir and I came second. And then, well, overall, I think he's a bit of a weirdo. Runce was quite openly involved in the manufacture of marijuana joints when I got there, so you'd think there'd be some more serious criminal activity going on.'

'Oh?'

'I actually don't think there was. They practically gave me a tour.'

He describes Pringle's domestic set-up – an Interview Room which is actually just a lounge, and an Incident Room which is actually just a caravan, with a Murder Wall, which is actually just gift wrap back-to-front, with some random bits of crap stuck to it, and Paphaedes thinks he should go on a Big Board Skills course, and I can tell this isn't heading anywhere reassuring.

'He's not normal. I mean, have you seen the film Se7en? It's like that – like he's a serial killer – but rather than killing people, he fantasises about being a detective.'

'Mmm?'

'Well, back in his Interview Room, which is actually just his–'

'Lounge, yes, you said – get on with it.'

'There's videos sir – of TV shows – which he calls his "case studies," and then he's got "files." On like, everyone in town.'

'Creepy. And probably illegal. What's in these files though? Nothing I assume? Pure dreamland stuff, right?'

'Ah, well that's the problem sir. I didn't see inside most of them. "Confidential," they said. Duke's clearly involved though – in some. At least one anyway. Mmm. Yes. Pulled one out, and she was stroking it and banging on about how "every name's an opportunity," like it was some sort of business lecture, and Runcie was talking about how I needed to "develop a tantric love of information." I don't know, they talk in riddles sir: probably all on something.'

I'm foolishly expecting more, but of course don't get it.

'Yes, Paphaedes? This file?'

'Yes. Well. I'm not sure I understand it sir – it's just that they seemed very keen for me to see this one file and mention it to you, "so that you know Pringle is a very good detective who needs to be involved in solving the crime," a file on a...where is it now...a Dr Mark Stoneman?'

Shit.

'Oh. Dr...?'

'Mark Stoneman sir. He had his appointments calendar, a photo and he'd measured how tall he was. Shall I Google him?'

'No! Don't bother. I think we're getting ourselves into a twist with this Paphaedes. A bit of a twist. And we better just, well, crack on. So off you go – back to work. Shut the door.'

Shit.

Shit. Shit. Shit. Shit. Shit.

Because Pringle knows I need the help of Dr Mark Stoneman. Because he's been psych-tested by him for the Social. Of course he has.

I call Stoneman, praying for a diagnosis that Pringle is as mad as a hedge, because, well – I'm under attack here. But no: Stoneman is apparently not of this opinion, and was only too happy to read from the letter he'd sent off to prove it.

' "He is clearly unconventional and displays some of the obsessive behaviours we associate with certain developmental and emotional problems. And he has a low IQ. But IQ measurements are notoriously linear. With help and support he can function, he's open about his motivations – this is significant – and is in many ways quite rational in how he goes about things. He has given me no cause to believe he cannot be a contributing member of society, in the right role." '

Like detective? Come off it! So why is he allowed to keep dole-bludging his way through life rather than getting a suitable job? It doesn't matter though. What matters, is that Stoneman is so fast and loose with Pringle's story – so much for the Hippocratic fucking oath – it makes me worry about the confidentiality of my own. That I'm struggling to be a contributing member of my own life, let alone society. Fit for work. Fit for anything. That I see Dr Mark Stoneman like clockwork every other Monday. That he calls me to make sure I'm not drinking too much, to check I'm not having panic attacks, fantasising about leaving my miserable wife = OK, fantasising about leaving my miserable life = not OK. It doesn't come cheap, it doesn't seem to help, and it doesn't look good when the brief from above is so crystal fucking clear: stop being "difficult" and play the game.

And as if by magic, by divine intervention, Hollis has phoned up to laugh at me.

Hollis. All I've ever wanted is to be as blithely, unflinchingly self-assured as he is, just so I could then choose not to be such a prick about it.

News travels fast: we're all suckers, I'm the biggest sucker of them all, and now I have to listen to his smug, gloating shit, knowing, worst of all, that he's right.

'You've been mugged off mate – literally by the sound of it! Trust me – keep playing along with this bollocks and you're opening the door to every wrong'un who wants a free cup of tea and a VIP tour. And you'll be paying lip service to any half-wit scheme the drips at regional come up with for the next two years. So, my advice – fuck him off, now.'

I'm tired. Hungover. Hungry. My body is weak. I have no energy for this – for anything.

'And how would you have me fuck him off then Mike? How?'

'I dunno – don't really care either. Baahahahaaaaa! Look, why do you think Mogford gives you this shit, not me? This is a chance for you to get yourself back on track. They're even irritating me. So if you don't find a way of handling this, you're the one who's mental: you've got a murder case. It's why we do the job for fuck's sake – where's your pride?'

I know I'm supposed to feel like that – excited – but I can't.

'The DCI's all over it though. Politics.'

'Politics, shmolitics. This guy's a loser jobbo mong – a classic bus station loony. And Runcie's a cocky little shit. At the very least they'll have your eye off the ball, but they're worse than that these two, they'll get you into some kind of stupid fucking nonsense, I guarantee it. Shit sticks – and I'll leave you with this, to help you out – like jizz on your work trousers.'

Hollis – vile.

'You'll thank me later when they've toddled off back to the shopping centre, or wherever it is the dribblers spend the winter these days. Fancy golf tomorrow with the Chief Super? Oh I forgot, you can't, you've got a special friend coming over. Bahahahhahaa!'

I'm left holding the phone against my forehead. One decent smash – really hard – and it's all over, the mayhem stabbing away behind my eyes gone forever. Pringle and his cronies have manoeuvred things to make sure I can't do a single thing to keep him out of the picture. Or have they? It feels like it.

So what next?

Stoneman tells me to think. Mogford tells me not to think. I close my eyes.

20

THE FUTURE

Police Testimony:
Stephen Patrick Runce

SR   'So everyone's left Chrissy to it. Fobbed off n forgotten about – set adrift on DHSS bliss.

N, well, yer can see now, that was a mistake. Coz when yer shove someone under the radar, yer give 'em time – all the time in the world to work up a fookin' mission, n then, well, anythin' can happen. N when yer as on-one n out-there n mad stubborn as Chrissy is – big things can happen.

It was still early days of course, n I wouldn't say he was happy, but yer know what – he was better. It was a new millennium, a new dawn, n he was under way. He's cobblin' together this set of rules, detective rules – from *the best in the business*. N he says his crash is his crime.

But it's just a gut, a guess, a fook knows? Now he's got to work out how.

Now, there weren't many about who could fill in the gaps about Frank, but Chrissy had a startin' point we didn't know about – he had Castlemorton.

He'd told me before about his dad comin' back – seein' him at raves. But it all just got forgotten after the crash. I didn't wanna bring it up. But now, with pushin' a decade down the line, n mission detective well under way, he tells me: he'd seen his old man at The Castle. N not just that: he'd seen him with them creepy Dutch psycho-nutters, the Heavy Boys. So now he's thinkin' about 'em – they were there, the last time he saw his dad. N he's rememberin': it weren't good. He was with 'em: just before he got in his car pissed, drove it off the road, n died.

But it was Julie who changed everythin'. See, back in the day, klepto Julie'd nicked this Dictaphone from old Dr Cripps – the old doc, long gone now – a Dictaphone yer now very familiar with? N with Chrissy startin' to talk about the Heavies, one day she just pops up with it. Presses play. N it's Doc Cripps, talkin' away, readin' his notes about this *interesting temporary patient*. N it was one of the Heffel brothers. Aka, the Heavy Boys.

N on this tape, he's sayin' how they've got this condition – an acute condition – which he calls A.D.D. N no, it's not that. It's *Aldehyde Dehydrogenase Deficiency*. I've not forgotten that one.

Student goes away n finds out what it is – shittin' it, lookin' over his shoulder, coz that's the hold these big, bad ghouls have on yer noggin if yer let 'em – n from the offski, summink about it snags in Chrissy's mad, fix-ated brain. Coz, the main thing about this condition is: yer can't drink. Yer drink, yer die. It sticks, right there in his noggin, n now he wants to know more – everythin' – about the Heavy Boys.

Now, it'd been a while, I was well out, but in the glory days, the Runce Dog was indeed a leadin' light of the scene, know what I mean? I knew people. Maybe I'd only been a coupla links away from other people – from the Heavies? I'd never wanted to know. I still didn't really wanna find out. But. If anyone had been a step or two closer? If anyone knew where they'd be now? It was me old thicky pals: the Maskells.'

21

NOW

Chris

Julie always tells me to be myself.

'My little horse is purple,' I say to PC Paphaedes. 'What's yours?'

He looks confused and peers at his rear view mirror.

'I'm Chris, you're PC Paphaedes. My little horse is purple, what colour is your little horse?'

'I don't have a little horse…but if I did, I guess it would be blue…like Chelsea?'

'Oh – I see.'

• • •

'I thought perhaps that today we'd step up your involvement a bit. Send you and PC Paphaedes down to look at the crime scene'.

That's what Inspector Kaye said this morning. The crime scene. I'm doing what I have waited to do for a long time. But I don't feel...happy.

'Will I be arresting anyone?'

'Definitely not.'

'Good. Because I don't know if anyone needs to be arrested. Yet. Also, it's important we don't get distracted by sex.'

PC Paphaedes looked worried as well as confused.

'Is that likely?'

'It's what happened at the Blue Moon agency, in the documentary Moonlighting. The police aren't very good – have you ever seen Murder She Wrote? And, I'm also like Jim Rockford. I'm being paid to clear up your mess.'

'Who are all these people? And actually – you're not being paid.'

• • •

We arrive at Brunswick Villas. Part of the building is black. It has no roof. It's cold. I feel cold – but fire is what I need to think about. Hot. No.7. There's a cordon – this could be the first time I walk past one.

'Right, stay in the car – keep the heating on. Do not touch anything. Just going to check the site's secure.'

'It would probably make sense to wash eggs.'

I have been thinking about this for a while and it seemed like a good time to bring it up. But only because I needed to slow PC Paphaedes down, so I could give him the benefit of my wise...ness.

'Uh?'

'You have to keep listening PC Paphaedes? Asking questions, see? And then, eventually...there will be one that someone can't answer.'

'Evidence Chris – that's what we need. Hours and hours of routine checks, eventually producing evidence – that's what solves crimes. That's what I'm always being told anyway. Stay here.'

I decide to do a bit of staking out. I look into my plastic detective bag. It contains binoculars, a note pad, The Heat Tracer™, a Scottish Man wig, biscuits and a sandwich. I asked Julie for "pastrami on rye" like the American detectives, but she just did ham and told me to fuck off.

•   •   •

It's boring in the car and I'm a very good detective, so I get out and feed a nice dog some biscuits, pat it gently, and then go and look at a door. When I knock on the door, there's a noise behind me, someone with a tickly throat: an "ahem." I'm not a quick turner. Oh, it's PC Paphaedes.

'I said stay in the car. Meeting the neighbours are we?'

'Interviewing them.'

'OK, well we've got something apparently, back at the station. I need to go back – to find out what it is.'

PC Paphaedes is trying to explain things, very clearly.

'Let me show you how this is done though first.'

Erm. OK? He tries to take over the knocking, but the door is already open.

'Oh! Good afternoon sir. PC Paphaedes. Come to talk to you about the fire.'

The man has hair on his face, but only on the top of his cheeks. Like little furry pebbles. He has an old cardigan on. He's holding a big newspaper. I peer past him, looking for further clues, always investigating. He has a lot of other big, old newspapers, piled up on his table. A gas fire is on. Hazard! He speaks.

'Oh – the murder.'

'Why do you say that sir?'

'Well you don't arson yourself to death, do you?'

'Right. Did you know the occupier?'

'I've spoken to your lot already. Where were you – indisposed?'

'Did you know the occupier?'

'He looked a state. Caught someone like him pissing in the street once.'

'Someone like him – or him?'

'How should I know? He was only here a month or two. Just appeared. Like they do in those flats. Landlords don't care. People appear. People disappear. Some of them piss in the streets – now some of them are dying, causing a fuss. It's a disgrace.'

'Do you think he had any enemies – or made any enemies in the local area?'

'What do you think? Probably had loads of pals didn't he, if he was pissing in the street everywhere and shouting nonsense in the middle of the night and getting murdered?'

'So you heard him shouting – when was this?'

'Oh, who knows? There's a lot of shouting comes out of those flats. It's a disgrace. Pissed in my disabled bay he did, or one of them. Took me 18 months to get that.'

'If someone's damaging your property sir, the best thing to do is report it, and let the professionals deal with it.'

The Professionals?

'Yeah well, this was a while back. And he didn't damage my property, did he?'

'Urinating on your car is—'

'I don't have a car – he just urinated in my bay. I sold my car – waste of money when the buses work, which they never do.'

PC Paphaedes thinks this is how it's done? I stay quiet. It's important to be nice.

'Right. So when did you last see the occupier?'

'The dead fella? Like I said – saw him earlier that night. Off out he was. Probably off to pick up drink. And a murderer.'

I look at my pad. I have a question.

'So, I have a question here, on my pad. Was he drunk when you saw him?'

PC Paphaedes is not keen on me asking my question, when he is supposed to be "showing me how it's done."

'Chris, it's—'

'Did you ever see him drunk?'

'Not really.'

'How about a description? This….is the Heat Tracer™. Murderers often look familiar, so using photos of hair and eyes and noses and chins from Heat magazine, you can flip through and create, erm, exactly the face what you…saw? This one looks like an egg, look. Or perhaps the hair was more…greasy?'

'No. Is there anything else you want, only I've got to go and watch telly?'

I love telly.

'What's on?'

The man stares at me and my tracksuit. PC Paphaedes puts on a new voice.

'If you think of anything else sir, here's a card with my name and number at the station on it – give me a call.'

I lean in and give him one of my cards as well.

'Or me – give me a call too.'

He shuts the door, looking all the way from my head to my toes and back again as he does so. We head back to the car. I walk around the disabled bay. PC Paphaedes walks straight through it. Oh dear.

● ● ●

We've gone back to the station. PC Paphaedes has typed up his report for Inspector Kaye. While we wait to find out the some-thing that we – the police featuring Detective Chris Pringle – have got, we've gone into Interview Room 2.

'I strongly recommend you take that wig off before DI Kaye comes in.'

'OK. Most people wear disguises though.'

'They don't.'

'They do. Just like most crooks have an M.O.'

PC Paphaedes is supposed to be practicing his interviewing on me, "for training purposes." Or it might be the other way round. We get started again, but now Inspector Kaye has turned up. I suck my pencil and look at PC Paphaedes.

'Can you tell me what you were doing at this time and date sir?'

'Yes sir, but first, can you tell me what you were doing at this time and date sir?'

'Yes sir, but–'

Inspector Kaye slams his hand down on the table. PC Paphaedes looks startled. My reactions are slower.

'Will you two stop whatever it is you're…doing…and stop calling each other sir. You both call me sir, because I am your superior officer. You don't call each other sir.'

I have a thought.

'OK. But. You're not getting anywhere.'

PC Paphaedes has a thought.

'You should say, "You're not getting anywhere, sir." '

'Yes, thanks for that Paphaedes. Look, Mr Pringle, will you–'

'It's Detective Pringle. Oh, also,' I tap my nose to point out the secret, very clearly, 'don't worry about "The Case of Dr Stone Man." I actually want to help solve problems, that's kind of my, erm…'

I show him my card.

'…thing. And apparently I'm mental myself anyway, so I would never tell anyone that you are too.'

Inspector Kaye goes awfully quiet. PC Paphaedes scratches his head. I think he wants to ask a question, but he can't, because I've got one.

'However. The thing is, to help you stop not getting anywhere, I have to do detecting – but I can't do detecting, if I'm not being given any clues? Detective Chief Inspector Mogford said–'

Inspector Kaye gives me a stare. I do my best hurty face. Inspector Kaye sighs. Puts his hands on the table. Has a think. Stands up.

'Look – OK. Just come to the Briefing Room then. Both of you. We've got news.'

• • •

'OK, listen up. We have a name. The landlord Mr Scott has finally decided that he really ought to act like he's done a halfway proper job of fulfilling his obligations, given he's got a dead body on his hands – so he's come up with a text from the tenant on which he'd called himself Francis Popper. Follow it up, now.'

There's murmuring. The police like murmuring. I make a note in my pad.

'Does anyone have anything to add?'

I don't know. Do I? I have a go.

'Rule 2: howdunnit? We have to find out…no, I have to find out…how someone done it…did it. Now, my enquiries, which started at my own detective agency and then included interviews today, attended by PC Paphaedes, have concluded that erm…'

Everyone is looking. At me. It's most peculiar. I look down. Then at my feet. Then over there. Then over there.

'…my enquiries…have concluded that there were two people at the property. When there was the death.'

The man called Chapman thinks this is funny. There's a laugh-murmur.

'Everyone got that? Two people at the scene when one guy was murdered by another guy.'

But Detective Chris Pringle is ready to continue.

'And one of them, was drunk. And he died. We just have to decide which one.'

• • •

Inspector Kaye ends the meeting quite quickly then.

Inspector Kaye takes PC Paphaedes and I back to his room and shuts the door. I don't think anyone else has been invited – this is going very well.

'What you just said about alcohol – how did you know that?'

'I didn't know it. I just thought it. But I know now. I just have to remember what it means.'

Right then. I better head off.

'Oi, where do you think you're going? We haven't fin–'

'Detecting, Inspector Kaye. I'm going detecting.'

• • •

Detecting. It's taken me to the library.

'Oh – it's you,' says the man at the library. My good friend Peter.

There's a metal bar that bleeps when you walk through it. I have to force it open, which isn't right. I look at my friend and he rolls his eyes and presses a button to make the bleeping stop. The bar opens and I give him a packet of Hob Nobs and a thumbs up – he looks surprised. I was surprised too when Mum gave them me – I have told her several times that nobody really likes Hob Nobs. Except Peter. Perhaps.

I see a woman looking at books. "A suspicious character." I practice surveillance. There are a lot of cracks you can surveillance through at the library. It's tiring though, so I sit in a soft seat near the papers and have a small sleep.

When I wake up I'm stuck on a thought: I must remember to remember. Remembering what I've got to remember is harder.

I'm staring at the suspicious woman I'd been surveillancing earlier.

'Can I help you?' she asks.

'No thanks.'

She rolls her eyes too – another friend? – and walks away. And I remember.

•   •   •

I go home. My bungalow.

Runcie is there.

I look at my Murder Wall. I go over to the picture of Inspector Frost on the loo door, touch him, and clear my throat.

'I just need to prove who…did what…to who. So I'm off to tell Inspector Kaye.'

'Right?'

'Yes. You see, the thing is Runce, you can do whatever you want. Celebrity chefs for example. Gordon? Ainsley? They're up here, cooking very well, but I'm just a bit lower down that's all, just because I haven't bothered trying, because my thing is detecting. And they could do detecting, if they watched enough cases, a lot. And I could do cooking. I'm already the same as Ainsley and Gordon really – no worse, no better.'

I hold my hands up to illustrate just how narrow the gap is between me and Gordon. Runcie has thoughts on this.

'Oh, yer definitely worse. I mean – definitely. Much worse. What was that gippin' soup thing yer did?'

I feel proud.

'Super Soup – discovered during "The Case of What's the Best Soup in the World?" '

'Remind me?'

'One tin cream of chicken, one tin tomato, mixed together, cheese on top, tell me you didn't like it.'

'Yer know I didn't like it. It looked like the pavement outside Wetherspoon's.'

'I don't remember you not liking Super Soup.'

'Yer mind's been on other things.'

● ● ●

It's dark outside. When it gets dark I like to be in my bungalow, looking at case studies, especially on Fridays, because I work very hard on Fridays, Action Day – very tiring. But now I am a detective: every day. Making notes. But when it gets dark, I should be at home. Learning. From Frost. Or Columbo. Or sometimes if I am eating pizza, Montalbano. But I also eat pizza on Mondays and Wednesdays. It's important to have a system. I have a system. The police have nothing.

I'm in Interview Room 2 again. Waiting. I wonder what it takes to get in Interview Room 1. Will I ever make it? Is it a good thing or a bad thing being in Interview Room 1? Is it better news for a murderer or a cop? I'm neither, so it doesn't really matter. I'd like a biscuit though. And then they take me to Inspector Kaye's office and I can begin.

'Back again then?'

'OK police man...Kaye. I am a detective and it's time to tell you my findings.'

I get up. I put my hand on my chin to show how hard I'm thinking. Then I put my hands behind my bottom and do the walk. I concentrate, looking at the ground. Which means I bump into the back of Inspector Kaye's chair.

'Ow. I've hurt my thigh a bit.'

I carry on walking though.

Inspector Kaye looks tired. He likes to sit down to hear news, probably so that if he doesn't like it, he can go all floppy.

'Go on.'

'Well. It's about this case. Someone died. That's bad. Am I right?'

Inspector Kaye does another one of the longest sighs I have ever seen. I pat my pockets. Stopwatch? No.

I look at Inspector Kaye.

He speaks.

'Yes Chris. Someone died in a fire which was started deliberately, so yes, I suppose you could say, that's pretty bad.'

'Yes. As I said. It's bad. But it isn't murder.'

He stares at me. He's listening. He has a feeling as well – I'm not good with feelings, but he has one, I can tell. He is either cross or worried. As well as still being sad and tired. But – and I think this is a good thing – every time I see him now, he looks a little bit more awake. Tired, but awake.

'You have to think: howdunnit? And I know…how. Sort of. And this isn't a murder case. But…I know a case which was.'

I have finished summing up. I walk to the door, put my hand on the handle and then stop. I turn. One more thing. I want to say, "One more thing." I look at Inspector Kaye.

'Chris. I'm really not in the mood for having my time wasted right now. So if you've got something to say – something about this case – you need to come to me with evidence. So. Have you got any? Have you got any evidence? For whatever it is you are going on about?'

I'm Chris. Detective Chris Pringle. And my little horse is purple.

'Yes. There's evidence Inspector Kaye. In fact, Inspector Kaye, better than that – there's proof.'

'What Chris? Where? Where is the proof?'

I know where. I know. I feel fiddly. And I say.

'1992.'

Inspector Kaye's phone rings. He is in such a rush to pick it up and be cross with whoever is calling him that he drops it and then has to pick it up again.

'Yes?!'

I hear a little voice in the phone. I can hear it outside of the phone too. I turn and look. It's Inspector Kaye's assistant. She waves at me as she talks to him.

'Hollis? Oh for fuck's sake – yes, yes, put him through.'

I turn around again and look at Inspector Kaye. "Hollis." I make a note on my pad.

'No, of course I haven't,' he says to the phone.

Inspector Kaye isn't looking at me, which means it's time to go and I successfully go, even though I am a very bad tiptoer.

22

THE FUTURE

Police Testimony:
Stephen Patrick Runce

SR   'Time then, to tap up the Maskells. What we had, in the Republic? It was special. Starry-eyed in a fookin' wonderland we were, half real, half a dream. N, well – I don't mean to get all misty, but we were there for the golden years.

After the crash though? The mission had been no more naughtiness, party for free: I love breakin' rules, but whether yer makin' 'em or breakin' 'em, yer can't let 'em take over yer life, so I'd taken a step back. But even so, it weren't the same. Things change innit.

It was already goin' to shite. Manchester, Bristol, London: guns. Castlemorton fooked everythin', the Criminal Justice Bill stuffed rave on the bonfire, n then it was Leah Betts they used to light the fuse. In the middle of every Shit Town there'd be a giant poster with her lookin' out at yer: *Sorted: just one Ecstasy tablet took Leah Betts*. But that's not what happened. Poor kid died coz she drank 15 pints of water – coz she thought she had to. The inquest said if she'd had the pill without the water, she'd have lived. So who allegedly paid a million quid to make that poster? The ad agency behind not just a lager bein' killed by fallin' bar sales, but an energy drink bein' marketed as the pill's legal alternative. It was a stitch-up – the Tories today didn't invent bein' cynical murderous bastards, it's been goin' on forever this shite – a stitch-up which fed a selfish, sanitised world with none of that shared, shimmerin' love in it.

The Maskells would no doubt have loved it – but the last thing I was gonna do, even after a decade, was go n find out – I'd always kept Chrissy well away. But at the same time, he was me duty, n I'd failed him, so Whitney Houston RIP, we had a problem. Enter once more, our secret weapon: Julie.

By this time Julie's got her job – puttin' her talents to use in the market place, reinventin' the telesales wheel, smashin' all targets – but she's still got her hobbies, n her mission to save us all with love in insights. Julie H Christ. So the Maskells don't know her, n she was quite happy to eat one for breakfast for the greater fookin' good. She chose Darren. She went hardcore. Hardcore, but he never, ever, knew the score. Coz all men are putty in her hands, little puppies in her hands – coz that's the power women have, n for Julie, it's a super-power. She takes pride – n the sheer volume we're talkin' about makes me proud n all, proud just to know her.

Soz – daydreamin'.

So anyway, we send Julie into the mad, bad, twisted, ultra-violence-lovin' world of Darren Maskell – no problem. *Mata Hari* Student calls her. She goes in, no doubt half-inches some keepsakes, but most importantly, nicks the Maskell secrets: what they knew about the proper nasty bastards they'd dealt with one step up the food chain. N yeah – as I thought, as I feared, it had been the Heavy Boys. But the story was, they'd gone now – same sorta time as the crash, same sorta time as I dropped out, off they went, back to Holland.

So suddenly Chris is gettin' ready to go to The Dam. Chrissy, fooked up, in The Dam though? That is a bad idea which would not end well, but I can't tell him that…s'not what we do. Luckily though, I don't have to. Coz while he's ramblin' on n makin' plans, I'm waitin' for him to remember – he hasn't got, has never had, a passport. I mean – me? Most of me holidays are mental – not mental as in bonkers, I mean I take 'em in me noggin, which is very liberatin', n it keeps me footprint down, yer get me? Mother Nature's tryin' to discard us right – gotta do yer bit. Chrissy though – he's just never been anywhere. So it was horses for courses: he's at home, I had connections, n whilst this weren't part of me retirement plan, really, a bit of Amsterdamage? Don't mind if I do, Blue.

So I get there, mooch around for a bit, chattin' to punters n askin' a few casual questions, n the Heavy Boys aren't that hard to track down. They do their business out of Rotterdam, like all the players, but even at the domestic, small-fry end of the industry – my world – they were known. Easy to find.

But actually, not quite. One of 'em was easy to find: Bobby. I saw him: same dodgy, shiny leather jacket n pressed trousers as before – that was as close as I was gettin'. The other one – Dirk – was nowhere. One Heavy Boy – present n correct. The other: who knows?

I make the call. Tell Chrissy. Chrissy, who's slowly becomin' this heavyweight armchair detective, buildin' his rules, obsessin' about his old man. Chrissy, who now has three leads to pursue. One Heavy Boy. One missin' Heavy Boy. N finally, this thought he's been stuck on back at home. A thought, he realises, which has always been there, but always been ignored: why hasn't he got a passport? N why, when he asks his ma for the birth certificate he needs to get one, is she completely unable to give him it?'

23

NOW

Runcie

Sunday dinner at Mo's – roastie, the famous gravy, all the bits n bobs – a childhood memory I get to re-live once in a while, all her boys in one place. Nearly. Church took over at one time of course, for years – but not these days. She's got Brendan now I suppose? He's asked me twice if I want an ale.

'Thanks; not me poison though B-Man – got any squash?'

'Ach, I'm sure.'

Chris is jumpy – in his own special quarter-speed way.

'Went to the shops – the arcade.'

'Right. OK Chrissy.'

Arrived. Then went to his old bedroom, lookin', detectin', maybe just coz it's a habit, especially when he's fiddly diddly as he calls it, which he is now, oh he really, really is.

Brendan keeps goin'.

'Fancy watching the rugby after lunch boys? Edinburgh-Munster?'

Chrissy: very jumpy.

'Monster? Rugby? No, no, no, no, no, no. Not keen. At all.'

He has got a monster on his mind n all – a monster who needs dealin' with. Julie's on it, I'm on it. We're makin' plans. But there's ghosts on his mind too, n that's what's spookin' him.

Brendan's eyes though, have been opened to summink else he didn't know about Chris. It happens every time.

'Oh. What's your beef with rugger then Chris?'

Chris is thinkin' about bigger issues, so I jump in.

'If I may Brendan, we think rugby is probably a sham, a cover-up, a farrago, a con, a beard.'

Brendan needs to put down his tankard to get his noggin round this.

'Is it?'

'What it is right, rugby, is just an excuse for dim, posh punters who hate homosexuals, to watch really dim posh punters who really hate homosexuals, rough each other up in a homoerotic way, coz, in actual fact, they're homosexuals. Which is pretty insultin' to committed, full-time homosexuals, who've actually made the effort, right?'

'Gosh. Well I must admit there was a hint of buggery floating around the 2nd XV at my school – but then again, there was a hint of buggery around most things back in those days, wasn't there? There's a really professional feel to the game nowadays though. Dieticians and the like. I'd be surprised if...although of course, the very best–'

'Brendan dear, I don't think the boys are very keen on rugby?'

Maureen squeezes his shoulder n he starts talkin' to me about Blackpool instead, coz it's summink we do have in common: where Jocks n Mancs holiday in sweet harmony. That's the sorta reasonable fella Brendan is.

Maureen is flutterin' around Chris as usual, feedin' the big fella up n then worryin' about his weight, while Chris sits, still, his eyes dartin' everywhere. The eyes are the giveaway – the brain is busy. Detectin'. Workin' on gettin' whatever's on the inside of his head, out.

'I'm getting closer Mum.'

'What's that Christopher?'

Looks-down-looks-left-looks-right-looks-down-looks-at Mo. His eyes settle n relax – mother n son, meltin' in love. It's sweet. But there's things that aren't bein' said n all.

'It's all happening.'

Maureen's not prepared for this – who would be? She grips her gravy ladle – too hard, n a bit goes on the carpet. A lucky diversion.

'Never mind. I've had this carpet for years.'

She has. Chris was curled up on it – his dad gone.

'I could get a new one down for yer Mo? I like repetitive manual labour. Whaddya reckon? Whassat the platitude-fans say Mo: a change is as good as a rest?'

'Oh no Stephen. I'd have to turn the place upside down. Brendan wouldn't like it.'

He winces nervously. He don't care: she knows it.

'I really wouldn't mind Maureen?'

'I went for one of those free health checks this week, one of those vans down at the arcade – went with your Uncle Phillip.'

Brendan's spotted her conversational get out clause, n knows his job now is to keep it goin'.

'Tell them what it involved Maureen.'

'Oh you know – cholesterol, blood pressure and all that. Worst bit was the blood test. Uncle Phillip needed six pricks before it would work.'

'That's a lotta pricks – even for Uncle Phillip.'

'Oh Stephen – stop it. He never found the right girl, that's all.'

'Well, girls with pricks are hard to find. Unless yer live in Thailand. Actually, didn't Uncle Phillip go on holiday to Thailand once?'

'No – Lanzarote.'

'Right. I don't think I got those two mixed up, but never mind. Poor Phil. All coz of yer rugby players see? N I don't like it. I could help him re-launch? I'm all over the *immutable laws of brandin'* me Mo. Julie could find him a fella – she can make men do anythin'. He'd be so much happier. It's a tragedy otherwise Maureen – a wasted life.'

'Mmm. Well. Maybe you're right. I don't like the idea that he's…lonely.'

Chrissy isn't even listenin'. On a normal Sunday lunch, Maureen'd be all *No detecting at the table*, but she knows we're past that now. He's thumbin' through his rule book n his note pad – a man on a mission. Hurtlin' towards summink. Possibly disaster. He stops, caught in the act of silently thinkin', plannin', detectin'. He looks at me, at Brendan – but he only really has eyes for Maureen.

'I just want everything to be OK Mum.'

• • •

It's like an olden days Sunday. Afternoon stretchin' on. Waitin' for the action. N waitin' for the Soft Lad, as always – in the Incident Room, where the Murder Wall n map are fillin' out with crap, n there's lists of registration numbers n phone numbers, n cuttins on the fire.

It's a rubbish wait though. Julie's here n there's been a crucial exchange of information, but now she's ignorin' me, so I've got no-one to talk to about me Blackstone's, n I'm not even supposed to touch stuff, coz these days if it's in here, *it could be evidence.* That's fookin' ridiculous of course – it's got to be, surely-to-me-favourite-Charlatan? – but it's a sign of how quickly everythin's become ridiculous. N I love a bit of ridiculousness as much as the next punter, but right now, I've had to pick up a ruler n start measurin' things, just to stop from fookin' dyin' of boredom.

'Eh, Julie? Talkin' dirty don't work in metric. *Oooh, I'm gonna give yer all 15 centimetres.* It just don't sound big enough. Even six inches sounds big right, compared to, what is it...15 summink centimetres? 15 inches though Julie? What about 15 inches?'

'Can't be done.'

Her eyes don't leave her mag, but she does think about it. 'Unless it's cumulative – couple of different cocks in a night, added up.'

'Ever done that – 15 inches in a night?'

Julie's good with numbers – I wonder if this is why.

'I've probably done about 25-30. Some didn't contribute much to that mind – but it all averages out.'

I'm reflectin' on the majestic wonder of this savage beauty, when there's the bumblin' crash of Chrissy fallin' up the caravan steps n in through the door.

'Alright Chrissy?'

He drags himself in on his hands n knees, all sweaty forehead n visible crack.

'Practice: keeping low and…checking for footprints.'

'Sure mate – n yer doin' a bangin' job.'

'I'm hot and I need a wee.'

He squeezes in to the caravan loo n sits down, but he's too big for the door to shut – as an Incident Room, it has its flaws. There's a moment's pause, he leans down n peers suspiciously out of the door to check that he can see us, which will mean we can see him, n then he gets up n waddles back out n down the steps.

Julie remains un-moved – her magazine contains all she needs right now. I consider the ruler n now empty lav, but decide that's for later. Coz Chrissy's back again n busy – a man who's bang up for smashin' through his To Do list. He often looks like this n then's asleep in a chair ten minutes later. Today's different.

'I am going to head off to Julie's. To stay at Julie's. She has access to the cases of detectives that I erm…don't.'

'Yer mean she's got a proper telly?'

'Mmm. My detective plan, is that I don't want Inspector Kaye to think about No.7 erm…Brunswick Villas. I want him to think about the crash.'

'Yer've got a plan then?'

'Yes. I am going to head off to Julie's.'

Julie has barely looked up from her mag. She hasn't, of course, offered her gaff as an option – but we don't say no to Chrissy.

'Need to do some "quiet detecting," I need to, erm, you know…think? Think.'

'Right dude. Gotcha.'

Two pudgy Pringle hands hold a note pad right up to me eyes – it's wide open, n a finger points at a name.

'Also, there might be the…visitors…so you know…if you could, erm, stay here and…erm…then I can get on with my… erm…'

'Course Chrissy – it's on. When am I expecting these visitors though? It is the Sabbath after all me fine friend?'

He has his things together – shrugs.

'No bother Big Man – I'll kip over.'

He goes n stands in front of Julie to show her they're leavin'.

'I'll be back.'

'No bother Arnie.'

'Because I need to join the erm….?'

'Dots?'

'Yes. Between people. Who belong together. One came back you see – I saw him. I saw him. And we're getting to the end of the story. The case.'

Mmm. I'm not a worrier – but this is a worry. Worryinly familiar.

'The end Chrissy? Right. Who'd yer see? Where'd yer see 'em?'

'Town. And if one was here, the other would be and then…'

He brings his fists together – two planets, collidin'. The planets explode. N then he fooks off.

• • •

Maureen

Dear Lord:

Not much to report about my day – since breakfast? I saw Christopher and Stephen? Did you? I saw some beautiful celandines? That was about it. Today was much the same as the day before, and the day before that – you probably nodded off when I told you then, you're probably nodding off now. If this was a programme, on the BBC, they'd have me straight off. Or they'd stick me on Sunday afternoons when most folk just want to nod off – no offence.

I don't know of course though, do I Lord? I don't know what you think. It's why I end up starting with something dull like "Thank you again for giving me my Brendan Lord." Thank you again for giving me my Brendan Lord. He's like when I had that nursing job at the weekend all those years ago, with that well-to-do family, the Digeys? Remember? In that run-down sort of place on the edge of town, all swallowed up by the new estates. It was probably getting that way even then, I used to see more of town going back and forth to church, but I don't remember a thing about anything these days. Anyway, they had me serving up meals which were well, I don't like to say "posh," because that sounds rude, like I'm saying something about them, which I'm not, but they were posh. Stuffed Marrow. Quail Mousse. Nan's Kipper Fish Pie. You'd never eat it out of choice Lord, and I couldn't wait to get back home to Crispy Pancakes. What sort of food do you like Lord? Mediterranean? You're prattling again.

Brendan's straightforward Lord – that's what I'm saying. A Crispy Pancake. Reliable. Dependable. It's not even anything he's done right or wrong actually though, because – Lord? He's just a good man. He'd never do anything stupid.

Stupid's what they used to say about Christopher – "you're stupid," and "he's stupid." He doesn't show things of course. And now…it's like those drawing games we used to play, you know, draw a bit, fold a bit, pass it on, draw a bit, fold a bit, pass it on. Everything's taking on a life of its own. I should expect that. I can't control it. But I've no idea how it's going to end. Did you ever play that game?

Of course he didn't.

Are you keeping well?

What am I talking about?!

Do you listen Lord? Do you have to? What with being all-seeing and all-hearing? Because I go on, every morning, every night. I talk a lot. But I say nothing Lord, don't I? Nothing at all. Does it matter?

I've made mistakes Lord. And one mistake follows another. And that's the key to life I suppose Lord: we all make mistakes, just try not to make more – or the same one, again and again and again. Because it's that simple isn't it Maureen? That simple – got it all worked out haven't you?

It's my fault. What he does now – what happens? It's my fault. I can't stop him. But can I ask you to protect him? Can I?

Do you hear me Lord?

Night Lord.

24

THE FUTURE

Police Testimony:
Stephen Patrick Runce

SR   'So: a missin' birth certificate. N a missin' Heavy Boy.

Now, I weren't gonna be stickin' me beak in the Heavies' business n gettin' meself kneecapped n lobbed in the Rotterdam docks with a concrete rucksack. That's no way to end yer holibobs, am I right? So I head home. When I get there, Chrissy's gone into overdrive. I mean, he was still a snail who'd had a pasta lunch, n set his sights on a leisurely slide to the sofa for a kip, but the point, the point is, he was on one: about his birth certificate. Summink was pushin' him back to it.

Now, yer've either found a birth certificate or yer haven't, n he hadn't – but he was pretty zen in his absolute, unstoppable focus on that bein' his one n only goal.

He slept. He ate. But the only other things he did were watch his detectives, n think about that piece of paper. Why didn't he have it? Where was it?

N I know whatcha thinkin', it's not exactly a 007 type challenge is it: just get a copy. But we didn't know about archives: it was a mythical piece of paper, the Holy Fookin' Grail. He needed Maureen's help – dates, places, whatever – n he weren't gettin' it. He had this vibe – that Maureen was holdin' summink back, summink that joined the dots – but he weren't gonna start pushin' her.

N we couldn't even send Julie in. I mean, Julie's sweet with Maureen – but like I say, she was wary. What we could do though, was learn from her – like when yer get the hackers in to sort yer cyber security? So we picked the Duke brains, about punters, stuff, treasures: if she was Chrissy's ma, n she wanted to keep summink hidden – a piece of paper, all about Chrissy – where would it go?

Well, it takes a bit of convincin' for Julie to play along: she had some good questions, like *Why are we saying she's hiding it, when she might just have lost it?* and *How do you know she hasn't chucked it?* Well, I didn't have any answers – but Chrissy did. He said it was somewhere. That chuckin' it, or actually hidin' summink from him, would hurt him – coz his ma knew he wanted it. N she would never do summink to hurt him. Not showin' him though – that's different. That's just…not-doin' summink. Like a white lie I suppose – compared to a biggun? There was no way she'd be hurtin' him – she'd just be protectin' him.

So Julie gets to thinkin'. Thinkin' hard. N yer can guess when n where she does her best thinkin' – it was a busy time for the bed springs n back seats of Shit Town. She's rackin' up the sovs at work, rackin' up the notches 24/7, n mullin' it – thinkin' it over. What a woman. N then she has her answer.

She's gone all out n followed Chrissy's theory: Mo loves him; Mo wants to protect him; she can't lie to him; n deep down, she wants him to know the truth – whatever the fook that is – n knows she can't keep it from him. She can't stop him, that's not what she'd do – but she's not gonna make it happen. He has to make it there: his own way.

So if, in her own screwy, nutty Pringle way, this was all about love? Then where would she hide summink, that she wanted him to find?

In a place that's close to his heart.

25

NOW

Detective Inspector Graham Kaye

Communication with Sandra is now allowed only through scrawled notes, pinched looks, and aggressive text messages from her bloody sister. Banished to the spare room. Saturday night. Sunday night. 1 am. 3 am. A couple of hours flicking through Mum's old photo albums. "You have to understand: a lot of what's going on makes no sense to her anymore, and that can be quite scary. Share some memories." That's what the nurse said. 5 am. That stupid travel clock, ticking, ticking, deafening; a murder case not ticking at all. And a madman who says it isn't a murder case, and wants to send me backwards – to 1992 – his stupid, vacant moon-face deadly serious, as he shares his latest bombshell, and then walks out again because he can.

When you don't sleep though, and there's no-one to talk to apart from yourself, no booze to quieten those voices, and no working day to stop your mind from wandering, you do at least get to think. And something's niggling me – but I have no choice but to keep my eye on the prize: Brunswick Villas. That's what this is all about – I've not forgotten that.

Monday morning.

At 5:27, I push out of bed in yesterday's vest and pants, to see if an early start and a change of tack will change my fortunes. Getting lighter, warmer, misty but cloudless: it's going to be OK.

But then I remember Hollis.

In a few hours he'll have been in. Will that be Pringle, away from this case, finally, for good?

And is that what I actually want?

• • •

Runcie

Visitors mean brews, n now I'm flyin'. I tidy away some paraphernalia I've been messin' with on an album cover, to help slow things down a bit – I keep me vinyl at Chrissy's, seein' as how I seem to live here – whilst talkin' Visitor Numero Uno (Papha) through me latest findins.

'Proof of possession. It says here, yer don't just need to prove I've got gear, yer need to prove I know I have, n that I know I shouldn't. Well good luck with that: I can be fookin' stupid when the need arises. See, for me, rules are like handrails – they're just there to get me where I wanna be. But to be a rozzer Papha, yer've got to swallow this bible whole – n I'll bet yer've only ever given it a little lick. It tells yer how to up yer conviction rate

– we're livin' in results-based world. Free advice this. *It's all about free stuff n freedom – which should always be free.* If I ever die – which I won't – I want that on me gravestone. As comfort n inspiration for the ladies of the future.'

PC Paphaedes looks glum. A minute ago he was sat here readin' How to Stop Worrying and Start Living. It was a nice little skive so I was pleased for him, but I guess I shoulda seen the signs.

'Y'alright Papha? Yer very quiet for a handsome young man with his whole life ahead of him.'

'I'm not too sure about the future really Runcie. We never seem to solve cases – not properly, the way they want them, all neat and tidy. You know? Me as a copper? Maybe I'm just not cut out for it.'

'Top tip: enjoy the rainbow, forget about the pot of gold – by the time yer find it, the shops will be closed, n everyone yer love will be dead.'

'You just talk Runcie, all the time. I can't keep up. I mean what are you actually saying?'

'Well–'

Ding dong, the doorbell – n he's suddenly all fidgety.

A second visitor…

N it's another rozzer alright. Meaty unit, dead threads. A '70s Bastard Cop: this must be him. But I'm prepared. Papha looks embarrassed – can't look me in the eye – he's a crap actor n it's a set up. But it's no bother. The unit speaks.

'Mr Runce? DI Mike Hollis.'

Oh yeah – deffo no bother.

'Call me Runcie, Chief. Or Runce Dog, Fella. Either of those is fine, Blue.'

'Mr Pringle not here then?'

'No. But PC Paphaedes is. N he's worried he might get struck down by the Gods of All Things Being in Good Order. N I was just about to say to him – shhhh, don't panic, they don't really exist? They're just a product of fearful, overactive, n actually quite talented imaginations, that could really be put to much better use. Neat n tidy's a prison Papha – but sometimes yer need a long sentence to be truly free. I mean look at Chrissy: he's a fat man, with a lotta VHS's, doggedly and obsessively faithful to his routine of watchin' 'em, while wearing a tracksuit – he's been doin' it for 20 years.'

Hooray-For-Hollis-Wood. He don't have room for the likes of me. That much is clear.

'Yeah well, we don't all have the luxury of sitting on our arses for 20 years doing one thing. Life moves faster than that.'

'Exactly. Blink n yer'll miss it, like yer missin' the point, right now: it's the 20, 40, 60 years doin' one thing – thinkin' – that makes the difference. There's no miracle moment. Checkit: the gatefold concept album here, is like a metaphor for the journey that is life – it goes on for fookin' ages, n at the end, yer'll probably wonder if it was worth it. Coz where's it got yer? But it's all on you Blue. N if yer heart n yer mind n yer ears are open, actually, it might just get yer up-close-n-personal with some answers.'

This chump's startin' to simmer already – easy.

'Fucking music. You think you're so superior don't you? But you're not so different from the rest of us. You and your "gatefold concept albums" and your dope. Your mate and his TV detectives. What's that about? You've just built your own little prisons there, that's all – hiding away from real life, buried in your bullshit, and your collections. You're deluded.'

'Ah, but that, yer see, is where yer makin' a tragic, life wastin' miscalculation. Sure, yer can bury yourself in anythin'. But it's a life without beauty that's a life un-lived – n there's endless beauty in what we're surroundin' ourselves with. Endless. We love it. Love, it. My tunes, his detectives, Julie's cock: they mean we're still alive, still searchin', still ready for love n misery n failure n success n ideas. It's not about pressin' mute on our emotions: it's about embracin' 'em, in Maximum Dobly. That's what bein' balanced is all about. Fella.'

Simmer. Simmer.

'When did you last see Mr Pringle?'

'In long-forgotten times Blue – simpler times. Some may say 'tis but a distant memory.'

70's Bastard Cop glares at me n then sits – uninvited – in the holy recliner. Spreads his manly thighs wide.

'As it happens it's you I wanted anyway Mr Runce. Seeing as how you, indirectly, are making yourself part of a murder investigation as well.'

'Has anyone ever told yer yer look like Pete Beale?'

'Try not to let your mind drift Mr Runce.'

'Yer like some kinda anti-hypnotist. *Don't relax*! Alright, soz Chief – crack on, I'm listenin'.'

I make a big show of sittin' up to attention, n give him me very best takin'-the-headmaster-seriously face.

'I've been having a look back through the records – a bit more thoroughly than some of the younger lads might. There's ways you learn.'

He gives poor Papha a look. I give him a supportive wink. I knew they'd try summink: knew that's what this would be all about.

'And hidden away there I've managed to find a conviction. From 1986. In Wythenshawe. Can you remember what that was for?'

Course I can. It was for me old man: coz he did it, not me. But for once I understood, so I took it. But that's my truth – it's not for this bleak twat, who couldn't get a hug in a pill factory. So I'll stick with the story.

'Oh, yeah, absolutely – it was for twattin' a fella on a skate-board. With a skateboard.'

'And why did you do that?'

'Well, look – we've all got summink that pushes our buttons. For yer mainstream, Alfie Boe-lovin' kind like yerself, it's stuff like men who wear hats. Or pot dealers. For me, it's shitebags who mess with the ones that matter to me. N this one had a skateboard.'

'And he did what?'

'Tried to have sex with me neighbour's half-brother's step-sister.'

He's lost. That's the trouble with these chumps – real life scares 'em. They're suspicious of it.

'She had learnin' difficulties – she could choose who she had sex with though, n she didn't choose him. He was snif-fin' around, caught him comin' out of hers with his board, so I showed him a coupla tricks.'

'It's interesting Mr Runce. It's with respect that I say this. This girl you describe, you say had some learning difficulties. Julie Duke – not the most, how would I put it, aspirational character around, is she? I mean she might have cleaned up her act, got a decent job by the looks of it but, well – come on?! And then you go around like some kind of bodyguard for Chris Pringle as well.

You're an irritant to men like me, a petty criminal, but it has to be said, you're not stupid…so why do you spend all your time with individuals who are vulnerable, perhaps even a bit…simple?'

'Julie? All her men n mementos? That's a higher callin'. N Chrissy: simple, yer say? Nah man – he's perfect.'

'He's not what most people would call perfect.'

'Most people are wrong. About so, so much.'

'But this whole detective business? He's obstructing a serious criminal investigation, and everywhere we look, you're there too in the background, poking away. What's going on Runcie?'

'Well he's Lovejoy, n I'm Tinker, except the wrong way round in terms of body shape n sex appeal. N what's goin' on right now is he's lookin' for evidence – proof.'

'Evidence? Oh I see. Good. Good. Because that's why I came funnily enough.'

He's building it up. The suspense. Like a regular tough guy.

'Perhaps you'd like to give us a sample Mr Runce?'

'Of what?'

'Urine.'

'Oh, right, thank God for that – I thought yer meant a freebie. No, I'm alright ta Chief.'

'Do I need to spell it out? You have a previous conviction. All we've got to do is find one little blim of evidence you've so much as been near gear, and you're going down.'

'You are so hot when yer being assertive. Immunity?'

'Not if you have a conviction or pending court appearance – just like it says in the small-print. That won't tell you everything.'

He gives me Blackstone's a smug look, n I keep crackin' me best *irritant* grin. Coz I'm not lookin' at the Blackstone's – I'm lookin' at Chrissy's H file. Coz I'm ready for yer Mr 70's Bastard Cop.

'Words can be wise Blue – but actions maketh the man.'

The anger bubbles up. The disdain.

'Listen to you.'

'Philosophy's all we've got Pal. It's all I need n all. Coz yer know what a great philosopher once wrote?'

'What?

'*Naughty naughty, very naughty.* Which brings us to the main item on the agenda. Inspector Hovis. Yer shouldn't always listen to Chris, on account of him bein' absolutely barkin' – but when he talks about say, Miss Marple, I listen. N he says, that when Miss Marple didn't know someone very well, she'd just think about someone she did know well, yer know, from the village, who'd done summink similar. She'd work out why that person had done it…n then she'd take this answer, n bingo, job's a good'un.'

'Yeah, that sounds like the kind of idea a nine-year-old would come up with.'

'I know – nonsense right? Or is it Captain Boggis? Just coz it's simple, doesn't mean he is, doesn't mean it's wrong. Coz in yer schemin' little world there, when was the last time yer came up with a better idea than a nine-year-old? Perhaps if it was since school, yer wouldn't need this salutary lesson on why yer need to think a bit more about all the different people yer reckon are stupid, like Chrissy, Julie, n yer wife.'

'Uh?'

'See, Detective Chris Pringle, he saw yer – sorry, pho-tographed yer – havin' a champagne brunch in the Horse n Feathers on a Monday mornin' with yer personal trainer – the one yer shaggin'? – n I'm just not sure yer missus knows yet.'

It's the sight of a gob bein' smacked. But worse is to come for DCI Mike Holistically a Cock-Knocker Hollis. Papha meanwhile looks terrified, like Mummy n Daddy are arguin'.

'But we don't need to worry her, do we Mike? Yer secrets could be safe with us – like what yer also doin' – back to Julie I'm afraid – in the extra special Duke Sex Diary. *Micro* – although Mrs Hollis probably don't need yer pet name explainin'. But anyway, sit tight Blue, coz I don't wanna tell the story like that, do I? The story of why you really need to pipe down. Coz I've got a better plan, see, all prepared. Have yer ever heard of MC Tunes?'

• • •

Detective Inspector Graham Kaye

'And? Then what?'

Paphaedes just gawps back at me – weighing up the pros and cons of trying to explain. But I have to hear it: how the bloody hell they got Mike Hollis out of their lives? I need to know the secret.

'Well?'

'It's just those files again sir. Pringle had done surveillance, you know, like he did with that…doctor? And it was to do with various women Hollis's wife didn't know about. With some stuff from Julie Duke too. About her and…Hollis.'

'What stuff?'

'I didn't understand all of it sir.'

'Why?'

'Because it was…well…'

'What? The filth that Duke gets up to a bit rich for you was it Paphaedes?'

'No sir. Well maybe. But it wasn't what Runcie was saying about Hollis that was hard to, er, follow – it was the way he was saying it. In a rap.'

'Say that again Paphaedes. Say what you just said – again.'

'A rap. By Runcie? He says he's..."The Third Great Mancunian Rapper," who goes by the name of–'

'Give me that. McChester?'

'That's M.C. Chester sir. Pronounced Chest-oh.'

'I see.'

I don't.

'And did you…?'

'Yes sir. I kept recording throughout. Neither of them even noticed – although I expect Runcie would have been delighted if he'd known sir.'

'Right. OK. Well what are we waiting for? Let's hear all about Hollis. In a rap.'

• • •

Afterwards, we sit in silence. There's nothing to say. There's a bond between Paphaedes and I now which can never be broken – now that we've both heard a Mancunian pot dealer's rap-based extortion of a repugnant copper on behalf of a pea-brain who thinks he's a detective. Christ. What next? Where do you go from there?

Hollis has gone quietly, his retreat a thing of such beauty, such relief, it's almost given me a lift – some justice at last. Pringle though is giving me no such customer satisfaction.

Not a murder. What – or who – is making him say it? The proof is in 1992. What proof? And why won't he tell us?

'Any idea where Pringle is now?'

'No sir, he either just appears, or is impossible to track down.'

'Mmm. OK then Paphaedes. I have a job for you. 1992?'

A long time ago. I could almost have been happy. Ambitious. Hopeful. With hair. And prospects. Heading down a cul-de-sac even then though no doubt – Mogford already way ahead of me.

'Pringle's mentioned it a couple of times sir, yes. Runcie said it's when his dad died.'

I take his printout back out of my top draw.

' "Parents Joan Maureen Pringle, Frank Christopher Pringle (died 1992)." How did he die?'

'Car crash apparently sir.'

Pringle's dad goes out in a car, never comes back. He's already a bit special – this sends him doolally. Still thinking about it now. Could make sense.

'Reckons that's his murder case then does he?'

'Well, he hasn't said as much sir, but well, you know, he never really, as such, says…'

'Anything? No, I know. I find myself agreeing with you PC Paphaedes. Check out this crash then. See what the paperwork can tell us – see if anything stands out.'

'OK sir. Will do.'

Well go on then man. Oh God – it's the confused look again.

'What Paphaedes?'

'Well it's just…sir? Why are we looking at that, not… Brunswick Villas?'

It's a reasonable question, but the answer is reassuring: instinct.

'Because, PC Paphaedes, a man with seemingly nothing to gain, is trying to get access to a murder investigation, and then saying it shouldn't be a murder investigation anyway, and bringing up something from nearly 30 years ago, when the only apparent link between then and now is himself. Apparent link – because there must be another one. Which leads us to a pretty big question Paphaedes. What – or who?'

•   •   •

Instinct. Scratching away at me.

I dial Mogford, and force myself to wear a relaxed, magnanimous smile. He answers, a clink of crystal glasses, braying voices.

'Inspector Kaye. Impress me.'

'I've got some better pictures of what Pringle's been up to sir.'

'I'm not your mum. I don't need you to talk me through the beautiful memories you're making together, I said impress me.'

'Yes, well I had a neat idea for the newsletter sir? A shot of Pringle, next to a shot of yourself: you know, show the Super how the scheme's working, top to bottom?'

'Now you're thinking. Tick the boxes man. Reach out to him. Who knows, maybe these dimwits have ideas – if he comes up with any, make it look like you're listening. Just show that C.L.E.A.R. works, clear? And the fire?'

'Reviewing the evidence list again today sir – going to really soak it all up.'

'Very good.'

'And there's a link to a past case we're exploring.'

Instinct.

'Mmm. Anything on the two persons who were at the property – victim or arsonist?'

'We have a witness who seems to know a bit about them. We're er…reaching out to him.'

Mogford's way is to keep the world in boxes. Hollis's way is to nail the lids down. And guess what, I have a way too after all: let everyone do what they want to do, and see what comes out in the wash. Instinct.

'Good, good. Well I better get on. Solve the case, keep Pringle looking involved, and imagine all three of us looking good in the local papers Kaye? Job done.'

I dig out my note book, open it to the first page and write the date. Pringle will be involved all right, somehow. I just need what no-one else can give me – proof. So I'm going to have to get it myself.

PART FOUR

DON'T WORRY

EVERYTHING IS GOING TO BE AMAZING

26

THE FUTURE

Police Testimony:
Stephen Patrick Runce

SR   'So Julie – pilferer, spy, force of nature n unstoppable professor of human behaviour – has delivered her verdict. If Chrissy's read it right, n Maureen's just protectin' him, then maybe that certificate can be found: somewhere *close to his heart.*

     I sit there, watchin' Chrissy think about it: huge, ever-increasin' yet slowly meltin' iceberg of a body, his eyes rollin' slowly. N then he's up, n we're out the door, n he's marchin', n I'm sayin' nothin' coz – what's there to say? We're off to Maureen's, I know that much, n well – yer never fookin' gonna be sprintin' to keep up with ma main man Prings, but he's on a mission, n I'm alongside him, chattin' away about shite, coz I'm not good with silences me, even when I'm gettin' nothin' back.

But – well, yer know the form by now – I just want the big man to be OK. There's a lot been left unspoken over the years – but I knew he was hurtin'. I'd always been there for him – since – but he didn't need any more disappointments, yer get me? So as we're walkin' along, a part of me is thinkin', *I hope Mo's not in, never in again.* Coz whatever's comin' up, someone's gettin' hurt. I love 'em both – but I'll be on Chrissy's side. Always. Always. I just don't wanna see any heartbreak.

Check out yer poor, sad, confused faces! Coz yer look at me, n all yer see is red-raw sexual power, right – n a crook yer'd like to bang up n pummel with a baseball bat? So who's this highly-developed emotional bein', wet as a fookin' flannel? Well it's not good for the street cred right – but these are the family I never really had, yer get me? I had to protect 'em.

So when we walk in, it's all a mare: coz there she is, Maureen, sittin', like she's waitin', as if she's been waitin' since the crash, since when we saw her, that very day, what, fifteen years earlier? Waitin' for summink. For someone. Waitin' for Chrissy. N finally, he's arrived.

N well, yer never know what's happenin' up top with Chrissy – but what happens next just leaves me with me own head in me hands. In despair. Coz he walks over n starts flickin' through a pile of vids, n then pulls out a Columbo box set he gave his ma back in the day – n I'm thinkin', *Jesus Chrissy, there's a time n a place dude.* But then he turns n nods at Mo, n Mo kinda nods back, slowly, n he sits down, opens up the VHS, pulls out the inner sleeve, n this piece of paper falls out. Folded up, neat, but clear enough, a fookin' birth certificate: n I'm gettin' a massive adrenaline buzz – never turn down a free buzz, me – wonderin' how this is gonna play out.

N then Maureen starts talkin'.

Not here.

N she says it – n it was just like Chrissy knew it would be.

Go home Christopher. I love you. But you must decide. You. What it means. And what you want to do about it.

When we were kids, n I was down for summers, we had this secret route we used to take to the Rec. Most of the time we were on our bikes, no bother – but if we were avoidin' the skins, or wanted to go off radar a bit, we'd head out the back lane behind his ma's, through this water pumpin' station yer'd get a bollockin' for bein' near, n into these crappy overgrown fields, now known as the Avalon Business Village. N halfway across the middle there was these big hedges, between the first field n the next, with a big dip down in the middle between 'em, where yer could mess around, n no-one would know yer were there – a little tunnel, a secret den, yer get me, with hedges archin' over the top? Just us, some rabbits, the odd mushroom. Puffball.

It weren't just our secret little hideaway – yer'd find the odd used johnny. But it was good for yer life-changin' moments: like checkin' out a porno yer'd found; or smokin' yer first fags; or findin' out yer weren't actually who yer thought yer were.

N that's where Chrissy wanted to be for this – between those hedges, back in his childhood, nice n safe…but with his birth certificate in his hand.

So we went.

We sat for a while.

N then he unfolds it – the certificate – n…wow.'

27

NOW

Runcie

Chrissy's time at Julie's is done. There were cases to be watched, rules to be recited, The Chronicle to be read n calls to be made. She says he went wanderin' too: watchin', lookin'. N all of it kept him away from Hollis, the Magic FM of basic bent coppers, a playlist of acceptable personalities and behaviours so limited, it blinkered him to the simple reality that we could off him, just like that, with nothin' more than a hint of rhyme, a dash of detection and a dollop of historical Julie Duke field work. *The Case of Mike's Naughty Willy* has been put to bed.

Next stop, back to Mo's. So soon after our roastie n all. Reunited. But not the way she'd like it. Not just stickin' faces together, blind nostalgia, ignorin' everythin' that's happened. Coz it can't be ignored any more. Chrissy won't let it. So we're all here, under one roof – Mo, Chrissy, Julie, me. Brendan ahem-in' his way to the shed, to get out of the way, to tinker, to leave us to it. N here we all are, sittin' at the old kitchen table, where Frank used to sit – mute, proud n damaged – all those years ago.

In his funny Chrissy way, it's a summit, a pow wow, a parlez, a meetin' of the minds: there weren't no summons to the summit mind, no coded messages, or meatheads come to escort us to where we needed to be. He moved, we followed, that's all. Just Chrissy keepin' goin', n the world being forced to keep up – Chrissy bein' the detective, to make sure he never misses anythin' again.

It's Julie though, who speaks first.

'The thing is see Maureen love – we all have to face the music sometimes.'

Julie's owned every second of her past to make sure every second of her present has meanin'. N that's all she wants for Chrissy, n all Chrissy needs for himself. Mo though? Mo's hidden from the past, omitted details. She's done what most people would do. *You can't live in the past,* she says. Well. Maybe yer can't – but yer have to. And this is Julie givin' her fair warnin': we don't know how n we don't know when, but it's comin'.

'You don't need to be afraid Mum.' He speaks. 'I'm a very good detective.'

She smiles her little Mo smile. The pain, the fear. The guts in Mo. It's all a part of it. Her mistake was entirely forgivable – but it has to be undone.

'Well I am afraid Chris. But I can see: it's time.'

●　●　●

Chris

In my bungalow. In my lounge. Which is also my Interview Room. Runcie is making teas.

'I see yer've got a matchin' mug from Diggers?'

'He's a very good friend of mine.'

'Just like yer said he would be dude – just like yer said.'

'Yes.'

Yes.

'To be a detective Runce, you have to know what it's like to be inside a detective?'

'Grim. Can't imagine it's much fun in Columbo's guts.'

'Everything is inside. He just has to get it out. When it's ready. When he understands. And right now, everything is inside…me?'

'OK?'

'Francis Popper. You see? Francis…erm…Popper. The erm…person…in the fire? Or not? It's one person. Or another person. You see?'

'Not really Chrissy, no.'

'No. Inspector Kay doesn't either. And I like Inspector Kaye. He's a very good friend of mine. So I am being very helpful.'

'Mmm. Maybe. Yer sure yer actually wanna be helpful? Yer sure that's what yer want?'

Runcie is learning to ask questions. This one is very tricky.

'Mmm. Oh. Did I say? Inspector Kaye is coming to my offices. To talk with me.'

'Is he?'

'Yes. He was surprised too.'

'Fook me, it's exhaustin' this; like buses these rozzers are – Pig-adilly Circus. Hold on – why was he surprised?'

'Well, because I called him up and invited him. It's a part of it see: as a detective, you can't…'

The sentence is on my note pad. I have prepared it and might use it on Detective Kaye too. I finish it off, presenting it to Runcie with both of my hands.

'…"hide from the truth." '

'Fook. Right. When's he comin' then?'

'Ooooh…gosh…I don't know…maybe he'll bring his mug… soon…erm…now?'

Runcie starts waving his arms around energetically. Opening windows.

'I'm waftin' coz they don't like the Runce Dog Chrissy, n I don't want you, me badass soul brother, to come a cropper with a copper. I mean, I heart giggles right, n I can see yer wanna help 'em, yer really do, n I've got a softy for Papha meself, I'm a Paphaedophile. But Boss Man? Well, you might want him here, but what's more worryin' is, he wants to come. Cops actin' predictably is one thing – when they start bein' unpredictable, they've woken up, n then yer've got a problem. N I know what yer gonna say next. Go on.'

'It's a part of it.'

'It's a part of it, right.'

Ding dong.

'Shite. N on that bombshell, I'm gonna hide in yer coat cupboard.'

•   •   •

Runcie

One of the things Maureen always says to us is – yer know, the way old sweeties have their sayins – *I never did teach you the rules of polite society.* N I think she means stuff like this: me hidin' in a cupboard watchin' Chrissy sittin' on a sofa next to a copper, clutchin' a note pad n starin' at him. That's probably rude, innit? The hidin' in a cupboard – the starin'? We're both guilty. But this is what happens with Chrissy. I should be out playin' in the fresh air, sayin' *Hello sunshine, where you been?* – but yer get sucked into all-sorts.

There's a bedside table I can sit on in the cupboard, n tiny dart holes in the door which I can peek through. I feel like one of them Stasi nutbars – just a bit more baked. N I start to wonder – is it the destination that matters to Chrissy, or the journey? Will there ever be an end point – does he expect there to be one? Maybe this is it now, forever – him thinkin' he's an actual detective, with me hidin' in cupboards. I'm not sure I like it.

Inspector Divorce breaks first.

'Chris. Thanks for having me over. What's that?'

'My Detective Rule Book.'

'There are no rules to being a detective.'

He looks around for me – he's been proven right.

'Yes! That's right Inspector Kaye, good – there are no rules to being a detective.'

There's a little pause, while Chrissy looks-down-looks-left-looks-right-looks-down-looks-at his lap, n then remembers.

'Except the ones in my Rule Book.'

He sighs contentedly, then confuses himself with a hiccup.

'Go on then: surprise me. Rule 1?'

'Oh – how did you know? There is a Rule 1. But we're not on that. There's three "golden rules" n we're already on to the best one.'

'Which is?'

'Rule 3: whodunnit? You have to find out who done it. And it's all in…'

He points a finger at his noggin, thinks better of it, moves it down to his gut, then kinda up to his heart.

'…here. Maybe?'

'Wow, OK. Thanks.'

Silence.

'Rule 3. Shouldn't it be wheredunnit though? Opportunity?'

Chrissy feels genuine sympathy for Inspector Kaye and his inferior detective mind.

'But I already know where.'

'Mmm, that's–'

'I need to know who. I mean, I need to prove who.'

Inspector Divorce nods solemnly n undoes his coat.

'Nice place you've got here.'

Not really. Awkward, this is – like a crime-solvin' blind date.

'Thanks – it's called a "bungalow." The council gave it me. And this is my Interview Room. Although, Inspector, erm… Graham…Kaye…now that I am almost running a successful, erm, detective agency, I will probably be able to buy a large house.'

Mmm.

'Are you still signing on Chris? As well as running a detective agency?'

Chris looks disappointed.

'I was just telling…'

He rotates a finger around in the direction of my cupboard, before rememberin' it's probably best not to name-check someone who's hidin', n then point to their hidin' place.

'...someone like, erm, my mum for example, she's a person...that I really like you. I am trying to help you. But the thing is – you see? – there is a problem.'

'Oh?'

'There's been a murder. And it needs to be solved.'

'Interesting. I'm well aware of that Chris – although the last I heard, you were saying there hadn't been a murder?'

Chris looks confused – like it's Inspector Divorce who's lost his mind.

'There's been a murder, but you are focusing on the wrong...things. It's what I was just saying to...R-, R-, R-, RRRRRRRRR...'

He can't lie. He just can't do it. But it's OK. Inspector Kaye has his own agenda.

'Right. Look, I'll cut to the chase Chris. I need you to help me out here. I'm talking to you mano à – actually let's try explaining it another way. When you say things, in a murder investigation, the police listen. So if those things don't mean anything, it can lead to...a considerable waste of time. And resources. And I feel like you're wasting my time Chris – and I'm not alone in thinking that Stephen Runce is involved. Behind it all.'

I can't help a little snort at that one – me, in charge of Chrissy?! Deep in his subconscious he hears it – maybe notices a flicker in Chrissy's eyes – but then the moment's gone.

'Where's Runcie right now? Are you sharing information with him about this case? Because you're strictly here as a passenger Chris. And he's not even a passenger – he's a passenger in a sidecar at best.'

There was way too much goin' on in that sentence – Chrissy's overwhelmed. There's a chance he might just stand up n scream *Runcie's in the cupboard* – but he looks OK. Calm.

'Do you know something? About the tenant of the flat maybe – who we assume to be the deceased? Francis Popper. That a name you recognize?'

'Mmm. Well, yes. I can tell you that I've never heard that name before in my life – apart from when you said it. And then when I read it in The Chronicle. And then when I said it to someone earlier. And then when you said it again just now. Apart from that – no, never heard it.'

'Ok. Do you know if they are dead or alive though?'

He thinks about that one. Considers gettin' up to do his walk. Doesn't – like it's too much effort.

'But either way, you're saying it's not murder?'

'Yes – that's what I'm saying.'

'Why?'

Pause.

'Because murder is…bad.'

'True.'

Chrissy strokes his chin in concentration n leans in to Inspector Kaye – they're in this together, two great criminologists chewin' the fat over a right fookin' bastard of a conundrum. He nods.

'But do you understand why this frustrates me Chris – unnerves me even? You keep talking about things which happened a long time ago – a crash, when your dad died…right? – and telling us not to think about what appears to be a murder now, the fire, because you say it wasn't a murder? And, you seem to know certain elements about that fire – yet you say you've never met the victim?'

Chris stops.

'Oh. Oh no. I never said I hadn't met the victim.'

'Have you met the victim before?'

'I don't know. I just never said I hadn't.'

'Have you though?'

'Well that depends who they are?'

'And who are they?'

Chris takes a loada nonsense notes from under his arm – rustles through 'em in search of, perhaps, crucial evidence.

'The…erm…"tenant"…was one "Francis Popper"…?'

Inspector Kaye looks finished. It can break yer bein' sent down a Pringle hole, if yer not used to it, n yer've got a busy schedule. For me, baked in a cupboard, it's fine.

'Would you like a cup of tea?'

Inspector Divorce looks at his watch. Checks his mobile. Grimaces. Rubs his forehead. He's considerin' his next move. The stress is oozin' off him. He's outta here now – he won't be able to cope with this. Notices a bit of fluff or summink on the back of the sofa behind Chrissy n picks it off. Chrissy sorta shudders, flaps like he's been bothered by a fly, n stands up.

Inspector Divorce sighs n sits back.

'OK then. Yes please Chris. A cup of tea would be OK.'

He's stayin'? What have I missed?

'Yes. OK. Tea. Runcie normally makes it but he's…not going to make this one. And I don't have any doughnuts. I've got biscuits though. Do you have a biscuit you rate most high…ly?'

'Do you mind me asking something Chris?'

Chris is happy again now – relaxed.

'Of course. Is it "Where's the loo?" '

'No Chris, I don't need–'

'No, neither do I. I did a big poo yesterday. At the station actually.'

'Right. Hold on? You were at the–'

'Do you want coffee?'

'Well, yes, but–'

'I don't have coffee. Only tea I'm afraid. No doughnuts either.'

'Tea's fine. Your TV detectives Chris? Why are you so…into them?'

Chris considers his wall of videos – the centre of his world, the project that's taken up 20 years of the crazy bastard's life. Sits to think. Stands to sum up.

'It's a whodunnit. But…it's never just about…one person. It's about a whole…picture. Like, I've got a Town jigsaw: 100 pieces? And you have to fit them all together? All of them? Murders aren't just about who's been…dead…ed, or who's done what. It's why it happened. How it happened. Who's still living. And what happens next.'

Big silence. He's choppin' n dividin' little boxes in the air, little invisible boxes, chopped into quarters, chopped again.

'All these bits see are mine, and they are all white? This is the only black bit left – and that's where the answers are. I might not get them all…'

He's lookin' at his imaginary squares, head on – he's got that last little black one in his sights.

'…but maybe, I can make this little black box…smaller.'

He's got stuck again. Part of me wants to click me fingers, but he'll get there. I don't know exactly what he's goin' on about, but he's a single-minded fooker. It may be a small mind – but it knows what it wants.

N then he's wide awake again.

'Can I ask you a question now Inspector Graham Kaye? Who's your favourite detective?'

'I don't have one.'

Chrissy stares for a bit then shrugs his shoulders – he's learned this from Columbo – as if to say, *Well, you must know what you're doing, I guess?*

'But again, can I ask: what do these programmes do for you Chris?'

'Help me catch murderers…is probably the main thing.'

A little edge of annoyance creeps into his very good friend the DI's tone.

'Look Chris. This is a murder enquiry. This. Today. Now. There are people out there who need to know the truth – friends, family. We don't know the victim's identity, we don't know the perpetrator's identity, and let me just say, it's almost like you want it that way.'

Chrissy ponders this n then decides.

'You don't.'

Inspector Divorce looks utterly defeated.

'What?'

'You don't know their identity.'

Our broken cop friend lets out a really big, angry sigh.

'Nor do you! You just said that!'

Chris considers this.

'There are two people: but which one was the who? Well, the fire you see was a fix and–'

Time to stop that sentence. I've already missed summink, I know it, n I can't stay in me cupboard n let Chrissy get himself in more bother than he's ready for. Not yet. I turn the handle, push the door open with me toes n hop down, dead legged, to stagger across his Interview Room, which let's not forget, is really just his lounge.

'Alright Chief – how's the noggin? Don't mind me – just need a quick waz.'

• • •

Detective Inspector Graham Kaye

Just when it was getting even more interesting, the jester in the court of Chris Pringle conjures himself out of a cupboard. But I got what I came for – even had the wherewithal to pick Runcie's mind, while it was on keeping my mind, away from the contents of Pringle's tiny mind. Or maybe not-so-tiny.

'Tell me something Runcie. You know crime. There's always a victim? So why does no-one seem to care about this one?'

'There's always someone who cares. I care. N look at him.'

'Then why isn't anyone coming forward? What are they afraid of?'

'The same things as all of us probably Blue.'

'Such as?'

At which point Pringle piped up with some more of his unique brand of absolutely nothing.

'The past. Erm. Understanding it. And what that does to the…erm…other one?'

'The future?'

'Yes. That's it. The future.'

Very deep, I'm sure.

So I nodded and left. Left trying to look like I wasn't in a hurry. Left trying to bottle the mixture of shame and excitement bubbling away beneath my tired, defeated and, quite probably once again fobbed-off exterior. Left, finally, with something they haven't given me.

Still though: Pringle? The fire was a fix? The more his chaos sucks me in, the more alive I feel, the more suspicious I am about him. You think you're on to something – he's about to spill the beans – and then, especially when Runcie's around to mix it all up, you end up talking about Shoestring, or why Pink Wafers aren't a biscuit.

One of the first things you learn on the force though – if you want to learn, and I did, I was hungry – is never to let a coincidence just sit there, unexamined. Because that way banana skins lie.

And with Pringle – everything's too much of a coincidence. He's a child really – a child in a man's body; lost his dad, found a mission. I understand that. I feel sorry for him – I really do. But there's a reason he's here, connecting himself to a live case, where someone knows what's happened, and that someone is probably a killer.

And because I've found myself waking up, from a paralysis, a fear, that I couldn't see the point any more, the point of me – I've found myself remembering that all the years I've been doing this, things do change, but what works never does. Proof works. You need proof: so you can do what's right. And if there is any? Then at least I might now have some.

28

THE FUTURE

Police Testimony:
Stephen Patrick Runce

SR   'We stared at the names. I didn't say anythin' – waited for him to talk.

My name isn't right. Half of my name is wrong.

Yeah. Well I knew it would be of course. Even Chrissy knew I suppose. But yeah…who's that?

Who's that?

Robert Hepfield. Robert Hepfield. Robert Hepfield?

It was disappointin'. If yer world's gonna be turned upside down, like Chrissy's was, yer'd wanna find out yer real dad was called Chuck or Biggie or Luke Skywalker. Not Robert.

But my dad was called Frank.

Punters think Chrissy's soft n all – a soft touch. They're wrong. That's the other mistake yer all made, apart from just ignorin' him – it's why we're here now. He's not soft. He's not weak. He'd decided yer see, there n then, for good: his dad, was Frank Christopher Pringle. That was his dad. Not Robert Fookin' Hepfield, or anyone else.

I stared at the name, n then stared at Chris. He'd gone into Powersave mode. He's got a low pulse at the best of times anyway, right? But now he's just stuck again – like someone's just, click, flicked a switch. After a while, his eyes flip to the side.

I have nothin' to add, so I'm thinkin', shit on a stick Chrissy, yer takin' all this very cool, calm n collected. N then he's grinnin', n it don't exactly seem like a grinnin' matter. I have no idea what kinda matter it is though, so I just sit there, 'til after about nine million years he just goes…

Dad's not dead. My dad's not dead.

Coz it kinda softens the blow dunnit, of discoverin' that yer whole life weren't what yer thought it was, when yer find out yer dad's not dead. N me noggin's tearin' through possibilities, tryin' to work out what it all could mean. But he's just sittin' there. N to be honest, he just looks kinda…happy.

Dad's not dead.

N seein' as I don't have answers for anythin', or any-thin' to offer at all on the matter, all I can think is: I hope yer right, Chrissy, boozin' like he did…I hope yer right.

But actually, Chrissy's thinkin' n all. He's been thinkin' – more than me. Coz then he says…

Don't tell anyone.

OK then. So I didn't. It was just us – Chrissy, me, Julie, Student.

Time goes by.

The late noughties.

He sits on it. He knows who his old man is n isn't – not that he agrees with the paperwork of course – n I've had me instructions: silence. Mum's the word. I wanted him to go back n talk to Maureen, but she'd already told him: decide. So he sits on it.

N at first, it was almost like he just wanted to enjoy the moment: daydreamy he was. The mission's still brewin', but everythin' he knows now begins n ends with his dad not dyin' in a car crash – n what can yer do with that? So he moves on to his so-called-real dad – Robert Hepfield.

He gets Student involved again – the man for the high-end research. Now, by this time, he's gone back to bein' a student, doin' some kinda Post-Nobbynobkins Double Doctoral Bunk-Off Graduate Degree Thingy, in Summinkology, yer know, for students who wanna be students all their life. N when he's not protestin', or drea-min' of noshin' off Jeremy Paxman, he's got some pretty big computers to play with he says, with databases n pass-words n free…whatever…I dunno, I stopped listenin'. But Chrissy listened, coz one day he turns up at his Uni to watch him.

Now, Student woulda been chuffed at this. Firstly, Chrissy isn't a big one for visitin' anyone. His ma, Julie – s'about it. It's an honour. N second, Student woulda loved demonstratin' his studentin' skills, coz me n Julie, obviously, just take the piss whenever we can. But it won't have lasted. Chrissy woulda come n sat right next to him, with his big body just there, breathin' heavily, starin' at the screen, n after a while poor old Student woulda realised that this weren't about him after all, n sure enough, Chrissy was soon ready with his instructions.

He'd spotted a possibility we never did. He gets Student diggin' around – usin', I dunno, dates, n places, n let's give 'em a little bit of credit, maybe some actual detective work, n eventually, they lock it down: sure enough, there is no Robert Hepfield. But where he isn't, where there's a black hole in the virtual universe, there, in his place, same age, same background, same everythin', is Robert *Bobby* Heffel. Brother of Dirk Heffel. Also known to the great don't-call-us-British ravin' Republic as - remember? - the Heavy Boys.'

29

NOW

Detective Inspector Graham Kaye

Nothing.

Waiting, waiting.

I look at the clock. Again. How long does it bloody take?

I can't think.

A watched pot never boils: so delegate the pot-watching to someone else.

I call Paphaedes.

'Where are you?'

'I'm on my way over to Pringle's sir.'

'OK. Well pause that and come here. I've got another job for you.'

'OK sir.'

'Any news on 1992 and this crash yet?'

'Well, yes sir, and no – I read all there was sir, which wasn't much, you know what these old, er, I mean olden day files are like. All looks fairly routine. Drunk driver, went off the road – no other passengers or vehicles involved or property damaged, so it was put to bed.'

Mmm. The paperwork never quite captures the personal loss though, does it?

'Oh – I tell you something funny I did find out when I was looking over the paperwork though sir. There wasn't much to it as I say, but the lead officer was DCI Mogford! Weird or what?! Wasn't a DCI at the time of course, but anyway.'

Fucking hell.

Pringle.

The letter. The follow-up call. He's bloody well hunted Mogford down!

• • •

Chris

There's a loud…slurping…noise.

I sit up suddenly. I open my eyes. I take a big breath. Very big, big enough so I can breathe again. Which is important. Because if you don't breathe…you…die. Even if you're a detective.

I'm on the sofa.

I'm on a case. The only case.

Runcie is on my recliner. He's looking at me. He has a plan now. He wanted to talk about the plan, but then I did a Super Snooze.

I start talking.

'Power meditation Runce. Two ten minute snoozes, every day. Prescribed by Dr Watts. I pretend there are, erm, whales. I close my eyes. I breathe in. I breathe out. I count down from 100 to 1, which is quite…well, I try. I think of the numbers. Each one looks different. And then what happens is, you're not thinking of any-thing...else? Apart from that. And that's when you get...?'

'An erection?'

I tap my head.

'...space...for answers. They just...appear.'

'Mmm. I've been here for yer ten minute snoozes Chrissy – like just now for example – n let me tell yer, sometimes they last two or three hours.'

'Yes – if a Power Meditation is too powerful, it's possible you might fall a little bit asleep.'

'Very possible.'

'But then when you wake up? You know what to do.'

'That's helpful then innit? Yer could call 'em Medi-Snoozes? Get it trademarked.'

He writes it in the sky. We both imagine it. But Runcie has changed his mind.

'Actually forget it – they sound like night keks for old folk. Anyway, back in the room right – brew?'

'Mmm. When I'm having a erm...thinking problem, I think, "What would Jason King think that Mark Cain would think?" It's double thinking. It's what you need when a thinking problem is twice as hard as normal.'

'See, I don't like to discourage yer Chrissy, yer know, be a negative force, but this is the danger? Gettin' all wrapped up in biz like double-thinkin', when yer everyday single-thinkin' could be sleepwalkin' yer into a world of grief. Which is why we need a plan, n why I've come up with a plan, n why it would be top-nana if we could activate that plan. Right? Coz to recap: when Inspector Divorce was here, summink happened...'

'Right?'

'N I couldn't work out what.'

'Right. Well. I'm going to go and see him today at his detective office, you know the police…place? One more time? So I can ask him then if you like? Or I could detect it? Can you make that happen by the way? With a…car? You're very good at making cars happen.'

'Great, thanks. Yep. If yer want. But the summink, see? The summink that happened? Well, it could be nothin'. But he shouldn't have been here. N he shouldn't have stayed. But he was. N he did. N that's why it was summink.'

'Oh.'

'N I wanna cover yer ass – yer know, a little bit better, OK, a medium-sized bit better, than we have so far. Y-Fronts, not a thong, yer get me? Startin' now.'

I look at my feet – wonder where my shoes are. Maybe I'll go in my slippers?

'Yes Runce. Because I'll be summing up soon.'

Ding dong again.

Runcie looks up, rubs his hands together.

'OK Chrissy. You'll be summin' up soon: sweet. But just sit tight for a min now Chrissy: it's another visitor, but trust me – yer'll like this one.'

• • •

Runcie

Chrissy. The madman in the attic, the sculptor channellin' God. He's chipped away at his masterpiece, minute-by-minute, hour-by-hour, for half his days. Yer get glimpses, but they don't make yer feel better. N soon he's gonna stop the traffic, unveil his life's work. N yer really, really want there to be a happy endin'. But. It's scary. And so…the plan.

I can't stop whatever pain's round the corner. But I can arrange protection. An intervention. The law.

'I've got someone to come in for a chinwag Chrissy.'

'Oh.'

'Nice lady. Friend of Julie's. She won't tread on yer toes Chrissy, just help yer…look after things a bit?'

Me judgement may be fooked though, coz I'm in love with her already. Just one power call was all it took. I wink at meself in Chrissy's mirror, fire a coupla cool cowboy pistols, n head to the door.

'Mr Runce?'

'Call me Runcie, please. This is Chris. Chrissy – this is Ms Patricia…?'

'Liversedge.'

\'I like your briefcase. I only have a plastic bag.'

They've hit it off.

'Call me Patricia. I'm a solicitor, Chris.'

'She's a solicitor Chrissy.'

'Well done.'

He looks happy enough – like this isn't really about him.

'Right, I understand the basics of the situation from your friend Mr Runce, Chris. May I give you my opinion?'

Chrissy starts to think about that, but she just carries on, n he lets her. Wow – she's good. That never happens.

'It's not complicated. First there's a minor matter. It sounds a little like the police are coming into this house whenever they want. They just need to be treated like children Chris – firm but fair – and then they'll know they can't be giving you any silly bother. We'll head in, and I'll simply tell them that my clients need a written and personalised assurance – signed from the top – that they will not be called to account for any irrelevant details which may come to light as a part of this process, and until then, they stay away. Because this scheme, C.L.E.A.R. – they can't be getting you and Mr Runce in under false pretences, can they? That won't do. We'll make immunity your binding right – it won't be up for discussion – otherwise we'll just trot off home.'

I've gone all gooey.

'You're amazin'.'

She gives me a pityin' pat on the leg – but her focus is Chrissy.

'True. And then there's the more serious matter, of whether you're giving them any reason – any reason at all, however inadvertently – to think that you might be obstructing or in any other way implicated in their enquiries.'

He looks at me. The sentence was too long for him. It was heavy going – so I try to lighten things up a bit.

'I have a question Patricia? So yer went to lawyer college, now yer a lawyer – what does yer boyfriend do?'

'I don't have a boyfriend and I don't intend on getting one.'

'No. Quite right. Keep yer options open.'

'My options are always open Mr Runce. Negotiations start for that very reason – to keep your options open and start closing down everyone else's.'

Mmm. Selfish but sexy. I like it.

'You have to have something to offer though – something tangible. What is it exactly you do for work Mr Runce?'

'Oh. Offer tangible things? Keep me options open?'

'Good.'

'Why d'yer wanna know?'

'Come to my "Closers" workshop. Little sideline I've got going on. Should help you with your deals. Have a flyer.'

'Don't be a loser, be a closer.'

Good catchphrase. Also sexy.

'What are yer other rules of negotiation then?'

I think I'm in love. She's almost as Goddess-like as Julie.

'Now – I wouldn't give all of those ideas away just like that, would I Stephen? I can put an end to your problems here, but I don't charge £600/hour for fun.'

Ah.

I look at Chrissy.

We won't be spending £600 on Patricia. Per hour. Not even for one hour. Coz I haven't got it – I've always stuck with a strict no trappins policy. Julie wouldn't give it – Chrissy's a hopeless case, not a charity case. N Chrissy wouldn't take it it. Give him six hundred quid's worth of Poirot DVDs to help him fine tune his rule book, and he'd grunt and waddle off with his note pad n a plate of Dodgers. End his problems for him though? Yer just can't.

Immunity means nothin' to him. I get it now. This is summink he's gotta do – n he's always had to do it alone. So I'll book that Hilltop's, n take him on his way in a bit.

Of course, it don't mean I can't stay in touch with Patricia Liversedge meself, yer know, just in case? Support local businesses n all that – winnin' smile!

'Give me yer card Patricia n I'll be in touch. Now – d'yer fancy a brew n a biscuit? The Runce Dog's fed up of hearin' all about us two – he'd like to hear all about you.'

• • •

Detective Inspector Graham Kaye

The strange mercurial magnetism of Chris Pringle, slowing everything down, but drawing us together. At the very moment he should be trusting me the least – and if he picked up anything along the way from eating crisps and watching telly, he'd surely realise that…but actually, what am I even talking about? – he comes in for a chat. It's unsettling.

He's marching slowly round the room, hands behind his back, waiting for his twisted brain to catch up maybe, to get some words out in any kind of an order. If he's expecting a bigger audience though, he isn't getting one. Paphaedes is chasing, trying to make things happen, while Chapman fulfils the inevitable request for tea and biscuits. Once delivered, he can fuck off – listening to Pringle is one thing, but I'm keeping this circus behind closed doors from now on, at least until I know, properly know, what we've got ourselves into.

'Would you say that you are the jealous type Inspector Kaye?'

Sigh.

'What?'

'Well. I really like you. You're a very nice police…man. It's important to be kind. And you are trying very hard and I feel… sorry for you.'

I'm being patronised by a man whose IQ is in danger of being overtaken by my age.

'Why are you asking if I'm jealous?'

'I saw someone else do it, another…detective…I can't remember…it's…'

He's flicking through his note pad again. Spends half his life flicking through note pads and rule books. I mean, is there even anything on that pad? I don't care man! I don't care! He looks up, spots me, remembers I'm there.

'Why are we here Chris?'

'Mmm?'

He stops, starts pacing in the other direction – still stroking his chin.

'Inspector Kaye. I think you want...proof. And this crime needs to be solved. Tick. Ish. But my good friend Stephen Runce – do you remember him?'

'Yes Chris. I remember him – very well.'

'He thinks I need proof too. So I..."understand," you see? That I need to show you, why you should listen to me...when I say that this – erm, fire – is, was, not a murder. Mmm?'

He stands there filling the room and pats me on the shoulder, the Godfather giving me his blessing – then wipes his hand nervously on his tracksuit bottoms.

'So...I am going to show you.'

Credit where credit's due, Pringle does have the ability to string out a conversation so it feels like it's going somewhere, but never is.

'Now.'

I take a deep breath, in, out.

'Are you OK if I take notes Chris?'

Gives me another Godfather smile. Benevolent.

'Of course – a good detective always takes notes.'

'And this is about Brunswick Villas, right?'

I retrieve my little Moleskine notebook – a gift from Sandra dating back to when she hated me a lot less – a lot. A pang of regret slices through me as I try and recall in a flash the little increments of that decline, and whether I could have done anything to stop it. But I'm not sure I could.

He's happily pacing. I click my pen, and he swings round to face me like he's caught me with my hands in the till.

I nod.

'Go on.'

He continues his slow march around the table. It's actually quite intimidating, such is my fragile state. I'm lucid, off the blockers, going easier on the booze. Will I crack?

'The deceased. The person who died. They had drink...in them. They were drunk. Drunk? But...'

My pen hovers.

'But they didn't want to be.'

And of course, that's when he leaves. Touches his nose – attempts a wink.

'I'm going...undercover.'

Chris Pringle clomps slowly out of sight, looking as if he's executed his public duty and genuinely helped me out. Maybe he has.

• • •

Paphaedes is back. Still no news.

I tell him about Pringle's visit.

'What you just said sir? Reminds me of something Pringle said a few days back – about his dad's crash? I just thought it was nonsense. But...well: he called that "proof" too. He said...what was it? I think he said, that his old man was a drinker, and the crash was to do with drinking – but it wasn't to do with driving.'

For fuck's sake. Riddle-me-fucking-Pringle. But perhaps we have a bye word – based on the mumblings of a lunatic, sure, but a bye word all the same. Our old friend, the booze: linking that bloody crash to my case. Just like Pringle seems to be.

Booze.

I send Paphaedes off to talk to the pubs, to find out what, if anything memorable, was going on on the night of. To be fair to him – and again, that's a sign of the times, as I've never cared about being fair to him before – it's a thankless task. He could come back with any amount of rambling rubbish – a total waste of time. But we have to keep moving. So Paphaedes is keeping us moving, by tapping up the town's most dedicated drinkers. I have to believe it will lead to something.

• • •

Five, six hours of thinking, precious thinking. About booze. And scenarios. And guns. One cleaned and empty. One loaded and not cleaned. Why?

It's 10 pm when Paphaedes calls.

'Well, it's extraordinary sir. You've been around a bit. Have you ever been in the Express Tavern for Steak Night? Packed. Apparently the landlady – big lady, been there 40 years? Apparently, when she was younger, she was pregnant, but so fat, she didn't know she was pregnant, until it just dropped out one day, right there behind the bar.'

Should the new me humour this nonsense? No.

'What did you find out PC Paphaedes – that's to do with the case?'

'How did you know sir? How did you know it would throw something up?'

Shit. The truth is, I wasn't expecting it to: was I?

'Express Tavern sir. Day of the fire. Odd fella sitting in the warm there all afternoon. Drinking tea as it happens – tea. It's all about the ciders in there really sir. Which was why he caught their eye. Think they were a bit annoyed. Anyway. He received a phone call at the bar about 6-6:30 pm. "Like he'd been waiting for it, it was" – that's what they said.'

Police Constable Paphaedes is proud of himself. He's got more too. He knows he's got more I'll want to hear. I don't want to appear desperate – but Dear God, I need to hear it. He looks back down at his pad.

'The fella calling sir? Went by the name of Pringle.'

'What?'

'Pringle sir. And then I went to the lab as you said sir – got the results.'

The adrenaline is pumping. I can't speak.

'The DNA results sir? On Pringle's hair, from his place?'

'Yes, yes, I'm aware of what you're talking about?'

'Well. They ran it through the system for the sake of it – no matches on the database. And then they ran it against the swabs from Brunswick Villas.'

And? And?

'And – well…we've got a match sir.'

Fuck. I knew it. I knew it!

'And the really interesting thing–'

'Tell me later, because…fuck!'

'Sir?'

'Overtime Paphaedes. I'll send Chapman too. Just find Pringle – and get him back here, now.'

30

THE FUTURE

Police Testimony:
Stephen Patrick Runce

SR   'Chrissy's got more gut than most, right? N we knew then, we shoulda trusted that gut all along: everythin', somehow, was connected to the Heavy Boys. N now he'd got to the huge fookin' dark heart of why: Bobby was his dad. Heavy times indeed.

So he's back to his ma – for the most bang-on weird, intimate conversation a mother n son could ever have, yer get me? Coz Maureen's got some explainin' to do: how could one half of the most rancid, ice-hearted, knife-edge, psycho double acts ever – who frankly felt too close for comfort even when they were just this paira mythical nightmares, stickin' a big fat downer on the vibe of our scene – be Chrissy's dad?

That's not how Chrissy saw it of course. I told yer – he was crystal about who his dad was: Frank. But, whisper it – how was Chrissy's so-called-real dad, a Heavy Boy?

N she tells the story: short, n not very sweet.

It happened. She hadn't wanted it to – but it had. Bobby? He was a horrible person. His brother was a horrible person. Paths crossin' at a difficult time. She didn't go into details. It was a mess. It made her very, very sad, afraid – but it also gave her the most precious thing in her life: little Christopher.

Frank was already on the scene, she was with him at the time. N she'd told him, n told Chrissy again now: *It wasn't all...my fault.* What a way to say it, yer get me – but she didn't wanna spell it out. Wanted that to be the end of it. I knew what it meant though, n Frank woulda known – but all he said was, *OK.* He swallowed the pain he felt for her, n never asked the questions she didn't want him to: he just said he'd stay, n he stayed.

'Avin' that hangin' over 'em though? That was horrible. Hard. On Frank. On Mo. Me ma was Mo's buddy for life. But she'd left n gone to Manc. I know we all had a few summers together before she died, me n Chrissy, buddies in Huggies – but she wasn't right there anymore, on Mo's doorstep, to listen...n she had problems of her own n all. So Mo couldn't ask for help, n Mo had no-one else she'd talk to. Not about that. Maybe if she had talked – found someone else – it woulda worked out different?

She never told Bobby Heffel she was pregnant. Never even told him about Frank. Just thought she'd let him disappear out of her life as quick as he'd arrived. Turns out though, once these proper bad punters get in yer face, they don't leave 'til they want to, or you make 'em. They'll feed off yer any way they can – off yer pain, yer discomfort. So, somehow, Bobby, he finds out.

He took no pleasure in it of course – just made it horrendous. Her, the baby, it was all just property to him, property he didn't want, but his property, all the same. He made her put him down – but not so it was exactly him – on the birth certificate. The Christopher was borrowed from his real old man, Frank Christopher Pringle – a secret little go fook yerself to Bobby. A mistake maybe? Coz after that, he took a loada pleasure in poppin' up, phonin': threats n malevolence, aimed at just one person. Frank: the – as he saw it – useless, blotchy, alchy loser, who'd had the nerve to keep his sheets warm.

So all this is drip, drip, drippin' away in Frank's head, n in his heart: he's tryin' his best to be a dad in his own way, tryin' to love Chrissy, tryin' to be there for Maureen, tryin' to provide, keep 'em safe. He's not a go-getter of course, n he's not John Wick – but he's there, n there's love, n that's enough for Maureen. But it's not enough for Bobby Fookin' Heffel.

They're psychos in a foreign land, him n his brother, n it was the '70s – a hard fookin' time right? But they just did what they wanted: sellin' smack, runnin' hooky goods, guns, everywhere from Bristol to Taunton to Oxford, they were all over it – n 'avin' some mousy little soft-cock stickin' around n bringin' up a Heffel kid, weren't a good look.

So Bobby started really terrorisin' 'em. Turnin' up. Frank's gettin' pushed around. Bobby exertin' his rights. Horrible shit.

N like I say: Frank was the gentlest soul yer'd ever meet. So what this all does to him? It's all on the inside. He's failed his family. He breaks. The booze is his escape. He can't be a husband any more. It's heartbreakin' for him. For Maureen. He weren't cut out for a war – he was cut out for a life of doin' no harm. But he knew it weren't enough, n it sent him over the edge. He was scared of what they might do.

So when Chris was about seven, he just started goin' away – enough that Heffel would leave 'em alone. N it worked at first. He was off gettin' jobs up on the rigs. Stayin' out of sight, but callin', sendin' the money home, comin' back for a few weeks, for as long as it felt safe, then off again.

But the drinkin' got worse, the jobs got scrappier, less well paid. He was a broken man, n the family was broken. Him n Maureen, they both knew: it was only a matter of time. Heffel had won.

N when Chrissy's well, like I say, about 14, Heffel turns up out the blue one day, n Frank's where he shouldn't be: sittin' at the kitchen table with Maureen. N Heffel left him in no doubt: go a long way away, don't come back, or someone will die: *Let's wait and see who.*

So the next day? He upped n left for good. N Maureen knew it.

No matter how big that sacrifice, how much love was behind it, well – the marriage was done. They still loved each other. But yer can't be married to a man scared out of his wits – so scared he's never there. He was just kind. Afraid. He only ever wanted Maureen n Chris to be OK.

Some people look at Mo – how she let Frank go, how she was with Chris after the crash – n think she's cold. Maybe they'll understand if they know – like I understood then? Mo was lovely. Think about it. All through when we were kids, with Frank comin' n goin', n then goin' for good: she was sittin' on this. She gutsed that out for years, n still, all she ever did, all she ever showed, was what she thought she could do for everyone else: for me even...but most of all for Chrissy.

The crash was her breakin' point. She couldn't take any more.

Judge her by what came before – coz it's not surprisin' what came later.

Mind if I?'

THERE IS A TEN MINUTE BREAK IN THE RECORDING FOR MR RUNCE TO SMOKE

A ROLLED-UP CIGARETTE, WITH A BRIEF ADDITIONAL DELAY FOR PC PAPHAEDES TO USE THE TOILET.

DIGK 'Continuing testimony of Stephen Patrick Runce. Present also Ms Patricia Liversedge; myself, Detective Inspector Graham Kaye; and, finally, PC Paphaedes. Let's get back to Mr Pringle?'

SR 'Right. So. So that's what Chrissy had to work with: his world from before he was born, 'til Frank heads off when he was 14. That's all Mo says she can give him for now: he has to work out what took Frank to that crash. It's back to her wantin' Chrissy to decide, not her: how much he wants to know?

N he's stickin' close to Julie. Coz yer understand now right, what Julie is to him? A safety blanket yeah, fillin' in a hole where his ma shoulda been I guess – but also, more than me even, in a way that really matters, his connection to the past. Coz only she can build those bridges to the past, get him closer to his dad, to the Heavy Boys – through the Maskells. Coz he thinks there's an answer in there. N of course, there is. On our long-forgotten Dictaphone.

So out of her stash it comes once more, n they listen back to it, again. The Heavy Boys don't drink. So how come the DNA, matched to Chrissy, says one of 'em – n me time in Rotterdam says it's Dirk – died in a boozed-up crash? Chrissy has no doubt – that crash was murder. But who cares, right? Well, of course, Chrissy cares. He desperately fookin' cares.

Partly coz maybe there's a way to Frank through all of this? N partly coz Frank was there at that crash, had to be, involved: so exactly what kinda person had he become?

More time goes by. I mean, it even looks like Chrissy's veered off course n kind of got off the point, like he's just goin' through the motions, watchin' his detectives, makin' notes – without anythin' bein' real. But he's just absorbin', absorbin'. N Julie's not forgotten either. None of us had. We were all on the payroll. We were all ready to help him – but he still hadn't had a breakthrough. 'Til Olympics year. 2012. I know that, coz he didn't watch any of it.

Julie, see, had shown him summink she found – just summink she thought he'd like. By this time of course there was some distance between the now, n the naughtiness of the old skool dayz...enough for punters to start sharin' all their happy memories, yer know, blogs of flyers, mixes, vids of free parties even, n lots n lots of raves: Gravity, Dreamscape, Perception, Fantazia, all the stuff we used to go to. Hold on – just rememberin'...*Your Love,* some big, orgasmic arena, the first thing we heard on 1ˢᵗ January, 1992...

OK.

Soz.

Where was I? Right...

So Chrissy gets wrapped up in it all. It's like reincarnation – like he can't remember bein' there, but he knows he was. N he sits there for hours, soakin' it all up. Makin' notes. But more just starin' –

like he knows. He knows: this is it. He's waitin' for a discovery. N eventually, he gets one.

He sees himself – at a rave. Yer'd never see me – camera shy, a gut feel for the implications if yer like. But Chris was – is – a slow mover. He weren't fast enough to hide, n there he was – swayin'.

N then he really can't let go. This is it for him. He's got to see more. It's real detective work. Him n Julie, they contact the guy who's stuck the video up. He's got more videos. *Yeah, come on over, have a watch.* Julie does her thing. *Yeah, I've got loads more I never stuck up because, well, you know – they've got dodgy dealings left, right and centre.* Chrissy watches it all, for days. N it's throwin' up fook all. So with my help, n Julie's, he starts honin' in on the raves he went to. He don't know what he's expectin' to find – but that's just it…put yerself in the situation, in the right place, the right zone, n there's always a chance that stories, punters, explanations…it can somehow start to fall into place.

N then sure enough, he sees himself again. N then again. N every time he sees himself, he starts that whole rave all over again, every little nanosecond, n he watches it. N every time, his dad's there too. N he's never far away. From Chris. N also there too, always at the same raves: the Heavy Boys. The Heffels. Summink's placin' all of 'em – just like he thought, Chrissy, his dad, his so-called-real dad – in the same place at the same time, five, six, seven years after they all went their separate ways when Chrissy was 14. N it ends with that crash: Frank disappearin'; a Heavy Boy dead.

So Julie's talkin' to Mr Documentary Evidence Filmmaker. He's a retired rave tourist with brains, not a proper scenester – coz yer'd have to have been right, yer weren't gettin' any documentaries made whilst gurnin' for queen n country. So anyway, this geezer's a proper grown-up now – runs some laundry business, borin' as fook. But Julie's windin' back the clock with him, talkin' about the Maskells, danglin' a hook, seein' what bites, and this fella pipes up that he never knew the Maskells back in the day, but he does now. One of 'em anyway. Karl. His bro's in the slammer. Karl ended up legit. Runs some delivery company – doin' well, all above board.

Now. I'm live n let live, me, but like I said, even after all that time, I had no wish to slap backs with the fookin' Maskells n have them connecting Chrissy to the Heavies – still gives me psychic shudders now, just thinkin' about it. So Julie heads off to pay Mr Legit Maskell a visit.

I doubt he'll commit to this if yer check him out, but that don't matter. This isn't about him. What matters is, Karl knew all about, not just the Heavy Boys of course, but when Julie dangles a name – old man Pringle – he knows all about him n all. Didn't know he was Chrissy's dad – didn't even know who Chrissy was, coz like I say, I'd kept him away from anythin' bad – but knew him as part of the Heavy Boys' set-up back in the day, '90, '91, '92: a whippin' boy.

Somehow, at some point, in the time between walkin' out on his family – to get away from 'em, to disappear – to that crash, they'd reeled Frank back in: some sorta fooked up situation. N this is what Karl Maskell said about it – about how they treated him. Bobby. But even worse, Dirk. *Ugly it was – like there was always violence in the air. Like it was obvious – it wasn't going to end well.*

N it didn't, did it?'

31

NOW

Detective Inspector Graham Kaye

Light early. No sleep. Paphaedes and Chapman knocking on doors until late. No sign of Pringle. Back out again this morning first thing – the same doors. More waiting, the unknown lingering over the hill, out of sight and out of reach – and I am unable to stop myself going to a pub. Not even a pub – the Harvester out on the ring road. Where nobody knows my name.

I sit at a pretend bar – normally occupied, I imagine, by loud sales arseholes – pondering the double vodka I asked a spotty, unquestioning teenager called Dean to put in front of me, too guilty to down it at 11 am, too desperate to enjoy the moral victory in not doing so.

I try to imagine Pringle as a kid – what he would have been like, what home meant, what happened when he lost his dad, what that might have done to him. And then the kids Sandra and I never had. That Sandra decided, late on, she'd never wanted. Feelings were lists of demands to Sandra – lists of her unmatched expectations. So I kept mine tucked away – about that, about everything really – to try and prove a point. What point? Stoneman said it – only yesterday.

'Don't fight battles you don't want to win. You're not defined by your feelings. But they are a part of you. Surrender to them. Hands up!'

The marriage is over – yet I'm in a Harvester before lunchtime, staring at vodka, with Sandra leading a chorus of voices telling me that I'm shit and I know I am. I push it away and head out.

The right people, in the right place, at the right time – that's all you need. Just keep moving the pieces, filling things in, one flicker at a time – that's the secret to cracking a case sometimes. Which is why it's so disappointing when Paphaedes calls and says he's coming back to the station, but Pringle won't be with him. He's gone AWOL.

'But about this DNA match sir. I really need to talk to you about this DNA match.'

'Go on…'

• • •

Chris

Alone.

• • •

I go and see Mum. And I tell her: it will be my birthday. We will be together.

• • •

Alone.

Sometimes at the start of the day – a normal day, in my bungalow, a last-20-years day – my head feels muffy. But if I fill up my sink with water and put my head in, I don't like the bits that run down my neck and shiver my shoulders, but the water covers the whole of my head. A million drops. Most fall off. But I am always left with the last hundred drops – different places all over my head, soaking in slowly. These drops are the important ones. They just sit there, and I don't think about them, but they are waking up the bits that need it most, and in the end, I understand.

• • •

I write down my five favourite detectives. I put on an item of clothing of each. (I do this in my head). I write down their rules. There are no rules. I close my eyes. I won't miss anything. There are two things left to do.

First thing is, I will have a meeting. After I have had the meeting I should be able to do the second thing, which is solve the case. And after that? I don't know what happens after that.

I don't know.

• • •

Maureen

Dear Lord:

I pray for Christopher, Lord. He needs protecting, from so many things – from himself.

Do you see him?

Do you see us all?

We spoke you and I – this morning. Didn't we? Like we always do? I'm losing my way here Lord. You were always my guide.

He came today Lord. And I wasn't expecting it. It makes me feel funny to think that: not expecting my own son.

When he was just a kid, he used to let bees crawl on his hands. "Eeky" I call it, that stuff that makes you go "Eek." On his fingers, crawling around. He used to stroke them – bees – can you imagine? But he's stayed like that Lord – he's still like it now, like he won't be scared, because if you're kind, what's there to be scared of?

He doesn't get it from me.

Sometimes you need to be scared Lord? He's going off see, getting himself closer and closer to something. Maybe to terrible things. Because I didn't make him understand. I started him off on this. I allowed it. And I haven't ever stopped him. I didn't feel I could. Or should?

I haven't talked to him.

And I haven't talked to you.

I talk gibberish yes, every morning, every night, like fail. I tell you about my day. I'd like to give though rather than just taking – but how? I offer you tea – but what use is tea when I can't see you. You've got holes in your feet anyway, you'd be like a bloody sieve.

I'm sorry Lord. I apologise. I deserve everything. I'm sorry for everything. I do believe – but I've made mistakes Lord…and now I have to change. I have to stop this – I have to.

Forgive me. But if you're there? I beg. I beg. I just want Christopher to be OK. I just want Christopher to be OK.

• • •

Detective Inspector Graham Kaye

Stoneman. Three times in a week now, the schedule thrown out of the window. My mind's whirring. It shouldn't be the right time – but…

'It never mattered if you held back to me – but you needed to stop holding back to yourself. A crutch is no good if you're not learning to walk again. The feeling you often described – a sense of encroachment, confusion clouding your thinking? That was coming from the inside, not the outside. The moment you stopped processing your emotions? That's when your illness began.'

Stoneman doesn't remind me of the moment, even if that rather goes against the spirit of facing up to things. The moment, when I spent New Year's Eve alone and Sandra fucked a person unknown in the loos at her "Rock Choir Ball." The vague story, the gleeful call from the witness to the truth (who I can no longer look in the eye), and the calm, shameless, blame-shifting admission of guilt.

He's in his element here Stoneman – the fitted suit, the ostentatiously large-framed glasses, the minimalist piles of paperwork – sorting out someone who isn't going to threaten him, or stink out his office, or only last as long as the NHS will keep footing the bill. Fingertips touched together, rocking gently in his chair, he's 100% confident: I've been turning a corner, and suddenly I've realised it.

'You described your marriage as "doomed for many years" – stresses over money etc? If you look at yourself there, objectively: what does it make you feel?'

Everything. And nothing. But mostly pity.

'I feel sorry for him.'

'That's terribly sad isn't it?'

No shit Sherlock. Fuck you Watson.

'All of that fog, anxiety, panic – it came not from the sadness itself, but from trying to bury it.'

I leave the sanctuary of Stoneman's office – just so, big windows, cool, calm, no shadows or distractions. I know I'll be back, I know that's OK, and I find myself thinking about my first term at John Hampden Grammar School: a young eleven. The first day and every day after that, terrifying, because it was never again going to be like it was before – like it was at little school, where you sat unaware, unquestioning, top of a pile of one. An unreal fear – nothing tangible to be afraid of. But simply, the worst fear: that everyone else thinks the same way, and you will never ever be able to. And I've lived all that again these last couple of years. Every day. That terror. I know it's there – that's the best that can be said. And you learn to spot the missed opportunities: where you were still out of control and afraid, but going against every survival instinct, you could have stuck your neck out a bit and just...seen what happened. And here, now, I'm sticking my neck out.

Because the problem, the future, the consequences – they're not mine alone.

Because of a DNA revelation too big – too mind-blowing – to sit on.

32

THE FUTURE

Police Testimony:
Stephen Patrick Runce

SR 'So Chrissy tells Maureen what he knows – Frank left, the Heavies followed, n one of 'em ended up dead as Dunkin' Donuts in a dodgy fookin' crash, with his name all over it. Chrissy ain't hidin' from any of it, Mo sees that – so now she tells him what she knows.

After Frank left, when Chrissy was what, 14, we'd all thought that was it – blackout. But it turns out, carefully, quietly, just so she knew he was OK, wherever he was, wherever the work took him, he was gettin' in touch. Nothin' – ever – to put Maureen or Chrissy in danger. Just phone calls, with a little system – yer know, two rings n then ring back, that kinda thing. Postcards from Yarmouth n Dover. N always summink for Mo to give to Chrissy on his birthday, like a bum bag from Portugal – Algarve 85 – little blind messages of love, n unspoken clues, which she'd never tell Chrissy the meanin' of, that he was still out there.

Sounds bad on Maureen now right, like I said? But think about it? From the moment they decided, when Chrissy was a kid, to protect him, to hide that birth certificate, there was no going back – there was never a right time to unpick the story. N now it was all on her. She was the first victim – n she was left on her own as the last. Coz how could she say it: he was out there somewhere, he was OK, but he couldn't come back coz...well, coz he weren't Chrissy's dad? Chrissy was already messed up in the head – breakin' cover wouldn't change that, it would just get 'em all in a load more strife. Yer get me?

N of course, out there, the more time goes by, Frank's not doin' well anyway – workin' less, movin' around less, drinkin' more n more, with a broken heart. But at some point around 1990, Bobby Heffel must've decided that him, out there somewhere, slowly killin' himself, weren't enough – must've decided that the most enjoyable aspect of the whole sorry-assed Maureen business, was 'avin a bit of sport with Frank. So he hunted him down.

They told him he had a new job – workin' for 'em. Pure spite. Usin' him. Coz they could. Dirk was somehow the worst. There was tension. N Frank was a barely walkin', barely talkin' driver, dogsbody, pills mule. No doubt tryin' to hide his pain, all the time. A one-way path to hell. N then, later, seein' Chrissy too – out on the scene, not bein' able to do anythin' – that was finishin' him off.

The last call Maureen'd had, he was cryin', drunk – said he just wanted to say hello to Chrissy, that's all. *To make things right.* That was just before Castlemorton. N then? The crash. She knew he'd not died there, not in that – but she'd never heard from him again.

So Chrissy goes back to his armchair; he's thinkin' about the end of Castlemorton, tryin' to replay a scene he's not sure he can remember, playin' it over n over in his head – yer know, if it was a VHS it'd be knackered, like that bit on me copy of The Delinquents when – actually, never mind.

He's like a military commander, playin' with his little toy soldiers, mappin' out the different ways a battle could've played out. He's not just re-livin' the memory though, lookin' round the faces he saw – he's tryin' to walk through it. A million times, from a million different angles. Yer think he's slow. But this is the score, right? Slow's OK. If yer spend more time thinkin', yer can take yerself to some incredible places. N one day? He gets to where he wants to be.

Since findin' that birth certificate, his whole idea of that crash, n what had happened, had gradually started to be shaped by fear. He remembered see, that in those last few months before Castlemorton, he'd felt like he'd got his old man back – out of nowhere there he was, messed up but, well, vaguely there. With Chrissy. Together. N what was the worst possible thing that could've happened? Losin' each other all over again. So Frank must've felt the same? Except Frank was bein' pushed to the edge by the Heavies. N Frank knew it was them who was gonna drive 'em apart. N Frank could do summink about it. N that was Chrissy's fear: he'd flipped.

But now he gets it. He'd seen it all wrong. His dad weren't a killer in that crash. One of the Heavies hadn't been shoutin' at Frank – he'd been shoutin' at his brother. Frank was bringin' 'em all down: watchin' 'em, watchin' Chrissy. N it was an implosion alright. But Frank didn't kill anyone. One killed the other, coz of Frank – coz of him.

Good news for Chrissy then right? Yeah, course – in one way. In another though? Maybe not.

Coz OK, Chrissy's old man weren't the victim in that crash. N now it's clear to Chrissy, he weren't the murderer either. But he was the witness. Which is why he had to disappear – n stay disappeared. For a long, long time.

But Chrissy? He felt…he was sure, Frank was still alive. So he had to be ready, see? He knew he'd have to be ready. N then a few months ago? He was back. He was about. He really had seen him. It's all in his files. N Chrissy knew, if Frank was back, he wouldn't be alone: the last survivin' Heavy Boy would be back soon n all.'

33

NOW

Detective Inspector Graham Kaye

Someone was dangerous, desperate or out of control enough to start a fire which killed one and could have killed more. The case stagnated, but one thing stood out: the presence of a damaged member of the public, contaminating, confusing, distracting, there because Mogford – the one man who should have known better – wants to go out looking progressive, on message, a team man.

Playing the game. I've always hated trying, hated failing. It's suffocating, debilitating, destructive. But when the truth is on its way? It has its place. I can see that now. Mogford's secretary is trying to look busy. Soon, she might be. Every good finger-pointer needs a paper trail, but I won't be a scapegoat in Mogford's – it's nearly 30 years short on detail.

He buzzes me through and she repeats the instruction, but I'm already on my way, strolling into his palatial office, being careful to check my phone like I don't have time for this, and making sure I don't wipe my feet on the mat – because fuck your new carpet. The look of strain and rage on his face almost makes me want to weep, and I'm tempted to milk it – feign a call to keep him hanging – but I must be patient: all good things come to those who wait.

'Inspector Kaye. An explanation is in order I think?'

I'm suddenly, spontaneously gripped with a vision of ramming a 99 Flake in his face – explain this you turd. I giggle – giggle! – then barely conceal it with a cough. He glares.

'I'm supposed to be on a golf course. Remember, if it helps me, it helps you – so right now, I'd like to know why I'm here? And how you are actually getting on with this murder case?'

'Yes, well sir. It's about the case actually, as I do have an update, which I rather thought you'd like to hear. About Pringle. Pringle? Remember Pringle sir? Chris Pringle?'

'Yes of course I remember him, why are you being odd? I hope you're not here to moan about C.L.E.A.R. again Inspector Kaye? If it's good for me, it's good for you.'

U-turn imminent. Take cover. The shit's about to hit the hypocrisy wind machine.

'Well. I did as you asked sir. Reached out. Even went to his house. Really worked hard to involve him.'

'Good, good, and?'

'And he's actually been useful. Just not as you might have expected. More in that, how should I say it, he seems to be directly involved…already?'

He frowns at me, impatient.

'What do you mean? What are you trying to say? Elucidate man!'

OK then you prick – I will.

'Well. You remember how all this came about sir? How he came to us – you – with his letter, and then he called – you – saying he knew stuff, that we were going to mess things up, how he had the answers?'

He cocks his head at me, interested now, but suspicious – like I'm withholding treats.

'Yeeees…?'

'And the Chief Super had his scheme, so you thought, "perfect," you sent him across with his acquaintances – all invited too, all offered immunity – and he well, carried on in the same vein, sticking his oar in?'

'Go on?'

'Well – now he's disappeared sir. Gone completely off radar.'

'Right. OK. Got what you wanted then haven't you? Did all you could, played the game, and now he's fucked off. You can focus on the case.'

'Yes, sir, absolutely. But we really want him back now sir, you see. Because there's been a development.'

'What development?'

'Well, a couple actually. We checked out the local pubs based on a lead we had, ran a couple of names by staff and punters, and there was a phone call that stood out on the evening of the fire – to a customer, unfamiliar face – from a "Mr Pringle." The customer headed off straight away sir. In the direction of Brunswick Villas. The times check out exactly. Slightly troubling.'

It's a bolt from the blue. He's worried. He just doesn't know why.

'In the direction of Brunswick Villas? Well that's very thin, surely Kaye: a name and a direction?'

'Of course sir.'

It's actually enjoyable, stringing the moment out…

'But here's the really interesting bit.'

…the truth dawning, that I'm still building to something.

'Go on, go on?'

'I thought we were getting rather a lot of coincidences sir. So we ran Pringle's DNA through the system…'

'Yes?'

'And there was a rather significant match up. To the scene. At Brunswick Villas.'

'Holy fuck!'

The panic has set in. He's trying to compute – trying but failing.

'How? How's that possible? Don't tell me. He can't be. Don't tell me…? Where? What?'

His eyebrows are in danger of creeping up to where his hair line should be.

'Not on the victim?'

'Well that's the funny thing sir. No, not on the victim. Which is a relief of sorts. But it really does open up a whole different side to the story. Which rather calls into question some of our work – your work – for quite a long period actually sir. All the way back to the early 1990s in fact. Because I listened to what he had to say, like you asked. And he said a lot about a car crash? When his dad died? Frank Christopher Pringle? I'll let you go and look that name up on the computer sir – 1992's the year. When you were climbing the ladder sir? Getting results?'

Still no clear recognition. His bullishness is flagging though. Fast. The best he can do now is hope – hope that I'm not about to ruin his day, no, worse, tarnish his legacy. But, sorry pal, I just can't help: it's your legacy they'll be after.

'So. You have in fact got two unsolved cases not one I'm afraid now sir, with a great big line stretching between them. Because Pringle's DNA wasn't on the victim at Brunswick Villas you see, no – it was in it.'

I savour the moment. Mogford, gasping like a goldfish, things not looking too clever.

'What does that mean? I mean – what does that mean? How can that be?'

It was an earthquake – his world of balls crumbling around him.

'I don't know. I will find out. But a word of warning – from a political point of view for you sir, I don't think it matters. Whatever's happened, it's bad.'

'What…well…I see…and who knows about this?'

'Who knows about it sir?'

This is fun. Fun!

'Well, everyone on the case sir, and the Chief Super's office – obviously I tried to get to you first sir, but you were busy, playing golf. And I knew you'd want me to let them know straight away sir – because of the C.L.E.A.R. connection?'

I dust off my very best shit-eating grin.

Mogford, eyes swivelling in his frazzled head, tries to blag it – but I can taste the panic in the air.

'Very good, Inspector Kaye. What's our next move?'

Meaning: how can we arrange things so that he doesn't look any worse than he already does? It's game over though. He knows that he needs me, and he knows there's nothing I can do.

'We move quick but steady, try and track him down, and see what he says or does next.'

I leave, and text Stoneman, for the first time ever.

'Everything is in turmoil.'

He replies straight away.

'Good.'

• • •

Chris

Rules are for fools.

Have I said that before?

I look at my pad. My detective pad. My Detective Chris Pringle pad. I stare at it.

I'm stuck on a thought. My pad helps me when I've forgotten. Or I'm trying to remember.

- You'll be home in your chair soon Chris.
- It's OK.
- Phone call.
- It's OK.
- Phone call.
- Don't worry, everything's going to be amazing.

Is it?

• • •

Runcie is here. In the café. In the arcade.

Runcie found me, the police didn't, so Runcie could be a detective. I tell him.

'Maybe. I'm a personal trainer for the soul though Chrissy. Natural introspection for sale, shiftin' just enough units to pay for yer licence fee.'

I look out of the window.

'Acorn used to be over there.'

'It did Chrissy – vape store this week I see. Simon would be turnin' in his indie grave.'

'Remember the phone box Runce? All the numbers?'

'All cleaned up now innit. Cleanest place in Shit Town. No-one uses 'em these days.'

No-one?

'Thanks Runce. For my detective agency. For being the Head of…erm?'

'Oh. Procurement maybe?'

He picks up the new phone he's just dropped off to me.

'You need stuff – I get it for yer. Easy. I don't need a business card though. My kind of procurement don't want advertisin' – or need it.'

He thinks of something.

'You know that number you asked me to stick in there – you know it isn't that phone box, right?'

I shrug.

'Right. Well. Anyway. Green to call – n just make sure yer press that red button when yer finish. No way of trackin' yer on that. Yer secret's safe with me.'

He gives me a Runcie smile and punches me on the shoulder – a love punch.

He's leaving. Julie's coming.

'OK Chrissy. I'll let yer get on. Stay sharp. Talk to Julie – I'm here, always. Good luck. Moonwalk.'

Runcie moonwalks out.

It's time to make a phone call.

$$\bullet \quad \bullet \quad \bullet$$

'Oh, hi PC Paphaedes, erm, Tim – please can I speak to your boss, my friend, Inspector…Graham.'

'Inspector Kaye speaking.'

'Hello?'

'Hello?'

'Hello?'

'Who is this?'

'It's me.'

'Who's me?'

'I am. You're you – I'm me. My little horse is purple?'

There's a muffled sound. Inspector Kaye is talking, but it's not to me. And then he's back.

'Is that you Chris?'

'Yes. It's me. I've already said that.'

'Where are you?'

'Here.'

'Right. Where's – perhaps we should meet up? Perhaps you should come down to the station? For a chat?'

This is no time for a chat. Doesn't Inspector Kaye understand?

'Well?'

'Well what?'

'Chris, listen to me: we think you may be able to help us with this murder case.'

'Well of course you think that: I'm a detective.'

'Yes.'

'And you put me on the case. So I wouldn't even need to be a detective to work out that you think I can help with the case. Or, in fact, solve it. But luckily I am a detective anyway. As you know, which is why–'

'Yes, Chris, but we believe you may have some important information, so we have some questions for you.'

'OK. Here's a question for you then. What are your questions?'

'We can come to you?'

This is very confusing

'No you can't.'

'Why not?'

'Because you don't know where I am.'

There's a muffled sound again, a bit angrier this time.

'Mr Pringle? This is Detective Chief Inspector Mogford. I'd really like to meet you. Would that be possible?'

'I'll think about it.'

I think about it. I get distracted.

'We've probably met before I believe Mr Pringle?'

'No – we never met.'

We never met.

'Can we come and meet you now Chris? It would be best for everyone.'

'I don't think it would. But I do have some information – for my friend, Inspector Kaye? Could you make him speak to me on the telephone again please Chief…man.'

'You can tell me.'

'No thanks.'

'Fine.'

He sounds sad. Or cross.

'Chris? Inspector Kaye here.'

'Hello my friend, Inspector Kaye.'

He doesn't call me friend back – yet.

'So. This is some "information" Inspector Kaye. Near No.7 Brunswick Villas, there will be a car. Probably. A car that hasn't gone away. A car that just came and didn't...go.'

'OK?'

'Yes. Find the car – go!'

I put the phone down. Maybe I could find the car if there is one – detect it. But I need to help the police leave me alone. And then everything will be...something.

I feel peculiar. I'm a detective – I have been for a while.

'Years,' Runcie said once. 'But, that's fine, I like the way the years slip by – like fields out of a train window, yer get me? That's what time is like to me. A cosy country scene, adventures when we were kids. Bit of sun on yer face, maybe some Football Crazies by a nice little stream.'

And then Julie said, 'Shut the fuck up Runcie.'

I remember things people say. I didn't used to remember. But I've tried really hard. Kept trying. And now I can understand things – most things.

But it's time to meet my dad.

• • •

Detective Inspector Graham Kaye

Pringle's dad. Dies in a crash. Comes back. Dies again. None of this looks like good news – yet he keeps talking. And this latest gift? That sounded like it matters. So here we are: me, Paphaedes, radios off, cruising the streets, while CCTV is scoured back at the station. And I believe we'll find whatever it is we're looking for.

'Never become like DCI Mogford, Paphaedes.'

'Sir?'

He looks confused. Nervous even. Like I may be about to grab the wheel and drive us into a hefty tree – his life just taking off, when his boss ended it all in a crazed suicide smash, and in his final moments, the young PC screams, 'I should have–'

Am I as mad as Pringle? Who's to say?

Stay focused. I am focused.

I've got Trim back, but I've left her at the station – because I never gave Police Constable Paphaedes the benefit of my considerable doubt. When people want to talk, make sure you listen.

'Why did you want to be a policeman Paphaedes?'

'Sir?'

'Why did you want to be a policeman? It's not a trick question.'

He looks embarrassed.

'To do good I suppose sir?'

'Mmm. To find out the truth.'

While Paphaedes shifts in his seat, I gaze at the cars parked up and down the street, logging colours, makes, number plates, examining my feelings to see if anything looks or feels wrong, wondering if one of these could be it. Everything's heightened, but nothing's coming to me yet.

'Give Trim a call.'

He puts it on speaker.

'It's Paphaedes. Any news?'

'Getting there. There's a couple of vehicles standing out already.'

'Trim? Inspector Kaye. That's the key here: what stands out?'

'Well, I've gone from the day before sir, and tracked through the day after and kept going – looking at Brunswick Road itself, Baker's Hill, which is the way in, and Hole Street, which is the only way out, it being one way. So far there's two vehicles that have come and not gone. One's a brown Transporter, looks like it's been in a bump – but it's the other one sir.'

'Why?'

'Dutch plates sir. Just struck me as unusual.'

• • •

That's how much process gets in the way – that when you do what your gut tells you is right, the feeling's so unfamiliar you start looking over your shoulder. Process can go screw itself though. 20 minutes for Trim to check who's stepped out of it, any other stand-out details – while we drive up and take a look. 20 minutes I gave her, and now Forensics are here, and we're in – because I've crowbarred the boot myself. Because what's the worst that can happen?

The swabbing starts.

Inside. The stench of cigarettes. A European Sat Nav in the glove compartment. A sleeping bag in the back. Trim's on to Border Control – they'll tell us where it came from and when, and who it belongs to hopefully.

But throughout, I have a feeling there's more to come from this search anyway. And I'm right. A man bag in the boot. Euros. Cigarettes. And then, bingo.

A passport.

• • •

Chris

Julie arrives and sits next to me. I have a piece of paper for her. She holds my hand and gives me some lardy cake. I am fiddly diddly. She gives me more lardy cake.

It's windy outside and warm. I think about drifting away, up over the houses and trees, looking down on the streets and oh look, there's Inspector Kaye, there's PC Paphaedes. They're shouting and waving, kind – oh, no, angry. I wave back and there's Mum and –

No. I have to stay here. The arcade.

It's so quiet sitting here with Julie. But it's time to decide.

'Am I really a detective Julie? I know people think I'm...stupid.'

'No-one proper thinks that Chrissy. Listen – I can stay if you want? I won't say a thing. Won't say anything at all – I promise.'

Julie wants me to be safe. Runcie. Student. Mum. But I need to do this alone. I give her my piece of paper. And Julie says goodbye.

'OK. But I'm gonna sit out on the road in my car Chrissy. Look – through the archway? You can see my car. And I'm getting Runcie. Any issues, call me. He's not gone after an hour, we're coming back in. OK?'

I don't speak. I'm arranging detective things on the table in the cafe. I wish I had a desk badge. Handing my card over won't seem right. He knows who I am – but I want to show him what I am. I know who he is. I need to find out what he is.

• • •

When the door opens and the bell jingles, at first I don't look up, or do anything – because I don't know the sound. I mean, I've heard it before, been here before. But it's not my door, not my bell. So it's a while before I remember. And then I am looking up at my dad.

We're both looking at each other's trousers. He's my real dad. We are the same. But are we...different?

I use my hand to show him the chair that I have prepared for him. I turn sideways and look carefully. He is still standing up.

'Do you want to sit down at this table?'

He does.

He looks around – like he's not used to being in normal places. He's my dad. Frank Christopher Pringle.

'Hello there Chris. Shall we have a cup of tea?'

• • •

I would like to sit next to him, but I don't know how. He's alive. And he's here.

But I'm still a detective.

I show him the back of my tracksuit.

He stirs his tea. He puts three spoons in. I remember. He lets the swirling slow down and stop, takes a deep breath and looks straight at me. He waits a little bit. We're both ready. He begins.

'First of all Chris, I think I need to say...sorry.'

Oh.

'I wasn't there for you. No matter why that was, I didn't do what I needed to – to be a dad.'

I'm fiddly diddly. I don't think I want this. He does though. Dad. And Detective Pringle does.

'Back then, I was drinking a lot. I was drinking, and I stopped being able to feel. That's why I did it, that's what I wanted. Because I was afraid. Still am actually. And he – well, then I, erm, had something to be afraid of, and that was probably…a good excuse?'

We don't say anything for a little bit.

'But it's not an excuse.'

My tummy rumbles, feelings trying to get out. I reach into my plastic bag to do a detective trick – click – and take a custard cream out, making sure the lady at the counter can't see me. I dip it slowly. No bits.

'And you know now of course that I'm…well…according to the paperwork, I'm not actually your dad!'

He laughs. He's fiddly diddly too! He made a joke. It wasn't a funny joke. But I don't really like jokes anyway.

'I will always feel like your dad though Chris. I always did. You understand that – right? I wanted to be your dad. Very much. But to him. Well…you were his.'

He's remembering. I can see the pain. I can feel it. I can feel what he's feeling.

He swallows.

'He wanted to control everything Chris. He wanted us to feel like we were nothing.'

He picks up his tea cup and stares into it. Puts it down again and slaps his knees.

'Going away? 1984 it was. It felt like dying. I've seen a few characters in hostels about the place – men who've had the word, that whatever they've got is going to take them? And something strange happens to them then – they just...retreat. Because... what's the point I suppose? That's where I was. It was bad enough. But then he came for me again.'

He looks nervously round at the door – as if Bobby Heffel's going to come in and get him. But he knows that's not going to happen – I know it too.

'I was in a terrible state by this time Chris. I moved around at first. But I'd become a serious alcoholic. No money. So I just got...stuck. And then I found out, up close, just how bad they really were. They wanted other people in the line of fire. So he hunted me down and I just did what they said. Got paid. Enough. Enough to carry on drinking myself to death Chris.'

He looks straight at me. My dad. I look back. I don't look at people like this. Ever. But he's my dad.

'But then I started seeing you and Stephen – at the raves. I was a mess. Surrounded by their hangers on – hard men, nasty people – an unnecessary precaution really, because no-one ever seemed to touch me, or them. They were on top of me, all the time, and they saw that something was happening. I must have thought I could give you something – show you I was OK? But they worked it out. Watched me, I guess: watched me, and saw me, watching you. And there we all were. You. Me. Them. Your real dad that is – Bobby Heffel – and his brother too, one big–'

No.

'No.'

'Sorry?'

'No. You're Dad.'

Our eyes are on the table between us. I will take some sugar sachets home, because they are a part of the cup of tea you buy. He tries to smile. But he's not ready.

'Thank you. Well. It was heading towards…I don't know? I got nervous. I was trying to watch them for signs…you know, of danger – to you, to Stephen? And it bugged them. Bugged Dirk. He hated me. He hated me more than Bobby did now. He was getting paranoid anyway – everyone was out to get them – didn't like anyone looking at them. They'd started calling me The Watcher – like a voyeur. I was nervous, I never had my glasses with me, so I couldn't see, squinting. But it wasn't a joke, the name. It hurt, because I'd stood by and allowed Bobby to take my life. The Watcher.'

He stops.

'They slapped me about Chris – in front of people. Second nature it was, to them. And then it was Castlemorton…'

He stops, again.

'They'd heard about it – heard it was going to be big, see? I don't know what we were doing there though. They'd gone mad, but–'

'Who died in the crash Dad?'

He takes a cigarette out, remembers where he is and puts it away again.

'Your uncle, I suppose we'd call him. Dirk.'

It's OK. It's just facts: for the detective. The detective has to make sure. Just facts. It's OK.

'There was a big argument. It had been coming. About me it was. About how I was getting in the way. And it was your birthday, see. And they knew – perhaps that's even why we were all there? Bobby, making some kind of…point? And they were all over me, even more than usual. Dirk didn't like it. The distraction I suppose. They were both angry.'

I remember.

'The fight started as we were leaving. You were there. But it felt wrong – like Bobby wanted it to happen. It was like he'd planned it. Like he wanted him dead. To be the boss.'

I was there.

'It carried on into the car. We drove on. And then we stopped. They got out, carried on at the side of the road. And then Dirk was on the ground, sort of knocked out. Bobby made me help pick him up, sit him back in the passenger seat, no seatbelt; sat me in the driver's seat holding a bottle. I was drunk anyway. Always drunk. He took photos – like Dirk was asleep and I was driving off. Took the bottle, poured the lot down his throat, there in the car. It was horrible. I couldn't understand. I mean I knew they didn't drink. He woke up, for just a few seconds, and he was choking – frothing.'

He looks scared – Dad – remembering.

'We were at the top of a hill. I was sat there, frozen. Bobby told me to get out. Pushed Dirk across in the front. His eyes were closed. Lifeless. Already dead maybe? Poured petrol in over everything – over him. Started the engine. They always put the car in my name. Put it in drive. I tried to stop it. I just couldn't. I tried. I was left lying on the road. It happened so quickly after that – off it went. It was a big hill, and it went so…straight, until there was an explosion, a big fire. Then a bike came along, a motorbike, and Bobby gets on the back. It was all pre-planned, must have been. Tells me, if I go far away – far away from him, from your mum and you – we'll never see each other again: there'll be no problem, as long as I remember he's got the pictures.'

Dad looks tired.

'You understand right, Chris? The idea was, either the police would just think I was dead – in which case, if anyone ever noticed Dirk had disappeared, there was no link to the crash, to Bobby at all. Or, if they worked out it was Dirk in there, then Bobby'd make sure I, the drunk driver, got the blame. Either way I was…finished. I had to disappear.'

Tired.

'I went to Scotland. Found out I was "dead"! It worked better than he could have hoped. To all but your mum, I was dead. My life was over.'

He looks into his tea. It's an empty cup.

'When you're at the bottom of the pit, and all you can see in front of your own eyes is shame, it's pretty scary. People talk about moments of clarity. They come again and again actually, where you realise you'd give anything for peace, stability. They don't mean anything though those moments. Nothing. You know what you want really. But you're lost. And there might not be a way out.'

It's quiet.

'I'd tried getting help before. They say drink is a prop Chris, to the alcoholic, that it props you up? But it wasn't like that for me. It was a manacle – you know, a chain that I'd put on myself? It wasn't my way of coping – it was my way of choosing not to cope. So I understood: I was the one that had to change. So the Steps? They didn't quite work for me. But the name's funny, because – well, they got me moving I suppose. The only thing you can do is put one foot in front of the other and start walking – climbing. You're stuck with your thoughts and that's quite…

tricky. And it takes a while…a long time…but one day you notice you've made a good decision without thinking about it. And, you panic at first – but then your gut tells you it's OK. It's OK to be a new version of yourself. There might even be a better new version of yourself? In the future?'

He's my dad – and he looks at me. We try hard to look at each other.

'Even gave myself a new name – just a little joke. Once I drank pop, I just couldn't stop. Well I did.'

I try not to be afraid.

'Spent a long time sure that I couldn't come back here though. But wanting to, every day. So that when, finally, my head felt clearer, I thought maybe I could come down this way again. Not too close. I just thought maybe enough time had passed. But it was stupid. Stupid, because I should have known it would never end.'

But it did end.

And I am very still now. I am a detective. Doing what detectives do.

'Did he come back to kill you Dad? Because you knew? Because you were the…witness?'

I am a detective.

'Yes.'

This is my dad.

'But that's not everything…'

• • •

Detective Inspector Graham Kaye

The car is key, just as Pringle said it would be – but at first I can't possibly understand why. Rented in Arnhem three days before the fire by, as the passport inside suggests, a man who the NCB and Europol confirm to be an elusive trafficker called Bobby Heffel – for whom they have no prints or DNA. So this gives me nothing at all, other than an eerie feeling again, of how much I don't know about Chris Pringle. Until I get back to the station, where, on my desk, is Chris Pringle's birth certificate, dropped off by Julie Duke.

● ● ●

Bobby Heffel – one half in fact, of a pair of gangland brothers, the other of whom disappeared in, guess when, 1992 – is Chris Pringle's father. Robert Hepfield. All records show it's the same person. And DNA in the hire car will prove he's Pringle's father – and prove he died at Brunswick Villas. I'm sure of that.

So now we know why Pringle cares – but also possibly why he is still AWOL. Because what could he tell us about the big questions remaining? Who's Frank Pringle? And how and why did Bobby Heffel die?

The whole situation has brought something out in Paphaedes. The disillusioned junior post boy, taught to work-to-rule in the depths of an immense, soulless regional depot, has suddenly been told that one of the boxes out back contains free sweets for life. He's alert. He's noticed that not knowing, drives Trim crazy: the pair of them have been in a room, pouring over 1992 and before and beyond, again and again, like, well – detectives. It's enough to bring a tear to the eye. As, sadly, is the confirmation that the DNA from the crash victim – which would, wild guess, show that it was Heffel's brother, Pringle's uncle – never made it past the mid '90s. Because did Mogford's team meticulously transfer everything over to the NDAD? Of course not.

And what I do next? They say it's the hope that kills you, but without hope, you're already dead.

And then I look up, and standing in front of me, is Chris Pringle.

I stand up too quickly, a rush of blood to the head, and I move across to shut the door behind him. I don't want to know how he has managed to walk straight in here – that will depress me all over again – but I need to hear what he's got to say.

He's donned in full detective gear, well, what for him is full detective gear – tracksuit, with a long raincoat on top, charity shop hat. More of a disguise than a get-up. And he looks like he's slept in a car. Pringle hasn't got a car though, please – one of the morals of this story is turning out to be to not judge, but this is a man that can never, ever be allowed to drive.

'Chris – you'd better take a seat. Can I get you a tea?'

'No thanks Inspector Kaye. I've come from a café. It had tea in it. And cake. And some biscuits. They're in this bag. Oh, actually – no they're not.'

'Right. Where have you been Chris? Do you want to start from the beginning?'

But where do things ever begin? I'll help him out.

'OK. So we know Frank didn't die Chris – in the car crash? And we know that your real dad, Bobby Heffel didn't die either.

Until Brunswick Villas. So who was in that fire with him? Who was it Chris? I need your help.'

I give him time. I'm desperate to wrestle the truth out of him but, as is so often the case, it's a slippery, deformed squid, which will birth itself only when its vessel is good and ready.

I think, for just a second, about wasted love.

'OK Inspector Kaye. I'm here to help you. My name is Detective Chris Pringle.'

I get my pen ready. He sits so still – I've never seen anyone so still. He can be fidgety, but when he is thinking, or at peace, he doesn't move. Then there's the tiniest of jerks into action, a double-take almost imperceptible to the naked eye. He sticks a hand into his plastic bag and pulls something out – puts it on the table.

'First, we need to listen to this.'

Because Detective Chris Pringle has got a Dictaphone…

34

THE DICTAPHONE

Frank Christopher Pringle: Secret Recording

FP   'But that's not everything.

I don't want to tell this to the police see Chris. I'm scared. But also…I want…I want to tell your mum. First.

I knew, no matter where I was, he could always find me, if he wanted to – but did he want to? It'd been a long time…a very long time – well of course, you know – so I wasn't even sure.

I'd moved down to Weston a couple of years back. I liked the air. I walked a lot. It felt close.

I wanted to see you. I'd been careful. But now I must have thought…maybe he'd gone…maybe I could, I don't know…see?

It was close enough that I started coming back here. I'd go around for an hour or two, carefully, just seeing everything was still OK, that you and your mum were OK, and everything in town was still as it was. But it didn't take long.

One day I head out of my place I rented over there – in Weston? – and go to the bus stop outside my front door. There's a guy sitting there, looks a bit out of place – you know, well-dressed. And he smiles at me, a bit too friendly. And I know, straight away, he's one of theirs – well, one of his. Goons. They were always a type – suited, something about their hair though, straight, but neither long nor short – brushed back. Smoking – you don't see that so much nowadays either.

And he gets on the bus after me, sits down and says it – plain as day. Bobby knows where I am. He wants to talk to me. "Don't try and run – he'll be in touch."

This was about two months before.

I didn't want to die.

It might sound odd to other people. Looking at my life, it won't seem much…but…I've reached a place where I'm quite happy. It's not what I want it to be, obviously. But you're safe, doing well, your mum's… got her life. I'm sober Chris. There's nothing bad, like there always was back then. I never used to say much did I? But I can talk now, and I wondered if there was someone I could tell? But who? Why? To do what? Of course I couldn't. I couldn't just reappear, because, you know, well – questions would be asked. I couldn't mess it all up again.

But for some reason, I moved back to town: here. I've thought hard about why. It didn't make sense as a thing to do; it's hard to explain. I can only imagine I wanted to be here, so that if he came after you or your mum, to cause trouble, I could be there? Or maybe just to get it all over with? Stupid eh?

It was strange being back. Seeing you. I tried to make sure you didn't see me – around? But you did didn't you, fair play? And I thought about it – and decided to leave my number, in the phone box. I knew you kids used it in the old days. It just felt…right…like you'd find it.

I rented the flat: Brunswick Villas. Lucky number seven. Erm. I'd been going to the pubs – just to keep warm. Cheaper. And I can do it now. It's OK. But really I did it so when he came, he'd have to meet me out – where it was safe. I'd had a note through my door already, see. They had this knack of always knowing exactly where you were. So I was waiting, waiting. The First and Last. Old haunts. New places like The Moon Under Water. Odd, it was, odd being there, seeing the same sorts of people I'd been myself. Not old faces – no-one I knew. I'm afraid they're probably all dead and gone, unless they've sort of, got out too? But the same type of people, following me home sometimes, trying to get me to carry on, didn't even notice I was on the tonic water.

But anyway – my idea didn't work. I went to the Express that afternoon. He didn't turn up though – he called. One step ahead of me. Called, using my name – Pringle. Tells me to meet him at the flat. My flat. It was dark. Cold. Again, I could have tried to run I suppose – but I realised, this was what I wanted too. I was so near to you again, and your mum, even though…well… you know?

I just wanted it to end.

He'd let himself in somehow. I'd wanted to walk round under the window and maybe, sort of creep up a bit – but there were no sounds or anything, so I just went in. And there he was.

The last time I'd seen him I was a mess, drunk, a bit crazy, terrified – his smell brought it all back. Strong cigarettes. But there was something else about the way he looked now. He looked ill – he was…haggard. And it was strange – I didn't feel afraid straight away. He was walking around, like he was trying to distract himself from some pain he was feeling, and he was – cancer he said, terminal.

He had a gun. Was wearing rubber gloves. Took my key off me – locked in, we were, so that's when I began to get scared. He hasn't even really said anything to me yet – just starts taking things out of this bag, strange things. A cooking pan he pours something into, some rope – thought I could guess what that was for. I was looking round. It was my own flat, but there was nothing in it really. What could I do? Perhaps I was scared? About what I might do?

So he's got a gun in his hand still and then he starts pouring petrol on the floor. I'm asking him what I've done, what he wants, and it's like he's using all his energy, all that he has left doing this – he can't talk as well. Petrol's everywhere, and he sits down on the sofa, tells me to sit down too.

He says he's dying – but he still has this rage. He said I was The Watcher. I'd seen it all. Erm…the crash, I guessed. And everyone thought it was me who'd died, and that was fine: so why did I come back? He was angry. Happy to make us both suffer one more time – just as long as he won.

And this was his plan. He was going to kill himself, make me watch it – and I'd get the blame, and maybe a broken leg jumping out the window or, if I was a coward, go up in flames before the fire engines got here. He was sure I was a coward. He was probably right. One final thing for me to watch he said – another chance for me to get the blame. I didn't really understand what he meant, I wasn't getting it.

I had a little table and chair – for my tea – and he puts the chair in the middle of the floor. He's got other things set up around it that I still didn't understand, and then he gets the rope.

He sits. Then he starts talking about you and your mum, and I didn't like it. He asked how we were. He's been told, through his people I guess, that I hadn't been in touch with you, but he didn't believe it.

He picks up the petrol can and pours the last few splashes down himself. He's laughing, like he thinks it's a joke. Then he pulls the rope round himself and gets me to tie him up, leaving one hand free, holding the gun. And then he tells me to look in the side pocket of the bag. And inside it is another gun, the same kind, and he tells me to pick it up.

"Finger prints," he says. "If we're lucky."

I've got this gun in my hand: it's a horrible feeling. He's laughing.

And then he sets his gun down quick, reaches down next to him and pulls this bottle up. It's cheap, nasty whisky – even I wouldn't have touched it in my day, but he didn't know, didn't care – it was just a poison to them, I worked that out. He just wanted to die. So he swigs it down – he just pours it, like he's desperate, all of it. I'm still holding this gun, but I can't think – he hands a gag to me and I put it on him, not so well. It's all happening quickly now and I still don't understand. He picks his gun up now and chucks it into the pan next to him and it fizzes and smokes, and I realise he's put some sort of acid in it. Drops in the key, something else, a wallet or phone or something, I can't remember. And he's sort of watching it all fizzing and smoking, and he's mumbling and gurgling and laughing at me beneath the gag.

"It didn't even have bullets…you fucking moron – no bullets!" he says.

And he's in agony now, something's happening to him, but he takes a match, strikes it on the zip of his top, chucks it into the petrol and sticks his hand into the ropes, so it's like they're both tied there.

We're just looking at each other. I'm frozen. He's kind of…wailing, in pain, quietly, scared I guess too, but just staring into my eyes, like he's enjoying it.

And it's funny. Not funny. But…well, he'd searched the place before I got there, top to bottom – I could see that. Professional – as always. Making sure nothing could get in the way. Not that there was much to search. But the alcoholic, like me, develops various little techniques…accommodations: to get through the day. You learn. And one thing you learn is: make sure you can always get to shelter. You never shake off those habits. So I always hide an extra key outside my front door, just in case. And I did there. And on my way in, I'd taken it, and put it in my shoe. I don't know why – I just felt I should. And right then, I remembered.

So I bend down and take it out, kind of look at it. And then his face changes: he starts screaming at me now through the gag, the flames are spreading really fast. He kicks out at me, kicks the bucket at me. I drop the gun. I run out. I unlock the door and I run out and I go. I don't look back. The fire brigade are there – quickly – I hear them, but it's too late. I went. I left him.'

35

NOW

Runcie

I wait outside the station in me Hilltop's, just over the road. Here, as always, for Chrissy – to embrace whatever madness he creates, n to do it with love. Any social occasion featurin' me main man Pringle interactin' with others, with me as company/bodyguard/documentarian, is always unmissable, but this one we're off to now, as he waddles out the cop shop, is all set to be a stone cold classic: the big class reunion, on his birthday, between him, Frank, n Maureen. In the old days I'd have baked a cake – not today though. This time it's Maureen's turn.

We pick up his old man en route. He gives me a hug – soft, childlike – an apology. It was sweet, n there did appear to be some kinda little lump in me throat, when he sorta looked to Chrissy for what's next – the role reversal yer get when a kid grows up I suppose, n it's the dad who no longer knows best, the dad who needs his hand holdin'.

The Hilltop's drove on, n then, there we were: Mo's.

Brendan's *popped to the shops* – to make this easier. He's a good sorta fella, cool as milk really, despite his dibsy bones.

Inside her little front room, window open, best tea set out; it's an emotional scene – the kind that should be captured in some kinda epic work of art, yer get me? Rap bein' me medium, I'm not the best man to do it on this occasion – I'm thinkin' more one of them deep, dark n murky oil paintins, coz give me credit right, I'm a Renaissance Man.

So the years gone by were sorta brushed over, n everyone understands each other, n everyone is sad but smilin' but a bit embarrassed, n everyone sees – yer can go proddin' around in the past for answers, lookin' for solutions, but all they really wanted was to look at each other now, n know they were alright. OK.

N in the middle of it all is Chrissy – son, detective, birthday boy. Sittin'. Calm. Happy. The lad was never unhappy these last few years. Bits were still missin' though – n now he's gathered 'em all in. Everythin' in one place. That's it. Anythin' else is just veggies from Waitrose innit – yer don't need it.

All that can be said is said, n it's time to go. Maureen did what she had to do: she saved herself n she saved Chrissy. Not easy if yer as much of a mouse-wife as everyone thinks – but she's not, see? N what have they all got at the end of it? Mo – poor Mo – has Shit Town lookin' at her in a brand new way, n she won't hide. Old Man Pringle? Well, he won't be comin' home – but he won't be goin' to prison or the boozer either. He'll be alright, yer know? Alright. He'll sleep at night. N Chrissy – he has his ma back n all, n it's been a long time. He looks peaceful.

Unmovin', paused, like always – but that little buzzin' fly inside, that tremblin', jitterin' glitch of energy, NRG – he's coughed it up, finally, n it's floated away. But still, he says, *There's jobs to be done.* One by Frank. One by me.

• • •

Maureen

Dear Lord:

Frank said today, that when you hear yourself talk out loud, to other people, a room of strangers, and for the first time you say – you tell them – everything? Said that's the turning point. Was for him anyway. That's what he said. He said that for him, that was the beginning. Realising you can do that – that you're allowed.

Frank.

Said you don't really change though, until you start coming up with answers – yourself.

That comes a lot later.

You talk to yourself, you keep talking to yourself, you don't lie, and maybe you get lucky.

Frank.

It's all wrong this isn't it? And it has to change. "Frank." It's like I don't even mention his name. To you? Hardly have really, have I? So what's the point? I've been talking out loud all these years – twice a day, never missed it have I, until now? But today's different. Things are different. A day which has been coming – for a long time. The start of something, for Frank, for Christopher: the start of something new, and steady.

Not for me though. Not yet.

I've often wondered what it would be like to be a Catholic. Talking to God is confessing I suppose. Confession's a bit more official – that's all really. And you get forgiveness into the bargain of course. But it's you yourself who has to do the forgiving in the end.

"Bobby."

Saying that name – it makes me feel light-headed.

Why didn't I share the shame?

What is the point in all this?

That's faith I suppose: you say nothing, you get nothing back, you still keep believing. And if you're not even there? Well it's hardly your fault is it? I don't even think I've stopped believing. But I suppose, if you keep talking and get nothing back, you come up with the answers yourself in the end. In the end. I mean, it's only taken me what, 50 years? 50 years to just…get started?

For now, I'm still hurting people.

I loved Frank. I really loved him – from when we were just kids really. He was kind – he was fun. He was happy back in the beginning. Until…Bobby. I just let Frank go down, down, wrapped up in his drink and his quiet.

The worst thing was, if he was ever just sitting, looking at Christopher, it was like he'd forget everything for a little while. I could see it – but then there's that split second, where he remembers? That broke my heart.

And that brings me on to Brendan. And you're entitled to worry that maybe I'm about to go off the rails here. Poor Frank never did anything to deserve any of this. And Christopher always thought we'd get him back. I could tell that. He's a determined little sod. And I'm so happy that Christopher is happy. With Brendan though: it isn't like Frank and I were back then, but it's what we all need. It's a love that I treasure, and I won't let anything wash it away. I told him everything – today – everything. And just like that, he doesn't care. Just like Frank. Two good men. He didn't care, he was sad for me – and now I have to promise to talk to him. I have to do that now Lord. Talk to him. Talk to Chris, to Stephen, Julie. And I will have to talk to Frank. I will have to sit down, again, talk more, spend more time with Frank.

He gave his life for me Lord, for Christopher. And we've learned the hard way, both of us, that we did it all wrong. But he's ahead of me now. He walks, he says – walks and talks. And when he speaks now, to others, it's the truth.

That sounds like you – like you're supposed to be. And maybe you are? I still believe.

But it's time to talk to real people for a bit. Night night.

• • •

Detective Inspector Graham Kaye

The end starts with the tale of the tape. A testimony from the person it matters to most: Frank Christopher Pringle. Aka Francis Popper. Chris Pringle's dad – not by blood, but by love. The car crash in 1992. Brunswick Villas. Everything in between. Barely believable. All making sense – adding up. But barely admissible. I told Chris Pringle: thanked him, but it's not enough. I need more. His dad didn't want to come in – my guess is he's already lost one life, he won't risk it happening again. And who could blame him? But Pringle says it will be OK and perversely, I trust him, he trusts me back, and there's pride in that.

The fact that Heffel travelled to the UK using his own passport suggests he came here to die – visibly. And he did. The DNA traces in the car match up with the victim – and with his son. No prints on the loaded gun Frank Pringle admits he held of course, which is lucky – because that means there's nothing concrete to link him to the death at all. Prints on the outside of his own front door: that's it.

Pringle Junior leaves, Paphaedes follows – to make sure his dad doesn't do a runner. And sure enough, he doesn't. They meet up, but just go straight to his mum's – just like that. To play happy families – who knows? And then Pringle brings him in anyway – and Frank Christopher Pringle says it all again. Complete. Brunswick Villas, on record, but from the horse's mouth: the fire was a fix. And you wonder: how, before his dad told him, did Chris Pringle know? How could he possibly know? So maybe he didn't. Maybe what he knew – what he had to believe – was that his dad was a good man?

Pringle Senior was of course, himself, absent for most of the back story, and Pringle Junior's statement is, of course, deranged nonsense – so guess who I get to invite into the station to fill in the gaps and, in all likelihood, be the hero who helps me put this case to bed? Runcie. As the man himself said on the phone: what a time to be alive.

And Mogford? I don't blame the game – I blame the player. Case solved and he's hit the papers, just like he wanted. Well, not quite. 1992's been raked over. Even back then he was only interested in moving onwards and upwards, but you can't always –

331

everyone has to take some hits. Shoddy police work helped cost Frank Pringle a life he could have lived. They even had Chris Pringle on file from Castlemorton the day before – and no-one even asked any questions. The words miscarriage and misconduct will be bandied about. Most pathetic and damning of all though? When Pringle went route one, straight back to him, straight after the fire? He didn't even recognise his name. Wasn't even on his radar.

In the meantime, off Pringle goes, into the night and I'm still left wondering. Against my better judgement I give in and look up the bloody Columbo case he'd wittered on about at the start…Any Old Port in a Storm. I'd written it down at the time, although I'd wondered why. And there seemed to be nothing there, of course. Booze was at the heart of it – not in the same way though. But then I see that the story ends with the great man sharing a fine wine with the murderer – pals, with the murderer! Panicking, I get him at home. He answers – "Detective Chris Pringle." Says his dad's still about, always will be.

I ask him what it means – Columbo.

'Columbo – he likes nice things. That's all. He likes things that are good.'

I see.

'I could eat food with you one day if you like Inspector Kaye? A very good friend of mine Peter, works in a place called Pizza Hut.'

He's got people looking after him everywhere. I can just imagine Chris Pringle causing havoc at the salad bar.

'OK then.'

A detective is a detective, however mad, deluded or lucky they may be. And Detective Chris Pringle wins. And I win too.

So the question now is: when this is all done, who bows out first: Pringle, the newly humiliated, happy ending denied, Detective Chief Inspector Mogford – or me?

· · ·

Chris

I made the brews – two cups of tea. Runcie taught me.

'Biscuit Dad?'

Watching case studies – Columbo. On my new DVD player. It's a new DVD too, given to me by a very good friend of mine Peter, who works at the library. He saw me in The Chronicle.

Watching Columbo. With Dad. Happy and kind. My real dad. No notes though. No rules. Because there are no rules.

My name is Chris Pringle – Detective Chris Pringle.

EPILOGUE

THE END

Runcie

To be quite honest with yer, I'm lookin' forward to some business-as-usual. Peace. Sunset over Shit Town. I specifically set out in life to be a chilled-out lazy bastard, n all this murder n mayhem is playin' havoc with me schedule. Just one more errand, n this cat is ready to curl up, yer get me? Have meself a nice big sleep, then maybe get showered and talced right up, put on some fresh threads n relaunch meself – keep the smokers smokin' n the ladies lovin', coz yer gotta be a giver, not just a taker. I've learnt that from the greatest.

N as for Chrissy? Well, it seems like he got what he came for.

'That man? He always did say it was going to be amazing.'

He did. N he was right. Coz things are good. N that's OK. The quest continues – always. But OK's all yer need – all Chrissy ever wanted. OK is pretty fookin' amazin'.

'What next Chrissy Bobs? Back to just watchin'? Or now that yer've started – carry on?'

No question is ever answered without careful consideration – that hasn't changed.

'What do you want me to solve?'

N that's where we left it: to be continued. N as much as the big mystery of Chrissy's life has been put to bed – case closed, almost, once this final errand of mine has been completed – the mystery of Detective Chris Pringle himself remains. I mean, I love the brother, but as a detective, what he's actually done? I don't know. Is he a man of good fortune n well-chosen catch-phrases nicked off the telly – or a fookin' genius? N the absolute bottom line is, it don't matter – if he thinks he's a detective, then he is to me. All those are just labels.

I give him n his old man a double thumbs up, leave 'em to their brews, n head back out to the cop car Papha's waitin' in. I'll miss him – he's alright. Kid's got a heart.

For now though, I have a business associate to meet, n then it's off to see Inspector Divorce: to finish this thing.

• • •

I'm here to fill in the gaps. For Boss Man – no beef. For Papha. For Julie, for Student even, who did his bit, bless his cottons, love him really. But most of all for Frank, for Mo, n for Chrissy. Coz for everythin' that Chrissy understands, there's almost as much he can't explain; n for everythin' Maureen n Frank have said, there's just as much that's missin' in between. So this isn't finished 'til a reliable witness like meself can furnish the dibsies with those all-important details.

'I get it Inspector Kaye – the detective work has ended, but the paperwork is only just beginnin'.'

He doesn't hate me like he did, but we're not in the clear just yet. The source of his disgruntlement is sittin' next to me, preparin' to bust his balls. Beautiful. Strong.

'Fair do's. So, Geez? This is Patricia. Don't call her Pat.'

'Ms Liversedge.'

'She's great isn't she? The barter system's a wonderful thing.'

I tap me nose n give him me most charismatic wink. I look at Patricia, who glares a little at me n then a little at Inspector Kaye.

'Anyway, Patricia will want me to stop talkin' now – so over to yer good self me man. If I fall asleep, don't take it personally Blue – the longer the day, the more I smoke to stay awake, n unfortunately, that makes me ability to actually stay awake, somewhat unpredictable.'

Patricia gives me another impatient look, n then bursts into action.

'May I remind you that you have now formally agreed that my client has immunity, and anything he says relating to any of his business activities past or present would be inadmissible, and must in fact be omitted from any and all records of conversations you have with him.'

'Agreed.'

'So I will be asking for a full transcript of this conversation, which will need to be signed by us both before we can talk again. If you really, that is, feel the need for that to happen.'

I wink conspirationally at him and offer Patricia Liversedge a fist bump. She glares back at me – again – but goes through with it.

'It might be better to record this Inspector Kaye.'

He gives Paphaedes the nod, n speaks.

'Police testimony of Stephen Patrick Runce. Those also present are: on behalf of Mr Runce, Ms Patricia Liversedge; myself, Detective Inspector Graham Kaye; and PC Tim Paphaedes. Please confirm your name for the tape Mr Runce and then we'll begin. Mr Runce?'

'Mmm?'

'Name?'

'Oh. Right. Sweet – an easy one. So: Stephen Patrick Runce, just like yer probably said Boss Man, but call me Runcie, or MC Chester, or President of the Republic of–'

'Date of birth?'

'Well, it was one of them years…yer know – back a bit?'

'Fine – have it your way. So, to confirm. Mr Runce: ahead of the inquest and any subsequent prosecution, you're here to tell us what you know about Chris Pringle, and events leading up to the fatal fire which occurred at No.7 Brunswick Villas. We know the basics. But there's a lot still missing. And for a number of reasons, Mr Pringle's accounts are…compromised. So that's where you come in: help us fill in the gaps. Take your time. There's no hurry. And please – let's start at the beginning.'

'Right Boss. Fillin' the gaps. Takin' me time. Tellin' the tale. Got it. It's a journey mind, so clunk click: there's a bit of now, a bit of then, now-then, now-then – but yer'd like that, right? See – he had to make a choice: between keepin' things buried, n diggin' 'em up? He didn't have the answers – course he didn't. But he did have a plan, a crazy, stupid, ridiculous plan: to get involved. The trouble was, yer let him – n we all know how that turned out. The beginnin' though, right? OK, let's go.'

I grapple me way slowly out of me slouched, relaxation pose, pullin' meself into an upright position at the desk, givin' Inspector Kaye me most earnest expression. I'm the Robin Hood of Rave me, the Pied Piper of Amblin', always ready to lead the rats on a chilled out trip to The Republic, when the Third Summer of Love finally arrives. But first I wanna get this right – so I'll deliver. Chrissy did the job – possibly – n we're all pretty proud of him. But investigations need to be thorough – I read all about it in me Blackstone's. Always learnin' see, I've learnt a lot. Like how maybe next time, I could be in charge...

Coming soon…
Friends On Benefits Mystery 2, starring Chris, Runcie, Julie, Student, Disco Sean, Tasty, DI Kaye and PC Paphaedes.

ACKNOWLEDGEMENTS

Thanks to: Jo, Emily, Nicky, Dan, Mark and Ben, for helping me find the answers; Alex Kirby, Delme Rosser and Amnet for cover design, web design and interior formatting; my mum for freedom and books, my dad for madness and maps, Howard for music and telly, Jo and my besties for the past and the future, and Alfred and Betsy, for every single second. Cover photo thanks to David Clode on Unsplash. Dedication thanks to Liam Howlett, the Prodigy and XL Recordings. Additional inspiration thanks to Joe Smooth, Primal Scream, The Shamen, Kicks Like A Mule, The Orb, FPI Project, PM Dawn, The Smiths, The Stone Roses, REM, Flowered Up, New Order, Captain Sensible, Rozalla, Happy Mondays, Altern-8, Beavis and Butt-Head, Viz and Blackstone's.

WHAT NEXT?

Keep going. Get in touch. If you're feeling kind leave a review. If you're feeling sinister, buy biscuits and administer. And don't worry – everything is going to be amazing.